Playing Cello for the Trees

Playing Cello for the Trees

by Amy Tatko

Real and Imagined Press
2017

First Printing: 2017

ISBN 978-1-365-99490-6

Real and Imagined Press
Montpelier, VT 05602

www.realandimagined.net

In memory of Elisha Hall,
beloved friend and passionate pilot

"Still the only certain thing for sure is what I do not know."

– Lyle Lovett, "Her First Mistake," *The Road to Ensenada*

"Choose to die well while you can;
wait too long, and it might become impossible to do so."

– Gaius Musonius Rufus, Roman Stoic Philosopher

Contents

THE LIST.. 1

TASK ONE: THE SEARCH FOR ANTHONY RIZZO 39

HIATUS 95

SIDETRIP TO NEW YORK.. 107

TASK TWO: SUNRISE AND SUNSET IN GREECE 135

TASK THREE: IN THE COCKPIT 161

THE LIST

I do not believe in much, but I have long held faith that beauty resides in unexpected places. The mind of Edith Small glowed with beauty.

Edith sat on the porch swing of her craftsman cottage with her hands resting on her lap and her eyes shifting from moist to dry and from dark to illuminated. In a long tunic and a matching skirt the shade of a ripe plum, and with gray and white hair that shimmered silver in the afternoon sunlight, she resembled a wizard. She was not afraid of silence. She knew how to cry. She had many opinions. The essence of life bubbled out of her like a magic potion that contained only essential ingredients: a dash of nostalgia, a pinch of hope, and a spoonful of clarity.

I had the unenviable task of interviewing her for a tribute piece about her dead husband. She answered each question with a sense of duty, if not with interest. In my four years as a newspaper reporter, she was the first person who paused before responding. She would look out across her front yard at the snowy peaks of the Cascade Mountains for a moment that stretched beyond what was considered acceptable in the social mores of our broken culture. Even through her veil of grief, I could see the mechanism of her mind at work. I imagined a gem, the only one of its kind, anchored at the center of her brain and emitting thoughts and observations that outshone everything else. I wanted to sit in its glow for a long, long time.

In the months after our interview, I saw Edith on her bicycle, at city council meetings, and in my editor's office, where she came to challenge the paper's editorial stance on the local battle over land use. The swirl of her purple skirts and the clarity of her voice identified her in an instant. The audacity of her convictions and the depth of her hope placed her alone among others. Something she had said during our interview haunted me whenever I saw her: "There are mysteries inside each human life that cannot be translated for others." Edith was a word lover's dream come true. When I commented on her fine English, she raised her eyebrows and said, "Our words reflect our worth and our truth, dear. We must choose them well."

A year later, on the anniversary of Henry Small's death by heart attack, my editor summoned me to his office. It was nine o'clock on a Monday morning in June. News was slow. I had a notebook and pen in my hands, city ordinances and census data in my brain, and despair in my heart from my decision earlier that morning to abandon what mattered to me most. As I rounded the corner and stepped into Cunningham's office, I smelled sparks and was not surprised to learn that the source of the fire was Edith Small.

"I have an unusual assignment," my editor said. "It's time for you to venture beyond City Hall." He slid a piece of paper across his desk toward me.

A LIFETIME LIST OF THINGS TO DO: TASKS FOR EDITH SMALL DURING HER TIME ON THIS PLANET
(written on the occasion of her fortieth birthday)

Handwritten on a single sheet of lined paper, the list was yellowed and creased but otherwise in sound condition. Item number one was perfectly legible in black ink and neat printed letters: "Play the violin and perform Vivaldi's *The Four Seasons* with an orchestra." A black check mark stood to the left of the numeral one. Below it, item number two also had a check mark: "Play the cello and learn the Bach cello suites." The violin and the cello, Vivaldi and Bach, would have been ample for one person and one lifetime, yet the list continued.

Next were several items pertaining to dance, pottery, painting, and other areas of the arts, followed by languages—Spanish, French, and Italian. The icing on the linguistic cake was item 11: "Learn Russian and read Dostoevsky and Tolstoy in the original." (Check.) After the languages came the reading of literature, including all of Shakespeare (check) and the Nobel laureates (check). Next was travel: "Stand on the equator," "Visit the South Pole," "Cross the United States by train" "and by bicycle." Each item had a check mark, and together they formed a long row of accomplishments.

Item 17 was the first without a check. "Watch a sunrise and a sunset on a Greek Island" was circled in the same red used by school teachers to correct homework and grade tests, as if Edith sought to make a correction by darting off to Greece. The boldness of red sounded an alarm after all the black check marks. Edith's red circle meant action. I glanced at Cunningham, and he raised his eyebrows. I looked back at the list and the enticing words "Greek Island." I imagined the Mediterranean sun glittering in Edith's silver hair. I saw Greek ruins, Greek beaches, Greek vineyards, and Greek men. Then I saw myself beside Edith, bearing witness to all. The aged heroine would fulfill her life's destiny as the fearless reporter followed along, notebook and pen in hand, to record the story of her final adventures.

"How is this news?" I asked.

Cunningham shrugged. "You'll figure that out soon enough, with a little help from Edith." Then he chuckled. "You know Edith Small. She's a hundred stories waiting to be told. And you're the writer to tell them."

City Hall was the only beat I had ever known, though the stories I wanted most to tell were not to be found within the pages of a newspaper. Cunningham knew this. One day about a year ago, he was pacing in the newsroom when I arrived an hour late for work. He had a press release from the city in his hand and a look of disappointment on his face. I hated to give up a part of myself, but I had no choice. I had to explain. Cunningham was not angry, he was hurt, and that was worse. "I lost track of time," I told him. "I write before work." He looked at me for a long time, and then he said, "You, too, huh?" He shook his head and grinned. I was not the only one with a secret novel on the side, plugging away at fiction in the dark quiet hours before and after work.

"There are three items left on Edith's list," Cunningham said. "She plans to finish them in a few months. She has a deadline, but she wants to tell you about that herself."

Cunningham was our city editor and a misplaced New Englander who moved through life without use of a first name. He had perennial smudges on his eyeglasses and made a conscious effort to seem tough on deadline. Toughness was not naturally in him. His only child had died, but nobody knew when or how or dared to ask. His wife left him after the funeral. We let Cunningham pretend he was tough, when in fact what kept us all working hard was the simple fact that we liked him and could not stand the thought of letting him down. He had grown up in Boston and was the city's best investigative reporter until his family vanished. He came to *The Bend Bugle* with a past and with tenderness when others would have gone bitter.

Now, a year after the death of Edith Small's husband, Cunningham was releasing me from daily deadline reporting to set me loose on my first special project. He was upgrading me from reporter to long-form feature writer, my idea of paradise. It was also a symbolic version of paramedics resuscitating me with the life-saving phenomenon known as hard work. Labor was a fine antidote to the inner nonsense that plagued us humans. My instinct was to ask Cunningham why he was giving me this opportunity. I had been content for five years covering city news and making it relevant and useful for readers. I had not asked for more. I had not complained. I worked hard, and I found purpose and satisfaction in my work. I liked serving the public as the news hound sniffing around City Hall. What I did on my own time with a pen and how I suffered in private from my own inner nonsense was my business. I had never asked Cunningham to rescue me, but now that he had, I was not sorry. I decided not to ask.

I glanced down at the list again. There was line after line of volunteer projects at the library, hospital, and schools. Then came the sports, including swimming, running, and basketball.

The second red circle appeared in item 28: "Learn to fly an airplane and get a private pilot's license."

The next category was nature adventures: "Climb every mountain in Oregon" and "Camp alone in the Deschutes National Forest for a month." Then there were tasks pertaining to meditation, religion, and the law.

Finally, on the very last line was the third unfinished task, #35, also ringed in red: "Find Anthony Rizzo."

Edith's destiny was a Greek island, aviation, and a search for a missing person. She had completed thirty-two tasks spread across the globe and throughout the years. Only a woman of great ambition, intelligence, and action could have conquered a list of that magnitude. No wonder Edith gave off sparks.

When I looked at Cunningham, he was grinning in a way that I had seen only once before—the day he hired me for a job that he believed would bring happiness to someone in love with truth, writing, and the marriage of the two. My exploits so far had included uncovering government corruption of the small-town sort, refereeing the land feud between developers and environmentalists with ink as my whistle, and traveling across the mountains to the capital to cover news of a higher caliber. Until now, pestering state legislators had qualified as high drama. My work life was good enough. Life was good enough, on the outside anyway. The inside of me was the problem. The truth that I kept to myself was a source of strife that nobody except Cunningham and my dad knew about. I was old-fashioned, a twenty-nine-year-old woman born a couple centuries too late. I believed that one's struggles should be concealed from others. Suffering alone was valiant—or in any case safer and less messy.

"Edith wants someone to record her final adventures," Cunningham said. "An old-fashioned scribe, as she put it." He paused to chuckle again and appreciate the awesome strangeness of Edith Small. "She said she tried the yellow pages, but there was no listing under 'writers' or 'scribes.'" We both laughed and shook our heads. "Then she remembered you."

Flattery was lovely, but my instinct knew better. "There's more to it, isn't there?"

Cunningham looked at me for a moment. Then he nodded.

"But she insisted on telling me herself?"

He nodded again.

Edith's list emitted power, promise, and mystery. The creator and pursuer of the list—the human being behind all those check marks—fascinated me. In a country obsessed with achievement, Edith appeared to be a reigning queen of excellence. I smirked a bit at the chance to write a parody of the Great American Dream, a.k.a. the obsessive American fixation on overachievement. Despite my tendency

7

to value character traits more than accomplishments, Edith impressed me.

And anyway, perhaps she was not the only one who would accomplish something great. Her unfinished tasks were a glue that could bind my severed halves. The reporter who craved more than local news and the aspiring novelist who had lost hope could meld into a single writer in pursuit of a compelling human story. I imagined my new business card with a black check mark beside "City Government Reporter" and a red circle around "Edith Small's Scribe."

* * *

The chime of Edith's doorbell echoed through her house as I stood on her front porch. The door swung open. She was dressed in purple from the hat on her head, to her tunic and her skirt, and down to the satin slippers on her feet. As she stepped forward to shake my hand, the silver bell on each slipper jingled a yuletide greeting—in June. Edith winked at me and clicked her heels together for a jingle-bell duet. In her hand was an old leather book with golden letters on the spine: Shakespeare. She smiled across the threshold and gestured for me to enter the house. Then she opened the book and read Ophelia's song right there in the foyer:

> *How should I your true-Love know*
> *From another one?*
> *By his cockle hat and staff,*
> *And his sandal shoon.*
>
> *He is dead and gone, lady,*
> *He is dead and gone;*
> *At his head a grass-green turf,*
> *At his heels a stone.*
>
> *White his shroud as mountain snow,*
> *Larded with sweet flowers; –*
> *Which bewept to the grave did not go*
> *With true-love showers.*

Edith pronounced each syllable with care and moved with measured pace from one line to the next. Her left hand held the open book, while her right hand swept back and forth, conducting the music of the words. With her grape garb flowing and her hair cropped short above ears bejeweled with sapphires and lapis lazuli, the glow of purples and blues illuminated her face. Her aura was mesmerizing. An arc of light hovered above her, or so I imagined.

She snapped the book shut. "The first time I met you, my husband had just died. I despise that foolish cliché, 'Time heals all wounds.' Rubbish! Time makes a scab. The wound never heals." She stared at me and then at the book in her hand. "I read all of Shakespeare, as you surely know." She leaned in, as if she were a Shakespearean character delivering as aside: "Those check marks are for real, dear." She winked and returned to her soliloquy. "I read aloud, as the bard intended. My children were in school, and the list was my work. Well, to be accurate, as one must when speaking on the record, I happened to be a professor of philosophy as well. I taught one class at the college each semester, to pay my own way and keep my brain fueled and firing. I had plenty of time and money to pursue the list. In the evenings, I read Shakespeare aloud to Henry and the children. We went to performances, too, usually as a family, but sometimes just the two of us. Our children were teenagers then. They didn't want anything to do with Shakespeare at first, but there was no way they could avoid it. My list was a part of our lives. Shakespeare—and the music and the foreign languages, all of it, really— was like vegetables: I would keep serving more, even if they complained. No good mother would let her children live without the arts. Literature, theater, music, painting, dance—our glorious human creations. After a while, Billy became a real fan of Shakespeare's comedies. He couldn't believe that something so old could be funny. Anyway, there were thirty-five items on my list, one for each year from age forty to seventy-five. I've been away from it for too long, and it's time to finish."

Most people needed time to warm up when they spoke to a reporter. Once they were rolling, I would keep my eyes on their face, nod my head for encouragement, reach a hand into my bag, and pull out my notebook and pen. My eyes never left them. As long as they had my eyes, my hands were invisible. Most did not notice my pen or notebook. Many would forget that I was a reporter, and they would tell me more than they had intended. Some told me their secrets. Others had an epiphany in my presence. At times that made me sad for what it meant about the lack of listeners in their lives, in anyone's life—mine, too, perhaps, though I claim not to want any. Everyone wants to be heard, and everyone aches for attention. I used that sad truth to my advantage. I was not proud of my sneaky ways, but they were necessary. Getting people to talk was mandatory in my line of work. Edith, however, was not like most people. Her mind and mouth were flying under her own control, and so was my pen across my notepad.

"I attacked the list with a ferocity and a focus that I didn't know I had. I started a new task each year, but there was also a lot of overlapping. Some of the skills and interests that I acquired became a regular part of my life. For years, I met with the local French group once a week to speak the language and discuss the culture. After I trained for a marathon, I still ran for years for exercise. I didn't do the list in order. I jumped around based on what inspired me most and which items fit best in my life from one year to the next. There were classes and lessons, practice and study, layered with the excitement of something new to learn, the next task to try. Some years I didn't have time for much else, like when I studied law and when I worked at the hospital. I always had a sense of purpose, and I enjoyed the satisfaction of checking each item off the list. It was a thrill to know that I had done what I set out to do. What I loved most, though, was the process. My whole life was about being in the process of doing—trying, learning, exploring the full potential of my mind and my body. The list gave me a sense of immediacy and intensity, and that has been a wonderful way to live."

My eyes fell from Edith's face down to my notebook under the weight of her speech, her enthusiasm, and too many grand proclamations too early in the day. We had slid away from the front door and further into the house. We were standing in a space that was not exactly a hallway but whose only purpose was to connect the rooms. I finished writing and looked up.

"Well, enough of that," Edith said. She stirred as if from a trance and shook her head to let the dust from her memories settle again. "Come in, dear. The kettle is about to whistle."

We stepped into her kitchen, where the scent of cloves and oranges greeted us. A floor of salmon-colored tiles and counters of pale yellow shone from the sunlight that drenched the room. Vases of fresh flowers stood on a shelf over the sink, on the counter beside the stove, and on the table. The bouquets exploded with color, splashes of beauty created with care. Two places were set at the table in the bay window on the far side of the kitchen that looked out onto the back yard. Edith grabbed the kettle and invited me with a wave of her hand to join her there. I looked around some more and wondered why anyone would go to the trouble to make such a lovely home for herself alone.

I sat down across from Edith and took a sip of tea. The scent of oranges and cloves melded with the taste of the same, plus a bit of cardamom and a touch of honey.

"I think of writers as strong and mysterious," she said. "I figured you would like something with pizzazz."

I sipped again, noting a hint of pepper. She pushed a plate toward me. The muffins were still warm and left buttery grease marks on my fingertips.

"You *do* consider yourself a writer, don't you?" Edith asked. "Something beyond a newspaper reporter? A modern-day scribe of sorts?"

I churned out sentences for a paycheck. I wrote for a living. Yet, I was also something beyond a newspaper reporter, as Edith had surmised. The writing that I did outside of the newsroom mattered to me most, yet a stack of rejection letters documented my failures. Perhaps the rejections meant that I was not worthy of the title "writer," but that was complicated and private. I looked at Edith and nodded.

"Excellent," she said. "I could tell from the way you wrote about Henry."

Edith sipped from a handmade ceramic cup, and her muffin rested on a matching plate. She wiped the crumbs from her mouth with a cloth napkin. The colors of the pottery glaze blended with the colors of the fabric. Edith cared about details. She planned the details. Something about that inspired me and saddened me. The simple cares that were once the hallmark of daily life had faded into the background as relics of times past. Nobody of my generation would match their napkins to their dishes. I traced my finger along the edge of the mug and imagined Edith in a pottery studio learning how to work with clay. The blue ceramic mugs in my kitchen cabinet were mass produced by machines on the other side of the world and sold in chain stores. Edith's hand-thrown mugs made me nostalgic for a time and a way of life that I had never known.

"Did you bring the list?" she asked. I nodded and reached for my bag. "I was reluctant to let it go," she said, "but your editor thought you would like the old faded paper and the creases."

I traded in the aged original for a photocopy that Edith handed me. The black lines and red circles were back with their rightful owner. I was sorry to see them go. My copy had no ruby red.

"There they are," Edith said. "Thirty-two completed tasks."

"It couldn't have been easy," I said. "You started in the late 1970s. Did you meet much resistance?"

"Oh, heavens, yes. Our small town was much smaller back in those days, and the thinking was small, too. Provincial, really. Feminism was seen by many as a threat rather than a correction of what was wrong and a part of basic human rights."

"I imagine that attending law school and riding a bicycle alone across the country were not typical activities for a middle-age woman in those days," I said.

Edith laughed. "I seem to have more tenacity than most people. I don't have an ounce of talent, but I am passionate and determined. Anyone who stood in my way gave up when they saw that I would not."

"Did you get tired of facing that?"

"I ignored it the best I could. The condescension annoyed me. The pejorative way that men speak to women disgusts me. In those days, women did it to one another, too. Many believed that our proper role was wife and mother and nothing more. Some accepted the choices of nurse, secretary, or school teacher. A lot of them treated me like an extraterrestrial. I don't take well to being seen as incapable or incompetent, and yet I'm not one to recite my credentials. You can't bully back, either. That gets you nowhere. I learned to mix patience with persistence, and grace with determination."

I had more questions, but Edith was done patting herself on the back.

"Enough of this," she said. "We have work to do. The time has come to finish." She looked through the window and exhaled a sigh full of meaning that I could not yet understand. Then she nodded her head and turned toward me.

"It all started the day I turned forty."

* * *

The Bend Bugle
"Local Woman Rediscovers Her Lifetime List"
By Lucy Hunt

On the morning of October 26, 1977, Edith Small sat at her desk overlooking the Deschutes River and savored the solitude that she had been craving for years. It was her fortieth birthday, and thoughts of the present and future consumed her. Her youngest child had started kindergarten. The house was empty for the first time since Edith had become a mother eight years earlier. Each weekday morning at eight o'clock, her children left for school. Each afternoon at three o'clock, they trickled home one at a time. For the seven hours in between, Edith was free. She had anticipated her new freedom with excitement, but when it arrived, it terrified her.

"I didn't know what to do," she recalled in a recent interview. "I didn't know how to spend my days. I couldn't even figure out what my career meant to me anymore."

Eventually, Edith knew exactly what to do, and she succeeded in doing it—or most of it, anyway. Now, at the age of seventy-five, Edith Small, long-time resident of Bend and retired professor of philosophy, plans to finish the work that she began thirty-five years ago. Yet, to understand where Edith is going, one must first know where she has been.

When her husband, Henry Small, had turned forty earlier that year, he experienced an existential itch that he scratched with a new job and a move across state borders. The Smalls packed their belongings and their children and followed the moving truck from their old hometown on the coast of northern California, where Henry had been the vice president of a college, to their new hometown at the base of the Cascade Mountains, where he became a college president. Henry's itch disappeared, and he got down to the business of living the second half of his life as first-in-command.

Months later, on the eve of her own fortieth birthday, Edith looked out at the second half of her life and saw only a void. Nothing in particular beckoned the woman who was a philosopher by training and a mother by choice. She could not decide whether to return to a career in academics or pursue something new.

"I thought about idling away the hours on the couch with a book and a cup of tea, going to town for manicures and massages, taking day trips to the coast to enjoy the view," Edith said. "I had earned it, after raising three fine children to school age, but, alas, the life of leisure was not for me."

She also considered pursuing something wild like skydiving or carefree like baking specialty cakes but decided that nothing frivolous would suit her. With no obligation to contribute to the family income, Edith was guided only by desire and her sense of moral obligation.

"I could not identify my purpose on this planet, but I wanted to live an interesting life and to find out what my mind and my body were capable of," she said. "Along the way, I wanted to do something useful, something of value to others."

Edith retold the story of her past during a series of interviews this week at her home on the Bend riverfront just outside of downtown. She lives alone in the same craftsman house that her family moved into thirty-five years ago.

Day after day, Edith sat at her desk in her upstairs bedroom and contemplated the meaning of life. She looked at the river, the sky, and the contents of her heart. By late October, with her birthday encroaching, she had not inched any closer to discovering her reason for being, but she was moving closer to the proverbial brink.

"I'd become one of those people whose thoughts eat away at their sanity, people who spend far too much time contemplating their own existence," she recalled.

On the morning of her birthday, Edith saw an advertisement for a full-time tenure-track position in the philosophy department at the college. She clipped the ad. The scrap of newsprint taunted her and begged her to consider and decide. Suddenly, a warm autumn breeze fluttered the papers on her desk, and the job announcement slipped through the window and floated into the great beyond like a miniature flying carpet bearing only words as its passenger. As Edith watched her future job fly away, she noticed a neighbor rushing along the sidewalk, briefcase in hand, glancing at her watch, late for her job at a law firm downtown. Stress was drawn in wrinkles at the edges of the woman's eyes and mouth, and her professional-height heels clicked against the concrete in a panic of tardiness.

"In each click I heard the answer to my dilemma: 'Don't do it,'" Edith said. "I imagined my own briefcase full of unfinished work, my own schedule crammed with meetings and seminars, and my own body stuffed into straight skirts and heeled shoes. No, thanks."

The lawyer hurried around the corner and disappeared. Yet, her mark was indelible. "I'll never forget her," Edith said. "She saved my life."

That was when Edith thought of the list. She took a sheet of paper from her desk drawer. She uncapped her fountain pen and placed it on the top line, like a runner taking her mark. Then she wrote, "A LIFETIME LIST OF THINGS TO DO: TASKS FOR EDITH SMALL DURING HER TIME ON THIS PLANET (written on the occasion of her fortieth birthday)."

A Canada goose flew past her window and landed with grace on the river, sending ripples outward. She still remembers the goose and believes it was divine intervention. Edith tapped her pen three times against her forehead and released the genie trapped within.

"I want to play the violin," she said out loud. "I want to learn how to read those notes and bring them to life. Certainly music is not frivolous."

As her pen hit the page, she thought of Vivaldi. She liked *The Four Seasons*, no matter what her husband and his colleagues thought. She stopped writing and flicked the pen back and forth between her thumb and forefinger with the even beat of a metronome. In her new life, censorship would be outlawed, and raw unmitigated desire would reign. The opinions of others would be exiled. Oh, to play God with a lump of creation clay that represented her own future, her own life. Edith discarded others' judgments and embraced her fondness of Vivaldi.

Yet, another horrible thought soon stopped her pen again: What if she could not do it? She waved her hand through the air to dismiss the very notion.

"So be it," she said to the goose on the river. "I may play badly, but play I will."

Edith decided that to do poorly was better than to do nothing. She would include anything that appealed to her and seemed feasible. She would not attempt to become President of the United States or the first woman to land on the moon. Parameters of reason would marry her dreams, and—voila!—the map of her future was born. She moved her pen to the next line, and wrote the numeral two. If she could learn to play the violin, then she could learn other instruments, too.

"I've always loved the cello," she said.

She spoke aloud to herself, to nobody, to the whole world, faster and faster as the excitement cresdendoed inside of her at the thought of the Bach cello suites. Music led her to ponder the other arts, including dance, which she had always admired but never attempted, and opera, which "baffled and even repelled me," she said. From dance she drifted into pottery and painting. Art inspired images of the great museums scattered about the world. If she wanted to see the art, she would need to speak the languages of the countries where the museums were located. Language led her to literature, which in turn stirred an interest in her local newspaper, world news, and the places around the globe that she most wanted to see.

As she paused again to watch the goose drift on the river, her thoughts narrowed to the community she lived in and its many needs. The list so far represented her truest desires. Standing on the equator could prove exhilarating, yet Edith remembered her wish to make a contribution. Her pen hit line number nineteen, and she committed herself to one volunteer job after another. The town's homeless population of a half-dozen or so may have gone unnoticed by others, but Edith would no longer ignore them.

"Under my watch, they would eat, they would bathe, and they would get off the streets," she recalled. "Most importantly, though, they would get back to work."

Edith wrote and wrote. She tapped her pen against her forehead when the ideas halted. For divine inspiration she gazed up at the river, where the grace and beauty of the lone goose—her unexpected muse—placed each new idea in her head. On she wrote, through sports, nature, law, religion, and more. Soon the list was complete.

"I had never felt so certain about anything in my life," Edith said.

In one sitting on her fortieth birthday, Edith Small outlined in no uncertain terms how she would spend the rest of her years. Later that evening, she determined how many years there would be.

* * *

My apartment was small. The bathroom had a shower stall, a pedestal sink, and a shelf large enough for my two beauty supplies: a hairbrush and a bottle of face lotion. The bedroom contained a doorless closet and a double bed that had never seen a second occupant. Most mornings I sat on the end of my bed and stared into the closet while I decided what to wear. If I leaned forward and reached down, I could grab a pair of shoes from where I sat. The rest of the apartment was a single room with a kitchen in the front corner, a counter with two stools where I ate and read the news, a two-person couch—the "loveless seat"—my mother's rocking chair, and my desk by the large window that looked out on the spruce trees behind the building.

Every Sunday morning, I read three newspapers cover to cover: the paper I worked for, the paper I grew up on, and the country's paper of record that had long set the bar for journalistic excellence. I started with *The Bugle* at the counter in my pajamas. After an hour of reading and drinking coffee on an empty stomach, my hands would tremble as I turned each page, and the rumbling in my gut would force me to break for food. I would eat at the counter as I began to read newspaper number two, the statewide daily from my home city of Portland on the other side of the mountains. By mid-morning, I was ready for the massive Sunday *New York Times* and headed for the loveless seat.

The Sunday morning after my first interviews with Edith, I started the coffee maker and trudged to the front door for the newspapers.

Playing Cello for the Trees

I opened the door and reached my hand toward the mat where the three papers lay side by side. My hand twitched, and I hesitated. I had seen my work on the front page numerous times, but this was different. This was my first full-length feature story and the first installment of my first special project. That was enough firsts to make anyone's hand twitch. The article had no statistics, no text quoted from city reports, no competing viewpoints from key sources, and no on-the-street reporting. All it had was Edith, uncensored and unprecedented, in her own words, and in my own words. My A1 Sunday story had a narrative voice. It had a main character, a theme, foreshadowing, symbolism, and other elements borrowed from the novel. The stakes were high, for reasons that only Cunningham, Edith, and I knew. Readers would be baited by the first article and then hit with a shocking truth a week later in the second article. Cunningham and I had talked it over and talked it through and talked it out umpteen times before the first story went to press. We believed that we were approaching Edith's unusual and unpredictable story with integrity and with our journalistic—and human—judgment intact. And yet, failure seemed dreadfully feasible. Criticism from readers seemed inevitable. There would be outrage. Edith would have enemies. I would, too. At last, I took the papers from the doormat and closed the door.

Although I had seen my writing in published form countless times before, I still tingled with delight and anxiety when my stories were on page one. There was something magical about running around town to report a story, then writing in the newsroom while the other reporters banged away at their computers, and finally seeing the finished product in ink on newsprint for thousands of people to read. To see it on the front page brought an extra thrill, along with extra nerves. There was nowhere to hide on A1. Our circulation was about forty thousand, and though that placed us in the category of a small daily, the notion of forty-thousand subscribers, plus more readers who bought a single copy or read someone else's copy, could worry me or impress me if I let it. Forty-thousand people was a football stadium filled to capacity as everyone sat holding *The Bend Bugle* and reading a news story written by yours truly.

The copy desk used the headline that I had suggested, a small but satisfying victory. The color photograph of Edith on her porch swing captured the vital details, right down to the bells on her plum slippers and the silvery highlights of her sun-soaked hair. I held my breath as I read and awaited my own verdict. I liked the lead sentence. The second sentence was fine, too. Everything on the front page was decent, a solid start for Edith and for me, the first step of a mighty long journey. I exhaled and allowed myself a smile, a wee celebration in the privacy of my own home. Yet, beyond the smile was a fear so intense that a tremor in my hands rattled the newspaper. In one week, the rest of the story would be out, and there would be no turning back.

I flipped to the rest of the story on A12 to see whether the editors had used Edith's photograph from her fortieth birthday. The telephone rang.

"Lucy, good morning. You up?"

"Of course I'm up, Dad."

"It's good to hear your voice. I was beginning to worry."

Six days had passed since Cunningham gave me the list, and this was the first time that I had thought of my dad. We usually talked every other day or so, and until that moment, I had not realized that I missed our phone calls. I walked to the kitchen counter and saw a blinking red 5 on the answering machine. I had spent hours at Edith's house, interviewing her and looking through her boxes of artifacts from her work on the list. Then I had holed up at my desk in the newsroom for two days to compile my notes, select quotations, outline the story, and write, rewrite, and rewrite again. At the end of each day, after deadline, when the newsroom was nearly empty, Cunningham and I would talk. He was as nervous as I was, and as we worked through our nerves, we worked out a plan.

In the evenings, I was exhausted and collapsed into bed after dinner to read. My alarm buzzed each morning at six o'clock, and I went straight to my desk in my pajamas and wrote for two hours. Then I showered, ate, and went to work. I began and ended each day with fiction, my first love, my true love, my secret—or maybe not-so-secret—love. In the hours between, Edith and her list monopolized me. I had forgotten my dad, the person I loved most.

"I guess you saw it," I said.

"Saw it? Are you kidding? I marveled over it. You haven't surprised me like that since the day you left for Bratislava."

"Marveled?"

"It's fantastic. *She's* fantastic. You brought her to life, kiddo. She's one old gal I'd like to meet. I've never seen anything like this in *The Bugle*. I know, I know—I've only been reading it for a year, but still, I know a good one when I see it."

"That's very generous, Dad. I think it came out alright. I'll get better with time."

"I figured you were just filling in. Are you off the city beat?"

"Cunningham put me on special assignment for a few months."

"To tell Edith's story? About the list?"

"That's the idea."

"It sounds like she's had quite a life. That is, if she actually did the list."

"Well, that's the interesting part," I said.

"I see. And I'll have to wait for the next installment to learn more, right?"

I wanted to tell him. I wanted his reassurance and approval. More than anything, I wanted my dad to be in on the secret so I would not feel so alone and scared. I did not budge, though.

"That's right," I told him.

My father chuckled on the other end of the phone. I could picture him in his sweatpants and T-shirt in his recliner with the newspaper spread open on his lap. He read the same three I did every Sunday. His golden retriever, Mango, was probably at his feet. My father was enjoying his retirement in Bend, as much as any widower enjoyed life. I wondered whether he would stay after I had moved on. I had no plan to move away, but I also suspected that I would not live the rest of my life in the same town.

"Well, I'll let you get back to your reading. Have you seen *The Times* yet?"

"Not yet."

"I'll be curious to hear your thoughts. Are you still coming tonight?"

"I wouldn't miss it for anything."

"You're always welcome to bring a friend."

"I know, Dad. Thank you. It'll be just me."

"Just you is perfect. See you later."

My dad's use of the word "friend" as code for "future husband" could not provoke me. His intentions were better than good. If he could have planted, harvested, and cooked happiness to serve to me three times each day, he would have spent the rest of his life doing so. I picked up the *Times*, and the front page froze me. A medical laboratory was doing breakthrough cancer research, and my brother, Charlie, at the age of thirty-two, was making significant contributions to the team. Their latest discovery was too important to be buried in the health section. There was my brother's name on the front page of the world's greatest newspaper.

Charlie and Lucy. Most people did not connect our names to the *Peanuts* comic strip. Those who did tended to assume it was a coincidence. The clever ones suggested that perhaps I was not aware that our names matched the names of the characters. When my mom was pregnant with me, she fell in love with the name Lucy. My father pointed out the *Peanuts* connection, and my mother found it amusing. They joked about it before I was born but figured they would agree on another name by the time I arrived. That never happened. When my mother held me for the first time, she knew me as Lucy and could not fathom any other name. She used the word "fathom" each time she and my dad retold the history of my name on my birthday every year. They claimed that if I had been a boy, they would have named me Linus. They also claimed that if they had been part-bold, part-goofy the day I was born, they would have named me Snoopy. I never believed that, but there was no way to get a straight answer when my parents felt playful. Even after my mom died, my dad would grin and say nothing when I asked about Snoopy. And so, my brother and I were not exactly named for Charlie Brown and Lucy Van Pelt, and yet, in the end, we sort of were. The guy I slept with in college would hum the *Peanuts* theme song every time he came to my dorm room. I found it endearing until he broke my heart.

The name Charlie Hunt stared at me from the front page of *The New York Times*. The name Lucy Hunt stared at me from the front page of *The Bend Bugle*. All I could do was sigh. Envy and competition may have been lurking in the dark recesses of my psyche, an inescapable truth for any siblings, perhaps. My conscious mind, however, knew only love and pride for my big brother. As I looked at our names on the covers of vastly different newspapers, the ticking of my internal clock grew louder in an aggressive way that made me uneasy. By my age, my brother had already been working to solve the world's medical problems and improve the lot of humankind. The milestone of my thirtieth birthday was drawing near, yet my dream seemed farther from my reach than ever, and the assignment that I had taken in its place was giving me physical symptoms.

* * *

That evening, I pedaled my bicycle across town to my dad's house about three miles away. He lived in a log cabin by the river. In the summer, he went fishing and walked the paths through the forest that lined both sides of the Deschutes River. In the winter, he heated his house with a woodstove and snowshoed along the same tree-lined paths. He volunteered at the local middle school, helping teachers any way they needed. He stayed in the classroom longer each day than he was scheduled to. He went into the school on the weekends, too, to help teachers get caught up on work, rearrange their rooms, and set up for new projects. He grew attached to his favorite students, as he always did when he was a teacher. For thirty-five years, his colleagues had warned him not to get attached to the kids. He would smile and say, "Then what's the point of teaching?"

During the warm months of the year, I rode my bike to my father's house every Sunday evening for our weekly dinner. We often hiked together on the weekends, too. In the winter, I drove to his house each Sunday, and sometimes I went early so we could snowshoe along the river trail before dinner. I went not out of pity because my mom was dead but because I wanted to. I depended on my dad and our friendship the way most people depended on their best friend or their sweetheart. For most of my life, I had not had either, but I always had a father whom I loved more than anyone. He was the rare kind of person that you could ask or tell anything. *Anything.*

One day in eighth grade, a bunch of girls in the bathroom were discussing blow jobs. They were giggling so much that I could not hear everything they said, and they failed to use the correct terminology, so I had to guess what certain words meant. Hidden in the last stall, I sat with my hand hovering above the toilet-paper dispenser and my private part air-drying as I listened with fascination and terror.

The girls' voices grew quieter, and the sense of scandal grew larger. As I strained to hear their whispers, I began to doubt that they were talking about how to blow-dry hair. After school that day, I asked my father, and he assured me with every necessary detail that hair dryers played no role in the process. I have since heard from other women that their mothers, sisters, and best friends used a banana or a cucumber for the lesson. My father used words. He did not want to turn my earnest inquiry into a joke. There was nothing odd about it for me or him. He told it straight and included the pertinent facts, as he did in response to every question that I ever asked him.

My mom never knew about that day. I did not intentionally exclude her from anything. I went to my dad not as a criticism of my mom's deficiencies or any other commentary about her but because he was the parent that I gravitated to in moments of need. My mother was a pediatrician at a busy medical practice downtown. My father was a seventh-grade math teacher at our neighborhood middle school. He was home with me and Charlie every day after school and every vacation and summer, fielding life's big and small questions as they arose. The three of us did well on our own, and the four of us were a fine combination, too. My family had a way of talking to one another that defined my childhood, our home, and love for me. No matter how difficult any situation or problem became, no matter how disappointed or angry we were at times, someone was able to offer up a bit of love and kindness to get us unstuck and talking our way toward resolution. This truth about my family made us different, and it made me different. I was the girl who liked her own parents, the girl with the older brother who held her hand on the way to school. I preferred to stay home on weekends to watch movies and play games with my family.

Nobody wants to hear about a happy family. I stuffed away my childhood and learned not to mention it. I spent my teenage years and early twenties looking for the kind of friend who might want to hear about my family and know who I am. I found one eventually, on the other side of the world, but not until after I had already survived the worst time of my life, the time when I had needed a friend most. My mom was killed in a car crash seven years ago. She was gone in an instant on her way to work one morning on a day like any other, or so she thought. A delivery-truck driver lost control of his truck, charged through a red light, and smashed head-on into my mom's car. Nobody in my family had ever thought for one second that we were immune to horrors and tragedies. We had escaped loss long enough to squeeze in a huge amount of joy. For twenty-two years, I had a loving, attentive, devoted, playful mother. Then she was gone, a concept that I do not pretend to understand. The pain stung most under my ribs. My heart felt as if it could not pump steadily like it used to. The blood seemed to surge at one moment and lag at the next. The ache lasted for a long, long time. I still feel it sometimes. I had just graduated from college and was living at home for the summer, getting ready for my next big move: my first apartment and my first job. After my mom died, though, I could not move. The pain of death means that you cannot work, make plans, or even read books, listen to music, or see the beauty in a sunset. My dad, my brother, and I clung to one another for months and wandered around in our grief like a litter of lost puppies bereft of its mama. Then one day, it was over. Charlie flew back to Boston after taking a semester off from medical school. Dad called the principal at his school and said he would be back the next week. I applied for volunteer work on the other side of the world and taught English to Slovaks in Bratislava, my favorite city on our planet, so far.

In Bratislava, at last I found a true friend, a soul mate, a lifelong forever friend. Ramona Kingsley was a reporter for the city's English-language newspaper, and she was everything I had ever dreamed of: kind, funny, quirky, strong, independent, full of surprises, and smarter than I could ever dream to be. She had the brightest red hair I had ever seen and the largest vocabulary I had ever heard. She liked to hug often and vigorously, and she held my hand in public in a schoolgirl kind of way, even though she was exactly my age. For two years, we told each other all there was to know about ourselves, our past, our childhoods, our families, our equally meager love lives, and our trials and tribulations with the Slovaks. When I visited Ramona at her office for the first time, I knew that I, too, was destined to be a newspaper reporter. As she typed under deadline and zipped across town with her notebook in hand, I watched with envy as she melded adventure with writing, interrogation with research, and turned the day's corrupt, heroic, dull, or riveting events into a valuable offering for the English-reading public in ink on paper. She was my own personal superhero and very best Best Friend. Then I returned to Oregon, and Ramona went back to England. We became pen pals in an age when nobody used paper and postage stamps anymore. On our last night in Bratislava, Ramona and I vowed to see one another at least once every two years on any continent. I went to London once, and she came to Oregon once. So far, we were living out our vows, even on the pittance that each of us earned as a newspaper reporter.

I thought about Ramona as I rode my bike to my dad's house for dinner the Sunday that my first Edith story appeared in *The Bugle*. I had not told her about Edith yet, and if I did not hurry, she would find out herself when she read the article on the paper's website. We always read each other's stories online, the one component of our friendship that relied on modern technology, for which I was grateful. Ramona covered the crime beat for a lesser-known daily outside of London. She worked nights and wrote gruesome stories of wicked events. I had avoided telling her about Edith because my confused emotions worried that she might not approve, which was a reflection of my own moral uncertainty and no reflection of Ramona. My brain knew that she would probably be envious and excited for me. This was the kind of story that made her fall in love with our profession all over again. Already I sensed that when I finished my Edith assignment, I would need a vacation. I was still thinking about where in the world Ramona and I could meet when I arrived at my dad's house.

The table on his back deck was already set for dinner. He still used our traditional family napkin rings that had been on the table during every dinner throughout my childhood. A cut-glass water pitcher that my mom had inherited from her grandmother stood in the center of the table. The ritual of making everything look the same as it always had comforted us both. I thought of Edith and the beautiful details that she cared for in her everyday life.

"This is gonna be good, Lucy," my dad yelled from the kitchen as I poked around the stacks of magazines and library books on the coffee table. The scent of baking salmon mixed with the crispness of lemon and an herb I could not identify. My dad loved to make me guess what spices and seasonings blessed each of his culinary master-pieces. I was often wrong, and that was part of the fun.

Soon we were seated across from one another on the deck. The river passed by below us. The swiftness of the water swished and sloshed as the icy Deschutes narrowed and pushed past the rocks that pervaded my dad's stretch. The river cooled the summer air, and the tall pines shielded the deck and the house from the sun. I preferred meadows, valleys, and mountain tops, but my father found great pleasure in his home beneath the trees. The mosquitoes fed on me, not him. I swatted at them throughout dinner each week and left with red bumps on my arms, legs, face, and neck.

"So, about Edith," he said.

My dad was savoring his salmon and deserved an entertaining story after his labor in the kitchen. I was not one to omit details, and yet, true to my dad's nature, when I finished an extended monologue, he asked a dozen questions anyway. When at last he had heard every fact, insight, and observation about Edith, her list, and my new as-signment—everything, that is, minus one detail, the critical one—he wiped his mouth and placed his napkin on the table.

"This is quite a change," he said. "Very different from the com-munity service of covering city government."

"Exactly," I said. I threw my napkin on the table. It hit my glass hard, and the water inside sloshed like a tidal wave in miniature. "That's the question. Is writing about Edith a public service? Do hu-man-interest stories serve the public, or does only hard news do that? And if this assignment has no public purpose, then what does that say about me? Maybe this is a frivolous pursuit."

Uncertainty made my voice crescendo, as if yelling questions at the universe could provoke the universe to yell answers back. My fa-ther looked at me for a long time.

"You've been thinking about this a lot," he said at last. "Even be-fore Edith came along?"

I nodded.

"You're asking two very different questions—one about the val-ue of art and the other about the life of an artist."

I looked at my dad. Then I looked at the river. I saw Edith's Ca-nadian goose. I saw the clipped job advertisement swirling through the air toward the ground. I saw the list with check marks of black and circles of red. I saw myself trotting around the world a few paces behind Edith, scribbling down what she saw and did and said, filtering her story and her ideas about life through my own mind and heart, and translating them into words that readers would then send through their own filters of mind, heart, and ideas about life. There would be no coup d'etat, no natural disaster, and no genocide. There was no crime, no corruption, no wrongdoing, no penalties or punishments. Quite possibly, nothing much would change as a result of Edith finishing her list, me writing her story, and others reading it.

Or would it?

I wanted to tell my dad everything—how Edith's story would end and what was really at stake for her, me, and our readers. I also wanted him to know that this battle of passion versus duty, of my true love versus my job, a paycheck, lofty notions of public service, and making a contribution to the world was not new. We had a silent understanding that he knew. I never told him. He just knew because that was who he was and who he was to me. Yet, telling him myself, openly and honestly, in my own words would have been different. The moment was upon us. I could have taken out my secret—*my* secret, about my novel, not Edith's secret—and shown it to him at last. Instead I let the moment pass. One's great passion could be fragile, and I could not risk seeing mine chipped or cracked by the person I loved most.

I left earlier than usual after dinner. As I hugged my dad and thanked him for another wonderful meal, I felt his eyes on me in the searching way of a parent. He could see the heaviness that clung to me. I pretended not to notice as I pedaled away.

I escaped past the juniper trees and rabbit brush along the open roads of the high desert out east. I took the long way home. The light was fading, and my muscles burned in an effort to cover too many miles in not enough time. My legs were chasing the same elusive answer as the rest of me. Edith was not news. There was no useful information in my articles. Her story would not matter, in the end. Readers would react, perhaps, but the public did not need to know. Her story was a mere tangent, extraneous material, filler, fluff. I could not be certain that anyone would learn anything, though I believed even then, at the beginning, that we always learn from every story, real or imagined.

My dad was right. The question was not about hard news versus feature stories. It was about the value of storytelling and the value of the life of a writer. My novel sat in my desk drawer. This was the truth that he knew without my telling him. Every day the manuscript asked me the same question, but it was a question that my father had not in fact posed, the other half of his equation that had remained unspoken: Was there any value to writing in obscurity? Was there inherent worth in the life of an unpublished novelist?

As the sun began to set, I turned and pointed my front tire west. I rode toward the blazing sky, homeward bound, destined soon for another day of work on a strange new journey whose purpose remained uncertain.

* * *

The Bend Bugle
"Edith Small Sets a Deadline"
By Lucy Hunt

When Edith Small's husband died a year ago, she made no major changes or decisions, and she kept his belongings for a full year.

"That's the widow's rule, and I obeyed it," she said.

Then, last month, she began to sort through Henry's belongings. While she was in the attic of their longtime Bend home, she came across the boxes from her "Lifetime List of Things To Do" that she had created thirty-five years earlier. The boxes contained notebooks from her language classes, boarding passes from her trips, pottery tools, ballet slippers, musical scores, librettos, telephone lists, maps, and more.

"When I pulled the lid off one of the boxes, the list was right on top," Edith said. "I knew I had to finish."

Edith had taken a break from work on her list a few years ago when Henry showed signs of poor health and old age. She did not forget about it, she said. She simply pushed it out of her thoughts for a time. Now, Edith has given *The Bugle* full access to the records and artifacts related to her list of thirty-five items, all but three of which she has completed. A *Bugle* reporter will follow Edith for the next few months as she attempts to complete her list. Interviews are underway with residents of Bend who were involved with projects from Edith's list, including her former language instructors, art teachers, and community leaders familiar with her charitable work.

During a series of long conversations earlier this week, Edith, now 75, reconstructed the events of her fortieth birthday and the creation of her list with the help of the detailed journals that she has kept since that day. Extensive dialogue from her family life is recorded in her journals. Edith read aloud to a reporter from the handwritten books in order to retell her story as accurately as possible.

Edith now lives alone as a widow in the same two-story craftsman where she lived with her husband and their three children. The house is located in the heart of historic Bend on the Deschutes River.

Throughout the afternoon and into the evening of October 26, 1977, Edith's list lay in hiding in her top desk drawer. She cooked and served her family her own birthday dinner: lasagna with homemade marinara sauce and fresh basil, a salad of iceberg lettuce and tomato wedges, Italian bread from her favorite bakery, and a flourless chocolate torte that she had baked and adorned with a single candle for symbolic reasons and for good luck. As she rinsed the basil and sliced the bread, and as she smiled through her family's rendition of the birthday song, the list tugged at Edith as if an invisible string connected it to her like an umbilical cord joining her to a vital new life source.

The evening proceeded according to routine. Yet, the ordinary activities of her family's daily life clashed with her new sense of the extraordinary that was awaiting her. The list pulled at her as she rinsed tomato sauce from plates and visited her children in their bedrooms to check on homework progress (Alice), paperdoll cutting (Rose), and block building (Billy). The household was settling down for the night. The children filed one by one into the bathroom to brush their teeth, and then they climbed into their beds. Edith and Henry tucked them in together each night, traipsing through the upstairs bedrooms with kisses, sweet-dream wishes, and the click of each light switch, one at a time, until all three children were nestled and peaceful.

Henry went downstairs to relax with the newspaper and a glass of brandy, while Edith stood alone in the dark in the upstairs hallway, contemplating the list. Then she hurried into her bedroom and to her desk. She slid open the top drawer, pulled out the single piece of paper, and entered the living room.

"I did something exciting today," Edith said.

The top half of the newspaper bent down to reveal her husband's face with raised eyebrows and a hint of a grin. "Ah-ha. Have you found the answer you've been seeking?"

Edith nodded as she sprang to Henry's side, removed the day's news from his clutch, and sat beside his slippered feet on the ottoman. She gave the list to Henry. As he read, his eyes remained still while his eyebrows moved up and down, wiggling and scrunching. Onward he read, with scrutiny and care, and an occasional "hmm" or "oh."

When he finished, he looked at Edith. "Excellent work, my dear."

His words were the reassurance that Edith needed as she stood at the crossroads of the unknown, this concocted and charted adventure that stood before her.

"You approve?" she asked.

"Absolutely, though the price tag will be mighty."

"I'll be teaching "An Introduction to Philosophy," every semester, one section only. It's all arranged with department. I don't want to work full-time, and I don't want a career, but I will cover my own costs, thank you very much," Edith said. "And anyway, let's not forget all the back pay that I'm still owed for raising three children, plus the bonuses for pregnancy, childbirth, and breastfeeding that I never collected."

Edith's long pause and stony face communicated her lack of humor on the subject. Henry did not dismiss or belittle her. He never had when it came to the work of motherhood. He took her hands.

"Edith, you are an extraordinary woman. If anyone can do this, it's you."

Edith squeezed his hands and grinned. "I'll need an assistant from time to time."

"Count me in."

Edith pulled Henry's hands to her face and pressed them against her cheeks. She closed her eyes and calculated a complex equation that measured the short-term benefit of stopping on a happy note against the long-term benefit of disclosing everything right up front. Every situation that she had ever navigated led her to the same answer: honesty was greater than the sum parts of everything else.

"There's more," she said at last.

He looked at her and nodded.

"We're both forty now," Edith said. "I wonder whether I'll live long enough to complete my list. I wonder how much time I have, how much time *we* have."

She stopped to breathe. She could see her words standing in formation beyond Henry's view, offstage, ready to appear from behind the curtain and take the spotlight.

"I don't want to wither away, and I don't want to watch you fall apart either," Edith said. "I can't stand the thought of us getting old and decrepit, or one of us sick and the other exhausted from caregiving. And heaven help us if we get stuck in a dreadful nursing home. What I'm trying to say, Henry, is that I don't want to grow any older than necessary. I don't want to be greedy about stealing extra years that I can't use well."

Night had arrived, and the darkness outside veiled the river and the Canadian goose that had guided Edith through the day. She imagined it asleep in the reeds at the river's edge, secluded and safe. She closed her eyes for a moment and conjured the sense of wonder and peace that had filled her that morning at her desk.

"Seventy-five years is perfect," Edith said. "If I make it to the age of seventy-five, then that will be all. I will make my exit, no matter what."

Henry rubbed his fingers up and down over his lips as he always did when he pondered dire consequences. Edith sat without a sound or a twitch and endured his pause.

"Seventy-five," he said. "Yes, I see. At seventy, there's still a bit left, one would hope, and yet, by eighty, we would have risked it all to illness, accidents, surgeries, the host of problems that torment the elderly. Yes, yes. Well done, Edith. Seventy-five it is."

"And you'll go with me?"

Henry closed his eyes. There was a time for silence, and this was it. Whatever visions were moving past Henry's inner eye were not for

Edith to know. Even inside the intimacy of marriage, the sacred had to be preserved.

Henry opened his eyes and nodded his head once. Then he said, "We'll need a plan. A careful and fool-proof plan. Something tidy that won't upset the children."

"I've thought of everything already."

Henry nodded. Edith stood, kissed him, and retired to the couch across the room.

As Edith recounted this memory from her present vantage point, she did not flinch at the thought of her impending death at her own hands. The fact that she is now seventy-five and in good health has not affected her decision, she said. She confirmed that she intends to end her life when she completes her lifetime list. She also said that she has had no serious health problems to date, she remains physically active, and she has experienced no signs of forgetfulness or the mental slowing process that is common among people her age.

"I'm healthier in mind and body than most people half my age," Edith said.An interview with Edith's physician of twenty-seven years confirmed that she is in excellent health mentally and physically. She has never taken medications or had any surgeries, said her doctor, who requested anonymity for the sake of doctor-patient confidentiality.

As a resident of the State of Oregon, Edith would be entitled to choose physician-assisted suicide under the state's "Death With Dignity Act" only if she were diagnosed with a terminal illness and given six months or less to live. The amendment is now under attack by groups from the extreme right and the extreme left.

On the right, Christian activists argue for the right to life and believe that suicide is an immoral act in all cases. They want to see the state amendment repealed.

"Our God-given life is not ours to throw away," said James Curtis, president of Oregon For Life. "Those doctors are killing God's people, and it needs to stop." A petition now circulating in the state's capital has the support of more than a thousand voters, according to Curtis.

Another group, called Choose God, Choose Life, based in Portland, is organizing rallies throughout this month to raise support for their position. They, too, are hoping to overthrow the amendment.

On the other side of the issue, right-to-die activists believe that the state law does not go far enough. They seek to broaden the amendment so that residents of Oregon could choose suicide with the assistance of a doctor under almost any circumstances.

"The right to die is the ultimate human right," said Nancy Henderson, founder of the national group Death With Dignity, which was a key player in the passage of the state amendment. "Suicide is the ultimate expression of free will, especially for the elderly when the final years can drag on and bring physical and emotional suffering. With limited quality of life, the right to die becomes the only peaceful way for many in our aging population."

When asked her position on Oregon's Death With Dignity Act, Edith declined to comment. She also declined to say whether, under an expanded right-to-die law, she would seek the assistance of a doctor to commit suicide in the absence of terminal illness.

"This is deeply personal for me. This is my life philosophy, as it has been for many before me, dating back to Ancient Greece," she said. Edith claims no religious affiliation but considers herself a practicing Stoic. "I won't let my life and my choice be turned into politics or smeared in a debate between extremists. Few people have the intellectual rigor and the compassion to appreciate views like mine."

That evening thirty-five years ago, as Edith's birthday approached its end, Henry returned to his newspaper and Edith disappeared into a Dickens novel. Together they read in silence. The evening ended as most did, when they turned off the living-room lights and went upstairs to bed together.

In the morning, everything would appear as it always had. Only Edith and Henry would know how very different, in fact, it was.

* * *

Edith reached out her hand and dipped her fingers into the goldfish pond in her back yard. The sunlight carved a path through the birch branches that canopied us, and a streak of rays settled on Edith's hair. When she turned her head to the side, the sun illuminated her face. Her joy did not require a smile. It anchored itself inside rather than outside. She pulled her hand out of the water and wiped her wet fingers across her cheeks. Her senses were wide open at all times, a condition that was proving contagious. Everything smelled rich, looked bright, and felt tingly in the presence of Edith.

My second story had appeared in the latest Sunday edition, yet when I arrived for our next interview on Monday afternoon, Edith did not say a word about it. She wiped her hand on her skirt and continued her story, picking up the tale where she had left off before the weekend. A notebook lay on my lap with a pen nestled beside it. We were between chapters. The newspaper's introduction to Edith's story had made her a figure of intrigue and outrage in the newsroom and around town. Many local residents had known her for years already, but the town was growing fast, and now the influx of newcomers was getting to know Edith, too. After the first two stories, evidence appeared that storytelling did perhaps serve the public in the form of stimulation and nourishment for the mind, the soul, the human spirit, the thinking-feeling-searching part of us that is known by many names. The stories had offered some old-fashioned reading pleasure mixed with a moral challenge that many seemed to welcome. As it turned out, people still craved this, even in our high-tech, fast-paced modern world.

The truth about how Edith's tale would end was now public information, and many people were incited. Cunningham told me to direct all calls from readers to him. My job was to report and write Edith's story, not to field complaints or threats from those who saw the story as pro-euthanasia propaganda. A small group of protesters had stood outside our building that morning. Others were at City Hall, and the paper in the state's capital had reported a large crowd outside the statehouse that morning, too, though it remained unclear whether they were responding to Edith's story. The left was responding, too, with comments posted to *The Bugle's* website and phone calls to me and Cunningham that morning. Nobody complained that the stories about Edith were bourgeois or frivolous. That criticism originated and ended inside my head. Even the wealthy new population of Bend, with their high-brow taste, higher education, and mansions high on the hillsides, found Edith captivating in ways that they deemed worthy of their time. People liked to read about other people. Our fascination with one another was limitless. Our fascination with death exceeded nearly everything.

The stories served another purpose, too, that was further proof of public service in my new role. The articles had engendered a sense of community through the mutual experience of reading the same story as it unfolded. I overheard readers discussing Edith and her list at local coffee shops, in the line at the grocery store, outside city hall, and even in city-council chambers when I filled in for the new city reporter to cover a meeting when he was sick.

Edith seemed not to notice or care that she had sudden local-celebrity/local-villain status. Maybe she was accustomed to it after decades as a champion for her own cause and a rabble-rouser in a small town. My research in the newsroom archive yielded more than fifty pieces, including letters to the editors, guest editorials, and articles, written by or about Edith.

In Edith's back yard that afternoon, I listened for almost three hours, through several glasses of iced tea and with one desperate dash for the bathroom when she reached a stopping point. She spoke like a natural storyteller, including every valuable detail and omitting the excess, using transitions to move from one scene to the next, and inserting the right pause, exclamation, or element of surprise as needed. Although she often read from her handwritten books and always spoke in eloquent sentences that seemed to have been revised in her head before she uttered them aloud, Edith had never before told her story straight through from beginning to end. We were somewhere in the middle now, as Edith told me one tale after another of each completed item on her list.

The sun reached its pinnacle in the summer sky, though the heat could not penetrate Edith's backyard haven. Evergreens and birches provided shade, and cool moist air drifted off the goldfish pond and its fountain as we sat on her patio. Between us stood a low table, and on the table stood an empty glass pitcher of tea and a plate of cucumber and cream cheese sandwiches with a single crustless sandwich remaining. When I returned from the bathroom, I felt weary from listening, reached for the sandwich, and devoured it. Edith was staring into the pond as I lingered near my chair, standing in an attempt to send a message that I was done. She read the cue as if she had expected it.

Then she stood and faced me. "The list is resurrected, and I am determined to finish it, but there is a deadline." She looked at me for a long time. She was asking me to be certain, to commit once and for all. "I'm already seventy-five years old. I have about four months to finish. My birthday, as you well know, is October twenty-sixth."

There could be no second thoughts or bowing out. I needed to leave then or remain until the end. There was nothing in between, no jumping off the train until it had reached its final destination.

"You must never try to influence me," Edith said. "I need your consent, Lucy, that you will not attempt to change my mind. You must not waste my time and energy, or your own, with debates or discussions of any type regarding my decision."

I wondered whether there could be legal ramifications. I felt like an accomplice already. The moral stakes stood clear before me, as did the possibility of reactions from readers becoming more aggressive and more personal. The fact remained that I was a newspaper reporter—a truth-seeker, a writer of others' tales, a presenter of information, an explainer of who, what, when, where, why, and how—and as such, I was duty-bound to the ethical code of my profession: neutrality at all times and any cost.

Edith waited. I took my time, just as Henry had. Yet, this was a question for which no pause could be long enough. Already I had agreed. I had written the story that announced Edith's intention to kill herself, but that was not enough. Now that the truth was out there, Edith needed to know whether I could handle the ramifications, the public attention, the anger, and the controversy. There was no right answer, but there was not necessarily a wrong answer either. I closed my eyes for a moment and then nodded my head once, my consent to Edith and a salute of sorts to Henry, whose place I felt I was taking in some way, though not that way. Edith reached forward and shook my hand without another word. Then I packed my bag and left.

When I arrived home, I found Edith's volume of Shakespeare in my bag, along with a note:

For Lucy – May your book leave readers smiling through tears and searching for real truths to replace the ones they thought they knew. – With gratitude, Edith.

I would never know which book she meant—the one that I had already written but never mentioned to her, or the one that she knew I was destined to write.

TASK ONE:
THE SEARCH FOR ANTHONY RIZZO

The house perched on a hillside surrounded by a meadow and framed by woods and a sky that changed throughout the day and the year. On a still day, if the children were playing in silence, absorbed in their drawing or their fascination with a bug, the trickle of the brook at the bottom of the hill traveled up and reached the porch. On most evenings, deer emerged from the woods, sauntered through the meadows, and leapt back into the forest when the shrill laughter of little girls or the appearance of a gardener startled them. Once or twice a year, a bear appeared and ate blueberries from the bushes behind the house. The family lived in the solitude of a country setting, and yet, a mere few miles down the road, the gold dome of the statehouse glistened in the summer sun as the bustle of modern life filled the tiny capital city.

We arrived in Vermont during the first week of July. Carpets of lush grass covered the hills, and the black and white of grazing dairy cows dotted the green. The smell of cow dung hung in the air, and its semi-sweet odor was more pleasing than offensive. The sky filled through the morning with the puffy clouds of summer. As we drove along the dirt road—the final mile of a three-thousand-mile journey over desert, mountains, prairie, and lakes—the house appeared in the distance, a red cape with a brick chimney sticking out of the roof.

In the shade of a lilac tree, Edith's middle child, Rose, sat on an Adirondack chair. On her lap was the younger of her two daughters, and to her left on the broad arm of the chair with bare feet tucked beneath her mother's thigh was the eldest child. Rose held a book in one hand and stroked the smaller girl's hair with her free hand. She read to a rapt audience until the rumble of a car broke their concentration.

41

The children leapt from the chair with declarations of, "It's Grandma! She's here!" and left behind the fantasy land of childhood stories and the haven of their mother's affection.

Daisy, age six, was oldest. Her strong lean legs carried her swiftly through the front yard and landed her beside the car first. Samantha was four and ran on legs still making the transition from babyhood to girlhood, with a trace of a waddle and the wiggle of toddler chub gracing each movement. Her sister may have been faster, but Samantha made up in sound for what she lacked in speed: "NO! WAIT! DAISY! STOP!"

Their mother took her time standing from the chair. She glanced at the open book in her hands and paused as if wondering whether to note the page number. She closed the book and dropped it on the pile of plastic-covered library books on the ground. She started across the yard to greet her mother and play the role of daughter. Her hands tightened her ponytail and smoothed the stray strands of hair. She closed her eyes and inhaled. Then she opened her eyes and exhaled, sending out a soft sigh that nobody was meant to hear. The arrival of one's mother could do that to the sturdiest of grown women. Rose looked determined to wear a peaceful face and a half-smile, perhaps as armor to deflect whatever she believed might soon be flung her way. Her hair was an array of copper and gold blazing in the sunlight. Her body was lean, and she held herself straight with her shoulders back.

Edith had disclosed only the names, ages, and hometowns of her three children, one living son-in-law, one dead son-in-law, and two grandchildren. The entirety of my background research amounted to a list of seven names, seven numbers, and three places. Edith would not answer my questions. Now that the history of her list's creation had been published, she put away her journals and narrowed the flow of information. She wanted me to tell her story in my own way, free from her biases and judgments, and guided by my own observations.

"I don't want to influence your palette of colors as you paint the portraits of my family with me in the role of matriarch adventurer." That was how she spoke from Oregon to Vermont for six hours on airplanes, three hours in airports, and two hours in the car.

Her rules were consistent. Her family knew nothing about me either, other than Edith's one mention of, "I'm bringing someone with me." The girls stared at me unabashedly, as children do, while their mother stole what she believed to be hidden glances, as adults do. Edith released the girls and reached out to embrace her daughter. Their last visit had been at Christmas, I later learned from Rose. The three siblings, plus Rose's husband and two children, had gathered at Billy's house in California so their mother would not be alone for her first Christmas as a widow. Edith and Henry had made many trips together to Vermont through the years. This was Edith's first without him.

"I'm Rose. Welcome." She stretched a hand out to me, and it was strong yet moist. My literary paintbrush had already begun to portray Rose in the colors of perfection.

"I'm Lucy, from *The Bend Bugle*. I'm writing about your mother."

Edith knelt before her grandchildren and whispered in their ears. The girls giggled. Then Edith stood, reached for their hands, and with one child on each side, began to walk with them toward the house.

Rose smiled at me and shook her head. "I hope you know what you're getting into."

"She fascinates me," I said.

"Oh yes. Me, too. And yet."

We watched the threesome cross the yard toward the house, all three skipping. "I hear every word," Edith called out over her shoulder. "I may be old, but I am not deaf."

Rose and I laughed. "My mother has told me nothing about you," she said. "We've read your first two stories about her, though. Mother mailed us copies of the Sunday paper. She doesn't quite understand about the internet. She sent them to my brother and sister, too. So, you'll be writing about her list?" I nodded, and Rose sighed. "Somehow my mother wears me out, even from a distance."

The journalist's code of neutrality was beginning to feel not only impossible but pointless. This was not a city-council meeting, after all. It was a family visit at a private home. "I understand," I said. "I've spent almost every day with her for the past couple weeks." Then I sighed, too. "I've spent many hours with her today."

Playing Cello for the Trees

Rose let out a small laugh of relief. "Thanks." She put her hand on my arm for the quickest of instants, a mere pat of acknowledgement. "Please come in. The girls and I made lemonade."

The afternoon lulled us along with a tour of the house and several glasses of fresh-squeezed lemonade in the shade of the towering maple tree in the back yard. When Edith and I finished unpacking our suitcases, Daisy and Samantha escorted us to the brook, where the icy water at last brought relief to my aching feet. All four of us stomped barefooted up and down the stream. Then Edith and I sat on rocks and watched the girls splash and frolic. When their clothes were soaked, they pulled them off and sat in the stream in their underwear. Time drifted along. There was no fading daylight to announce the onset of evening. The grumble of stomachs sent us home for dinner.

Edith's clan shared her fascination with my work as a writer. From the start of our journey, when Edith knocked on my door at five o'clock in the morning for our taxi ride to the airport, I was assumed to be an expert in grammar, punctuation, usage, word origin, pronunciation, spelling, world literature, the publishing business, print journalism, the history of the printing press, and the relationship between the media and society. Edith expected me to know every text ever written and every author ever published. On the airplane, when I opened the Henry James novel that I had been slogging through, she interrogated me about his biography, reputation, and prose style, and the works of his contemporaries. When we reached Vermont and the last leg of our trip, I turned on the radio very loudly.

During our first day at Rose's house, the assumptions about my knowledge as a writer stacked even higher, with references to my presumed expertise on every language spoken on the planet (Daisy), inquiries about the role of local feature stories in the changing world of technology and online news (Rose), and consultation about the best magic marker or colored pencil for making letters with a plastic stencil (Samantha). Daisy had instant faith in my grammar skills and asked me to join her mother in an effort to fix her past-tense verbs. "I used to say 'goed,'" she told me on our walk home from the brook. "Mama tried for months to get me to stop. One day last winter, she stomped through the snow right behind me and said 'went went went went' a billion times. She was fed up. It didn't work, though. I still said 'goed.' Not on purpose. I couldn't remember. Now I remember, though, 'cause now I'm six. Back then I was only five." Still, she was finding certain past-tense verbs tricky, even for a six-year-old. "Since you're an expert, you can help me."

We were sitting down to dinner on the porch when the back door swung open, and Rose's husband, Carter, appeared. His lips were on his wife, but his eyes were on me. Rose beat her mother to the introduction.

"This is Lucy Hunt from Bend, Oregon." Rose smiled at me and then looked back at her husband, passing over Edith. "She's the reporter at *The Bend Bugle* who's writing about Mother and her list."

"Of course she is," Carter said. "I recognize the name from her byline."

Carter Emerson, the missing piece of Rose's family, had spent the day in a kayak on the Winooski River and returned home for dinner with a sun-kissed glow and the serenity of a man who had built his life with care and now had nothing better to do than enjoy it. From September until May, he lectured undergraduates in the lessons of early American history, the riveting tales of revolutionary principles and our so-called founding fathers. From May until September, and during vacations, weekends, and days when he had no classes, he ventured into the wild playgrounds throughout the state that he had selected for precisely that purpose. He kayaked, hiked, biked on dirt trails and asphalt, snowshoed, skied downhill and cross-country, and spent every moment possible in the forests, fields, mountains, rivers, and lakes of Vermont.

Rose muttered about the pot on the stove, and Carter went to get it. He returned with a large bowl of steaming corn-on-the-cob and sat down beside me. The thick scent of sweat, river water, and sunshine fell off him like invisible slabs of testosterone-infused male. His was the scent of Man with a capital M, and it brought out the woman in me faster than you could say "libido"—or "inappropriate." My face flushed in a way that it should not have while I was on duty or thinking about someone else's husband. I inhaled to snap myself back to my senses and gazed past Carter at the distant scenery. The views provided a stunning backdrop to a table full of the summer's bounty: lettuce and spinach from the garden, steamed asparagus from Rose's last harvest, and a wild-rice salad chock full of nuts and freshly picked berries.

"So you wrote the articles about Edith," Carter said.

I wiped the buttery corn kernels from my face and nodded. Edith sat across from me with a granddaughter on either side, and I was sandwiched between Rose and Carter.

"You have quite a mission," he said. He looked at his wife. "Rose told me about the list on our first date." Then his eyes shifted to me. "You're ambitious. I imagine this story will cause a stir."

He glanced at Edith, who gazed over her corncob, kept chomping, and winked. I was on my own. I preferred to do my explaining on paper, but five people, including two small ones with large eyes, were looking at me for a live response in spoken English.

"We've gotten a lot of responses from readers already," I said. "People are interested in the list, and Edith's plan for after the list has already stirred a debate. For the next few months, this is my assignment. I covered city government for five years, but now Edith is my beat."

Edith howled and clasped her hands together at her heart. "I'm her beat! Oh, heavens, what fun! What a fabulous word. I never imagined the day that I'd be a reporter's beat all by my little old self." On and on she hooted, hands pressed against her chest.

"You'll need to be impartial to Edith and her ideas," Carter said. "That sounds tough, especially at the end."

I stabbed a tomato, shoved it in my mouth, and waited for divine intervention or someone in the flesh and blood to rescue me.

"Goodness gracious, it's not as serious as all that," Edith said. "I have resurrected my list, and I plan to finish the last three items. Then I'll bid you all adieu, and that will be that. In the meantime, Lucy is here to record my adventures. She is acutely, phenomenally well suited for the job."

Daisy said, "What's adoo? What's Grandma talking about?"

We all pretended not to hear her. I could not lift my eyes from my plate, and Rose did not lift hers either, because we knew what was coming. We had heard the wind-up before, and we knew the delivery, too. The girls looked around the table. Carter stared at Edith and waited.

"I prefer to think of Lucy as a scribe, in the tradition of authentic writers, not in the pejorative sense of someone who handwrites copies of texts." Thus began the speech. All we could do was pray that it would not include song or verse. "I admire her profession to the point of envy. I knew the first time I met her that she was capable of human insights and literary creations of the highest caliber. Lucy wrote the tribute piece on Henry. It's a shame to see talent like hers stuck at a daily newspaper. Don't bother to defend yourself, dear. I understand that you do it for the public service and the paycheck, but I suspect that a book must be in the works. How could it be any other way, with your mind and your feel for language? Now Lucy is free, out in the world, witnessing life without the shackles of a newsroom and daily deadlines, as an ambitious young thinker and writer ought to. She's a modern-day Thoreau with a bit of Homer thrown in. And for the next few months, she will be my traveling companion and my scribe."

Edith's description may have been absurd, but her words held the promise of my greatest potential and described a noble target to aim for. The choice was mine: toil in pursuit of the noble target, or cower and fail.

"So, my mother is your long-term assignment?" Rose asked. "Wherever she goes, you go? Whatever she does, you write it and print it?"

I shrugged and nodded. "I'll follow her wherever the final three tasks take her, and I'll file weekly stories for the Sunday paper. I'll also write shorter daily stories about the items from the list that she has already done. And we've planned a special section at the end as a tribute and wrap-up."

Carter slammed a fist on the table, and I jumped. "Who said the newspaper is dead, huh? Alive and well. What a gig. I bet your colleagues are burning with envy."

"Some are. Others cringe at the thought of writing a big Sunday story every week for three months. And then there are those who—" I half-smiled, half-frowned, and ate some more salad. "Well, not everyone is envious."

"So, what are the three tasks, Mother?" Rose asked. "Does Lucy know? Did you bother to tell her what she was getting into?"

"Of course she knows." Edith turned to me and raised her eyebrows.

"Edith wants to do them in the order that makes the most sense to her, so we're actually starting with the last item, number thirty-five, which is to find Anthony Rizzo. He was Edith's high-school sweetheart, and she hasn't seen or heard from him since she was seventeen. I wasn't able to find much background on him, but he lives about twenty-five miles from here in the Mad River Valley."

"No kidding," Carter said. He looked at Edith. "Have you contacted him yet?"

"I called him last week," I said, as their heads swung from Edith back to me. "I explained that I was writing an article about Edith Small, formerly Edith Nelson of Tolt, Washington. He couldn't believe that she remembered him. Anyway, Edith wanted it to be a surprise, so I told him that I'd be in touch again soon."

"Let me guess. You're going to drive to his house and ring his doorbell, unannounced," Rose said.

"Precisely," Edith said.

"You'll give him a heart attack, Mother."

"Can we come, Grandma?" Daisy said. "Are you going to get married? Are we going to have a new grandpa? What's that called again, Mama? Wait. I know. A step-grandpa, right?"

We all laughed, and Samantha clapped her hands and yelled, "I want a new grandpa!"

Rose glanced at her watch. "OK, silly girls. Say goodnight to Grandma and Lucy. It's past your bedtime."

Carter scooped up Samantha, dangled her upside-down above Edith's face for a good-night kiss, and then dangled her in front of me to say good-night. As he carried her into the house, Rose picked up Daisy, whose predictable response to her sister's squealing fun in her father's arms was to ask her mother for the same. As the family disappeared inside and clamored up the stairs, their laughter drifted through the screen porch door. The sisters shared the larger of the two second-floor bedrooms, with their twin beds parallel and separated by a window and a nightstand. Bedtime was a family routine, complete with giggling, singing, and stories.

Rose emerged about thirty minutes later wearing cut-off jean shorts and a faded cotton camisole. Her hair was pulled back in a high ponytail, and she was shoving earphones into her pocket. "I'm going out to the garden. Don't touch the dishes, Mother. Carter will do them after he showers." If I ever found myself with a husband anything like hers, I reckoned I would not be out weeding while he was in the shower and the children were tucked into their beds for the night. Rose stepped off the porch and walked across the grass as Edith announced that she was retiring for the evening.

I was alone for the first time since dawn. The stillness of the evening air and the beauty of the distant views tugged at me. I stood and walked across the porch. There was an old wicker chair in the corner, but I sat instead on the top stair and gazed out at the back woods as a family of deer emerged. The mama lowered her head to the tall grasses beyond the house, and the fawn behind her did the same. The other young one stood at high alert. Her ears twitched. I heard something, too, a high-pitched shout of sorts. The mother raised her head and straightened her large ears. Another yell sounded out, and the doe turned and leapt into the forest with her children at her heels.

Rose was crouched in the garden with a black cord stretching from her shorts pocket to her ears. She was grinning, and her eyes were closed. Her head moved from side to side, and her shoulders began to wiggle. Her lips formed each syllable. A trowel sliced through the air in one hand, while the other gloved hand was free to do its own dance moves. Then her eyes opened, and her hands returned to the dirt, pulling up a weed and then another. The metal bucket was full, and she stood, walked to the end of the row, and dumped the contents over the fence. On her way back down the row of carrot tops and pea plants, she dropped the bucket and raised her face to the sky. Her hands flew upward, her feet lifted and pounded in the soil, and away she went, up and down the rows of her garden, skipping, leaping, shaking her hips, and jiggling her rear end. As I leaned forward to see her in the back rows of the garden, I lost my balance and almost lost my seat on the edge of the porch just as the door slammed.

"More dancing than weeding, from your reaction," Carter said. "I've never known anyone to get more pleasure from music than she does."

"What is it?"

"Someone whose music reaches her soul. That's what she tells me. She calls him her muse."

"Goodness."

"Right. I don't get it either, but it's fun to watch. It's a wild love affair."

"The first of its kind?"

"Oh, yes. And the last, too, according to her, seeing as he's one of a kind, 'a unique talent never to be matched.' That's another direct quote from my obsessed wife." He was gazing across the yard at her. The way she danced on her knees as she pulled weeds made him smile. "She calls it her little island of joy. No matter what's happening with the girls or her writing, she can always find solace in his music."

Carter grabbed the bowl of corncobs and a stack of dirty plates and started toward the door. Then stopped and looked at me. "Rose has an amazing ability to lose herself in something. Everything bad, her worries, life's struggles—none of it exists for her when she's lost in the music or in her poetry or out working in the garden. There's this visible serenity that washes right through her." He glanced out at the garden. "Pure human joy is a thing of beauty."

Rose blew kisses and flung them to the heavens with both hands. "I love you! I do, I really do!" she yelled. Then she crouched back down in the dirt, pulled out another weed, and waited for the next song to begin.

Later that evening, I was still alone on the back porch as the sun faded into night. My notebook lay on my lap, and my pen was poised and ready. I tried to capture in words what I had seen. *Pure human joy is a thing of beauty.* I understood Carter's awe and his envy. I wanted what Rose had, too.

* * *

Early the next morning, the girls were at the porch door about a hundred feet from where my tent stood out in the yard.

"Do you think she's scared?"

"Nope. Grown-ups don't get scared. Just imtimpidated."

"Mama's afraid of the dark. She told me."

"She probably just said that to make you feel better."

"No she did not! She IS afraid of the dark. It's the actual real truth."

"Shh! You're supposed to be quiet when people are sleeping. It's disrespectful to wake up a sleeping person."

"I AM being quiet. YOU'RE the one who's yelling."

"Now look who's yelling. I wonder if she knows that bears live in the woods."

"Yeah, and mooses and foxes and dragons."

"Yeah, but not the fire-breathing kind. They only live in England."

"We should tell her about the bears. What if one eats her?"

"Yeah, and we come out in the morning and she's gone because the bears ate her. I bet they could digest her bones in one hour flat."

"She can sleep in my bed, and I'll sleep with Grandma."

"Grandma snores."

"I don't care."

"Well, how come you get to sleep with Grandma? I don't want to sleep with *her*."

"Shh! You're supposed to whisper."

"Stop telling me what to do. I'm older than you."

"Stop calling her 'her.' We're apposed to call people their names. Mama says that's part of manners. What's her name again?"

"Lucy."

"But Grandma calls her something else."

"That's because Grandma has big ideas and big words and gets worked up about stuff. She gets all excited about how she's a really really good writer."

"Grandma's a really good writer?"

"No, you big dummy. HER. The writer."

"Oh. What's her name again?"

(Audible sigh.) "Lucy."

"Do you think she eats pancakes?"

"Everyone eats pancakes."

"But Mama said she isn't our friend. She's here for working. Maybe working people can't eat pancakes. They definitely can't eat maple syrup. It's too much sugar and it will make her crazy and then she can't focus."

"She probably drinks coffee the whole entire day. Once Auntie Alice said news people drink too much coffee and it makes them jittery and mean so they go after people with their pens."

"That's really bad. Coffee has caffeem."

"Yeah, but it's OK for grown-ups. Just kids aren't allowed to have it."

"Mama said it's a drug."

"Nuh-uh. Alcyuhol is a drug. Caffeem is only coffee."

I lay in my sleeping bag and listened to the song of their voices and the words that I imagined most kids their age did not know. If they were precocious, then precocious was good. That word had suffered an undeserved bad reputation along the way. Daisy and Samantha were deliciously, deliriously precocious, and I could have listened to their banter for hours. When I unzipped the tent and climbed out, they ran through the house.

"Mama! She's awake!"

"Grandma! Grandma! Your writer woke up! What's her name again?"

I brushed my hands through my hair as the morning dew chilled my toes. The wet grass stuck to my bare feet. I was wearing a T-shirt and pajama shorts. The official statement on me was that I was here to work, and if I was not even allowed to eat pancakes, I should not have entered through the back door barefooted and in pajamas.

Rose held a spatula in one hand and was flipping the flapjacks on the stove. "How was it out there? I'm jealous."

"Perfect," I said. "The stars are incredible here."

"Did you sleep outside your tent?" She seemed excited by the possibility, and I was sorry to disappoint her.

"No, but I lay on my back in the field for a long time before I went to sleep. Did you hear the owl last night?"

"I listen to it every night as I'm falling asleep."

Daisy and Samantha were nudging one another and yelling frantic whispers back and forth at the far end of the kitchen. When they finished their negotiations, the little one stepped forward.

"Mama, we need to tell her about the bears."

"You're worried that Lucy doesn't know that bears live near our house?"

Daisy nodded and bit her bottom lip. Samantha said, "Yes. Even though she's not our friend, we should tell her."

"Who isn't our friend?" Rose said.

"Her. Grandma's skibe. She's here for working, but we should still tell her about the bears."

Rose looked at me and winked while she loaded pancakes onto a plate. "It's true that Lucy is here to work, but she's also our new friend. Even though she's watching and listening to Grandma, we can all be friendly and get to know one another. Did I get that right, Lucy?" I nodded. "Papa and I told Lucy last night about the bears. We were concerned about her safety, too. Since she's a grown-up, she makes decisions for herself, and we respect her choice to sleep outside."

"Mama, is 'respect' the same as 'like'?" Daisy said.

I laughed even though I knew I was not supposed to. Non-parents always laugh at children when they are not supposed to.

"Respect is different from like," Rose said. "Respect is when you are accepting and polite about someone's choice even if you don't agree with it. You keep your own opinion quiet and let the other person do what she wants."

"So, we shouldn't tell Lucy how big and scary the bears are?" Samantha said. "And that they can make you dead?"

Now Rose laughed. "Lucy knows that bears are big and scary, but she also knows that they aren't likely to bother her while she's sleeping in her tent."

"I have a can of bear spray just in case," I said.

"Does it make them dead?" Samantha asked.

I glanced at Rose, and she nodded. "No," I said. "It surprises them and stings their eyes, so they run away instead of hurting you."

Edith appeared from the guest room dressed, coifed, and smelling of lavender and talcum powder. "Good morning, my dears. What a day! Look at that sunshine. And to think that I get to see dear sweet Anthony Rizzo today."

Rose placed the kettle on the burner. "He may be more wrinkled and crotchety than sweet, Mother. You're really going to just show up at his door?"

"Yes, indeed."

Edith sat at the long farmhouse-style table that appeared to be made from reclaimed wood. A bowl of fresh berries was on the table, a cup of tea and a pot of coffee were on the way, and the maple syrup was heating in the microwave oven.

"When was the last time he saw you?" Rose asked.

"September 2, 1953," Edith said. "A few days before my senior year of high school began. A month before my eighteenth birthday. That was the day he left for college out East. He graduated first in his high-school class, though there were never more than a dozen kids in each class and most of them were discouraged from paying attention to their school work. Their families needed them on the farm."

Rose carried a plate of steaming pancakes to the table. Then she stood over one daughter and then the other as she cut their pancakes and supervised the pouring of maple syrup.

"Anthony was the first person in his family to go to college," Edith continued. "He broke with tradition, left the family farm that three generations of men had run, and turned his back on everyone he knew. He had to. There could be no other way, or he would have thrown his life away. Now don't get me wrong. Farming is vital and respectable work, but a man knows whether he was built to use his hands or his mind. Anthony was destined for other work. Farming would have destroyed his spirit and left him bitter and resentful. Anthony prepared me during our two years together, and I gave him my blessing. I knew he would never be back, not for Christmas, not in the summer, not after he graduated. We wrote each other a pile of letters during the first few months, but then we stopped. We had to. I never forgot him, though. I haven't seen him in fifty-eight years, and still I wear his imprint on my heart."

Rose glanced at me and shook her head. "She wears his imprint on her heart. I hope your notebook is nearby. The story of my mother comes with its own polish and shine, free of charge. She thinks she is poetic."

"Oh, Rose, why must you be so critical? I am what I am, and I happen to adore our beautiful language. That, at the very least, is something we three have in common."

"True enough, Mother, though the purple in your words and your attire is a bit much for me."

"Goodness, this is a lot for a mother to bear so early in the morning. And before I've even had my tea." Edith sighed and fluttered her eyelashes playfully at her daughter, though I saw a flicker of pain beneath her antics.

Rose poured boiling water into the mug without a word to her mother. The tag that hung against the outside of the hand-made ceramic mug advertised "organic fair-trade black tea." Edith caressed the paper tag between two fingers and stared at it. Her long silences were as characteristic as her long speeches, a truth about Edith that, like so much else about her, made her unusual. The sting of Rose's words hung in the air, muted only by the happy chatter of the children as they chewed their pancakes soaked with butter and syrup.

Rose placed the kettle back on the burner and returned to the table, where she stopped behind her mother and kissed the top of her head. "I'm just jealous, Ma. I wish I wrote half as well as you speak." This was the first time that Rose had called Edith something other than Mother. Edith grinned, and her eyes changed back to normal.

Carter had referred to Rose's writing, but I had not dared ask. There was reporting, and then there was prying. I knew the difference. "You write?" I asked. My gut also told me when to break the rules.

Rose nodded but said nothing. Melancholy seemed to wash over her.

"She's a poet," Edith said. Yet, the poet was gone, vanished around the corner and into the bathroom with her sticky-fingered children. "And she's excellent, but she refuses to publish."

"Refuses to publish" was a phrase I had not heard. Fails to get published, remains unpublished, dreams of being published—those were familiar, and not only to me. That was the standard: to try and fail, and try again and again in pursuit of the nearly impossible. Yet, the assumption that Rose would be a published poet if she so desired was a puzzling notion.

The girls and their mother reemerged and sat at the table again.

"Grandma, can we be flower girls?" Samantha said. "We made a plan so there won't be any bickering."

Daisy shifted her eyes between her grandmother and her younger sister. At age four, Samantha dared to ask what Daisy at age six could only wonder. As the silence lingered, Daisy whisper-screamed across the table, "You're not supposed to ask. Grandma didn't even pronounce her marriage yet."

Edith tossed her head back and hooted, and Rose and I could not help but smile. Daisy's face withered with embarrassment, and her mother's face changed, too.

"You understand perfectly, Daisy," Rose said. "You surprised us with how much you know. How can a six-year-old know so much?" Rose looked at me and Edith for reinforcement. We nodded in support, but Daisy frowned and kept her eyes on her plate. "We're not laughing at you. We're delighted by you. Grown-ups aren't used to hearing words like that from a child. Should we ask Grandma about her intentions with Anthony?"

Daisy's head remained down as she shook it. "It's not our business, Mama. It's private."

"So, should we wait and see what happens? And let Grandma decide whether to tell us?"

Daisy nodded and slipped off her chair to carry her plate to the kitchen. "I'm full. Can I go play on the swing?"

Rose kissed her on the cheek. "Of course. I'll come push you in a minute."

Samantha clapped her hands and bounced in her chair. "Grandma, I think you should marry him. It's too sad to live all by yourself. I'll let Daisy be the flower girl, and I'll be the audience with Mama."

A ceramic plate crashed in the metal sink, and Daisy reappeared with her arms folded across her chest. "Stop talking about grandma's private business. Mama, tell her to stop. That is *not* OK. It's none of your business."

"It is too, because she's *my* grandma, and I don't want her to be alone. I want her to have a husband. That is too my business. Right, Mama?"

Rose stood from the table, wiped her mouth, and reached out a hand for each of her daughters. They recognized the cue. Daisy took one hand while Samantha slid off her chair and took the other. They walked out the door, across the porch, and into the yard. Rose's voice traveled through the screen door, and her words were not about rules and manners, or even about weddings and matters of the heart.

"I see red in the strawberry patch and red on the raspberry bushes. The berry plants were working hard during the night while we were asleep. Sammy, do you think berries go to sleep? Daise, what do you think? How do they manage to get red, red, red by morning?"

She released the tiny hands, and the girls fled to the garden in search of ripe strawberries and raspberries, yelling out theories about sleeping berries and the Red Garden Fairy as they flew through the grass in bare summer feet. Rose followed them to the garden's edge and talked to them over the top of the fence as they picked the ripe strawberries. I wanted to join them. I wanted to be one of them, a member of the family, maybe an older sister or an aunt, someone with a claim on them that would entitle me full access to their minds, their hearts, and the maternal nurturing that Rose offered and that everyone on the planet secretly wanted even in adulthood. I wanted to write the story before me rather than the one that I had been hired to tell. I wanted to stick my nose right between the mother and her daughters, the better to sniff the intoxicating scent of the truest affection on earth. I wanted to follow Rose through every second of her day and see with my own eyes how a woman of her intellect and creativity managed to stay engaged in the often thankless and tedious work of raising humans. One by one, the strings that attached her to Daisy and Samantha would fray or be cut. In the end, though, the invisible threads of their bond would outlast the forces that would act upon them in the years to come. Rose cocked her head and watched Daisy teach her sister the difference between a weed and a vegetable seedling. Then she listened to Samantha concoct a plan for counting the slugs captured in the beer cups throughout the garden.

I stood alone in the yard and watched them unnoticed. My work required me to stay in neutral territory. If I entered the garden, I would alter its magic. While I sat at the breakfast table, the truth of my identity separated me from the family that surrounded me. I stood alone in the grass and felt the weight of my own aloneness. My mother was gone, Ramona was across the ocean, and Charlie was imprisoned in a laboratory by choice. I relied on my father as a substitute for all the other people who should have filled my life. I remembered Edith. She would soon be ready to start the day. She would come looking for me and herd me into the car with the determination of a work dog. Alas, I was here to work, and it was time to go. I turned my back to the garden and walked toward the house.

"Are you leaving already?" Rose called out. I stopped and looked at her. The girls were at her feet, handing her one strawberry after another.

"Mama, take this one. It's HUGE!" Daisy said.

"And this one, too, Mama. It's red, red, red. The most reddest in the whole entire garden," Samantha said.

I nodded and waved. She waved back at me. "She can't drag you to Anthony Rizzo's house every day," Rose said. "We'll be sure you get a day off. Right, girls?" Daisy and Samantha looked across the yard at me as if trying to recall where they had seen me before as they popped berries into their mouths.

When I stepped inside the house, Edith was singing in the guest room downstairs. The tune was the same one that she had hummed when I took too long to pay for my snacks in the airport or while I was waiting for my suitcase to appear on the baggage-claim conveyor belt after hers had already arrived. The happy tune that sang out her kindness and bliss for all the world to hear had for me become an alarm ringing out another deadline and a warning to hurry up, lest I delay the next chapter in Edith's story.

I showered on turbo, pulled on a summer dress that I hoped would announce me as professional but friendly, and checked my bag for notebooks and pens. The last time I had used a tape recorder was at graduate school, my year at journalism boot camp. Daily deadlines and weekly assignments had dominated my schedule that year. The professors taught us to rely only on paper, pens, and our own powers of observation. For my long-form master's project, however, the rules changed. The advisor told us to use a tape recorder for back-up during interviews of our main subjects. I still had the tapes of the three novelists that I interviewed for my thirty-page piece about immigrant writers and multi-culturalism in publishing. My fate was clear even back then, but I kept turning away from it and toward my resume. Solid credentials would lead me to a paycheck. Literature may have been my true love, but my upbringing and a sense of duty and independence told me to follow the path to a normal job and the stability it would bring. A novel would lead only to dead ends. Even now, though, I could still hear the voice of the novelist who had been that year's literary star: "Toil!" Work as hard as you can at what you love, he had said. Work to make the writing the best it can be. Work to transcend yourself; the work itself is all that matters.

"Ready?"

Edith was calling to me from the living room. I had my tape recorder in one hand, my bag beside me, and my head full of distant memories. My abandoned manuscript was stowed in a desk on the other side of the country. I wondered what Rose wrote. I was curious about the themes and the words visited by a woman who credited her flamboyant mother with English superior to her own, and yet whose mother in return claimed that the daughter refused to publish publishable poetry.

"Lucy, dear, are you ready?" Her voice was closer now. I looked up, and she was standing in the doorway with her head cocked as she watched me place the tape recorder in my bag and close the buckle.

"Ready," I told her. "For anything."

* * *

We drove along one dirt road after another, moving deeper into the countryside and deeper into silence. I tried to enjoy the quiet but found it more unsettling than peaceful. I had never seen Edith nervous and did not know how severe the symptoms could become. We wound through the woods until at last we turned into a driveway with a mailbox marked Rizzo. The engine fell silent, but Edith's hands continued to grip the steering wheel. She inhaled and closed her eyes. Then she exhaled, opened the car door, and stepped out. I stumbled out of the car and hurried down the path behind her. She rang the doorbell and waited without a glance my way. The heroine had taken center stage, and I was left with a notebook, a pen, and a seat in the back row, my perennial location. She rang the bell again, and the front door swung open.

A man of average height and bulky weight with shaggy white hair and boxy black glasses stood before us. He made no effort at a friendly welcome, nor did he appear surprised or confused. He looked at Edith and then over her shoulder at me as if waiting to learn what product we were peddling or which politician we endorsed.

"Hello, Anthony. I hope you'll pardon this unannounced intrusion. I'm Edith Small. You knew me as Edith Nelson of Tolt, Washington. From high school, Anthony. It's me, Edith."

Only his eyeballs betrayed him. They darted maniacally as the machine of his memory turned the wheels of time back through the years in search of the girl that had grown into the old woman who stood before him on the front step of his retirement home.

Edith showed even less of a reaction. Action was her forte. With her prepared lines and poised stance, she loomed too large to allow space for anyone else, including the person that she had chosen as her leading man. She wanted him to look at her. She wanted to be the star of her own show. Then I saw the quiver along her jaw line and the shaking hands at her sides. To shake was human. Edith was, alas, one of us.

"Edith Nelson. Of Tolt, Washington. Well. I'll be…"

His voice was steady even as it dropped off into nothing. Edith broadened her smile and interlocked her hands at her chest like a soprano preparing to launch into song. For Edith song, sonnet, or soliloquy was possible at any moment. Anything was possible, anything except the wild card that was not hers to play. She had rehearsed for this moment. She had composed and practiced her lines with the theatrical finesse true to her nature. Yet, nothing could prepare her or anyone else for the unknown that was another human being's reaction. Her hands and face trembled beneath a false smile of nerves.

"I always hoped that you'd come looking for me," Anthony said.

Edith opened her mouth and then closed it. The smile was gone, along with the quiver and the shaking. The man that she had remembered with fondness for more than half a century had wanted her to find him.

"Nobody has called me Anthony since high school," he said. "Anthony was the boy my mother raised, the boy destined to run the family farm and read Scripture every Sunday. I'm afraid you won't find him here. Tony is the man I've been since I left all that behind."

He gazed out over our heads into a distance that contained the images of an abandoned past, as if the snapshots of his youth were hanging behind us from the branches of the birches and pines that lined his property, and his squinting could bring them into focus. He wiped one hand across his mouth and then scratched his forehead at an itch that did not exist. When at last he emerged from the past, he remembered his manners in the way that one suddenly remembered a pot boiling on the stove. He looked at Edith, really looked at her.

"Forgive me," he said. "This is unexpected. This... recalling the past. Somewhere along the way I turned into a grouchy old recluse. I can't imagine why you've come. Is there something you need?"

Edith cleared her throat. It was a soft and gentle clearing, the sort that did not fix a clogged passageway but meant she was preparing. I surveyed the lilac bushes and the woods for a hiding place. There was no stopping her once she got started.

"If your heartaches seem to hang around too long
And your blues keep getting bluer with each song
Remember sunshine can be found behind the cloudy skies
So let your hair down and go on and cry."

I scribbled the lyrics in my notebook and drew a question mark in the margin. I had never heard the song and could not guess whether her crooning and slow syllables were an imitation of the original recording or her signature touch. As Edith warbled on, the question mark came to represent not only my idle curiosity about the song but also my perplexity regarding the singer. I lifted my eyes and took a peek. She was plowing ahead with her scheduled program with utter disregard for her audience, unaware of the discomfort in his eyes and the awkwardness in his lopsided stance. As she sang, his eyes grew cloudy. When she finished, he dabbed at them with a thick dirty hand.

"That song was all I heard during my first semester at college," he said. "I imagined you sitting at your bedroom window during the last warm nights of summer and staring at the moonlight on the hills as you cried. I cried every night for weeks. I waited until my room-mate was asleep, and then I turned toward the wall and let it out. God, I wanted you there with me, Edith. I wanted you so badly, but where would that have gotten us? Married as teenagers? Parents before we reached the age of twenty? I wanted to see you, but that would have made a bigger mess, so I stuffed it down, and I convinced myself that it was for the best. I told myself to forget you, that you had forgotten me, that it was silly kids' stuff. And it was, wasn't it, Edith? Wasn't it just a bunch of silly kids' stuff? Going to the drive-in. Dancing to the hits on the radio. Smoking our cigarettes and strolling through town arm-in-arm as if we were someone and being together meant some-thing. First love, Edith. That's all it was. We were right to move on and let it go. You were smart to stop writing to me, to forget about me and make a life for yourself. You did make a life for yourself, didn't you? I always figured you would. That's the kind of girl you were."

Anthony stepped forward and opened his arms, an eighteen-year-old trapped in an old man's shell. He took another step toward her. Edith walked into his arms, and he whispered, "Sing it again." And so she did, as her sweet Anthony held her in his arms as she had dreamed he would. He started to sing, too, and they swayed to the melody of their gentle duet. Edith's skirt clung to the leg of his trousers and re-vealed a patch of withered pearly-white skin below her knee. They danced as though they had been dancing together through the decades. They sang together as if this were the next in a long series of concerts. They were a princess and her prince in wrinkles and gray hair united in the magic of their fairy-tale. I thought of Henry and wondered whether Edith was thinking about him, too. He had stood by her through graduate school and pregnancies, childbirth and family, the creation of her list, and years of Shakespeare, foreign-language tapes, a trip to the equator, and much more. While the romance of resurrect-ed teenage love swayed before me, the less flashy love of marriage stayed fixed in my mind. The concept of adultery died along with the husband, and yet something felt not quite right. I slipped backward one step at a time and sat on an old tree stump nestled at the edge of the woods. Swarming around me and crowding my head, beckoning me and battling for my attention, I saw words. They floated by on the clouds and roosted in the branches of the trees. All I had to do was reach up and take the ones that I liked best and needed most. Here at last was a story, a real-life tale, that was theirs to live but mine to write.

* * *

We walked in the woods behind Anthony's house for more than an hour. He and Edith tossed biographical facts back and forth, and he identified nearly every tree, plant, flower, vegetable, and fruit growing on his ten acres. Then he invited us inside for refreshments, and we settled into armchairs in his living room. We sipped ginger ale over ice with sprigs of mint from the garden, and Anthony passed around a plate of oatmeal cookies that he had baked that morning. The house was tidy and spotless, a fact that Edith noted. Anthony responded with the honesty of a man who was too worn out to put on airs: "A cleaning lady comes every Friday. Sometimes she's the only soul I see all week." His despair plopped itself down in the middle of the room with a resounding thud. We stared in awkward silence and wondered what to do with it. Edith smiled onward. I fumbled through my notebook for the next blank page and pressed the record button on the digital recorder that my father had given me as a parting gift.

"My wife died twenty years ago of breast cancer," Anthony began. "I buried myself in work, and by the time I came up for air, I was too old, fat, and sad to bother with women and dating. My sons, Jeffrey and Raymond, were already grown and living their own lives when their mother died. Jeff flew in from Tokyo, where he had been teaching English for a couple years. He stayed with me for a week, and then he was gone again. I was still in Maine then, in the house the boys grew up in on the coast. During their college years, the ocean kept them around in the summers. They both liked to kayak, and they'd be gone paddling for hours, each in his own boat but always together. Every year, they became more and more different from each other, but the ocean was their mutual love. The kayaks kept bringing them back together, even when they fought about politics and careers and women.

"After college, Jeff traveled the world and fell in love with Japan and a Japanese woman. I'm lucky if I see him once every couple of years. Japan. Who would have thought that a middle-class white kid from Maine with a degree in philosophy would land in Tokyo and stay forever? He has two children. My grandchildren are Japanese. I never would have guessed it.

"Ray graduated with an economics degree, went straight into an MBA program, bought a one-way ticket to Wall Street, and never looked back. That was the end of him, as far as I'm concerned. He fell in love with money and eventually got himself a wife and three kids, plus a nanny and a housekeeper to do the work that the rest of us call life. I see him twice a year. He doesn't come here. Once a year I drive down, and he takes me to fancy restaurants and expensive performances. His maid does my laundry every day. *Every* day. I don't know what that is. I don't know how that could be my son. A live-in maid and a nanny raising his kids. His wife works for a magazine, puts in sixty hours a week, and glues the cell phone to her ear the whole time she's home. She's the deputy editor of some fashion magazine. I forget which one. I know it matters, but I can't remember. When their children were babies, they would see them for an hour at dinner time, kiss them good night, and hand them back to the nanny. Every winter for the past ten years they've sent me a plane ticket to meet them on some foreign beach for pina coladas and lobsters. Lobsters from Maine. It's the goddamn saddest funny thing I ever heard of, going to their island resort to eat a lobster that was caught in the town where I lived half my life. They never saw the humor. They aren't the types to see humor.

"All I ever wanted was to play with my grandchildren, but now they're too old, and when they were little, I couldn't get them away from the nanny long enough to find out who they were and what they liked. Two little girls, now two young women with nothing to offer their aging grandfather other than the yearly Christmas photo of their smiling faces."

Anthony stopped and sipped his ginger ale. He smacked his lips and shook his head after each swallow. Edith watched him with folded hands and a face that encouraged him to continue.

"I worked in management for forty years, at an insurance company. Forty years. I can't believe that was me, sitting at a desk, talking on a telephone, leading meetings, day after day. I did it for the same reason that everyone has ever done it and is still doing it. I thought I had to. I did it to pay the bills and keep up with the mortgage and make sure there were vacations and music lessons and summer camps and a nice dinner out with my wife on our anniversary and her birthday. I did it because I had stopped thinking about anything else. I stopped believing that there was anything else. I couldn't see anything except the road before me as I commuted to work every morning and back home every evening. I was a mouse moving through the maze to try to get the cheese. In the end, though, the cheese was nothing. The cheese was another paycheck, and another after that. There I sat at my sons' high-school graduations and college graduations, clapping and grinning at their success, which I believed, as every parent does, to be my own success, a mark of my self-worth and a job well done in raising them. I slapped them on the back and escorted them down the path to their own future cheese. Another day, another dollar, another life wasted on the empty dream of success and family, mortgage and vacation, bonuses and retirement planning. Was I happy? Was I ever happy? Yes, I was. I was happy for one brief moment before I understood what my life was. That is the only moment that any of us is ever happy—the instant before everything becomes clear, before we see what we really are."

He looked at Edith. He looked at me. He drank the rest of his ginger ale.

"When my wife died, I started listening to music. I listened for hours. I wanted to know what I was hearing, see the notes, understand what the composers and the musicians were expressing. The music became my cheese, and I got through each day with the goal of getting home to my music—symphonies, quartets, concertos, opera, all of it. The day I retired, I bought a cello, and the next day I took my first lesson. I have been playing ever since. For eleven years, I've lived alone in this house and played the cello. I open the windows, even in the winter, even in the snowstorms, and I play music for the trees. I imagine the pines and the maples and the birches bending their trunks to lean in closer and listen. The veins in their leaves and the spikes of their needles drink in each measure of Mozart and Bach in silent appreciation. They are nourished by the sweet melodies and transformed by the thundering overtures. Some days I play as loudly as I can to reach more of them, farther out, deep in the woods. Some days I play quietly, and they must lean their spines and stretch their limbs as they strain to listen. Of course I know that trees cannot hear. What imbecile cannot see that trees lack ears. I think they sense it, though. I really do. I think the trees have some sort of experience of the music, and this is the belief—the dream, the beautiful idea—that has carried me through each day for all these years. Playing cello for the trees has become the one true joy of my life. My bliss. My peace. This is how I spend my time. I'm not chasing anything anymore. This is what I am. Playing cello for the trees."

In the months that followed, I read Anthony's words again and again. Somewhere along the way I entitled his long monologue, "Playing Cello for the Trees." Art imitates life, yet life itself is an unlimited artistic masterpiece, beautiful with its infinite and unique imperfections. Whenever I read Anthony's speech, I thought of the writers who had come long before me and of the novelists in particular. I scoffed at them, and I felt shame before them. They invented their characters, composed lines for them to speak, and created lives for them to live. Anthony, however, was real. All I had to do was type his words and write my name at the top. I did not know what that made me.

When forty-seven seconds had passed—my digital recorder kept time—Edith broke the silence. "Play for us," she said. "And if you feel too shy, then we will walk off and disappear among the trees, and you may play for your trees and forget about us."

Anthony ate another cookie. I waited for the usual routine where the musician feigns humility or claims his talent insufficient to please the audience. I waited for him to need to be begged or to reject the request and steer us in another direction. He sipped some more ginger ale. Then he stood, left the room, and returned a moment later with his cello and bow. He gestured with a sideways tip of his head toward the patio, and we followed him through the French doors into the haven of gardens, meadow, and forest. He sat alone in a straight-back wooden chair, and he seemed no longer to need us or even to notice us. Edith wandered off through the apple trees and perennial gardens that exploded with pink peony blossoms and white daisies. I scanned the back yard until I found a stone wall along the left side that separated the grass from the forest. I sat alone. My notebook, pen, and tape recorder were inside the house.

I recognized the opening notes right away not because I was a connoisseur of classical music but because Edith had played her cello for me before our trip. In the early years of her list, she learned to play the violin, and once she had mastered the basics, she tackled the cello. Years later, she abandoned the violin after she achieved her goal of performing Vivaldi's *The Four Seasons*. By all accounts, she played badly. The video of the concert proved that she had made a prudent choice when she retired her violin. Yet, in the cello she discovered lasting joy. For more than thirty years, she had played most mornings for an hour. A firm believer in the power of practice and the need to put in one's time, Edith claimed that she had played the cello "abominably" for the first ten years. After she had accumulated the requisite number of practice hours, however, her ability improved, and her playing had an ease that sounded natural. She argued against the idea of being a natural at anything. There was only discipline, commitment, and work, she insisted. The first time that she played her cello for me, her introductory speech was twice as long as the Bach suite that followed. She expressed her disdain for the notion of an overnight success in the arts. "An overnight sensation," she said, in fact meant that the artist had spent ten years, or perhaps twenty, mastering and refining her work until one day someone happened to notice it, like it, and admire it publically in order to draw others' attention to it. The intersection of the public and the private made no sense to Edith when it came to the arts. She was content to play her cello for her own satisfaction. The music had started to sound good sometime around the fifteen-year mark, and her sense that she was skilled and accomplished pleased her without any need to make the experience public. Edith's theory disturbed me. There was no way to apply it to literature and land in a peaceful place. An unpublished novelist was not much of anything except a person with a bunch of pages that she happened to have written. I wanted to crumple the word "accomplished" like a failed page of a first draft and throw it out a figurative window. Writing was my only accomplishment, and yet unpublished novelist was the only title I could claim outside of newspaper reporter.

Playing Cello for the Trees

Anthony moved the bow across the strings of his cello, and I lifted my head to gaze at him. My thoughts had carried me far away from the music. We could never regain the time that we lost while we wandered through our own thoughts. I was glad to be back. I watched his face and listened to the mournful song. The last note drifted up from the patio, down across the wildflowers, and out into the trees. My eyes stopped on a distant birch whose limbs swayed in the soft summer wind like the delicate hovering arms of a ballerina. The papery white trunk had a slight bend in its middle, and the tree's tip seemed to lean inward toward the yard and the patio, as if searching for the source of the fading notes. A burst of air ruffled the branches, and the rushing and tapping of one leaf against another resembled the applause of an admiring audience.

Anthony looked up from his cello and out at the birch tree. He watched the leaves dance and bowed his head in recognition.

* * *

Our drive back to Rose's house was quiet. When we arrived at the little red house on the hill, two car doors opened, two weary travelers exited, two car doors closed. "Hello, and good night," were Edith's only words to Rose when she crossed the threshold and vanished into her room for the night. Rose's face betrayed no curiosity. She would not give her mother that satisfaction.

The children were asleep upstairs in their beds. Saxophone music wafted through the screen porch door. The silhouette of a hand lifted a stemmed glass to lips.

"Will you join us?"

Rose stood at the kitchen counter with an empty wine glass in one hand and a full bottle in the other. I nodded, and she got another glass. Like a child trailing the Pied Piper, I followed her through the house and out to the porch, magnetized by the wine, the jazz playing in the darkness, and the silhouetted hand. As I sat on a cushioned wicker chair, my age made itself known, and I struggled to get comfortable under the weight of four older eyes. I had nothing of value or interest to offer a married couple whose wisdom and experience dwarfed mine by a decade. I felt like an exchange student from a foreign land known as Confused Humans On The Brink Of Age Thirty. Our chairs formed a triangle that placed us equidistant from each other, though equality of any sort was impossible. I expected them to laugh and tell me to get the hell off their porch. I gazed at the star-dotted sky and the woods a hundred feet away. Rose filled a glass and handed it to me.

"Cheers," she said.

"Cheers," I muttered.

"Here's to checking the first mission off your list," Carter said. He clinked my glass and smiled. I tingled despite myself and prayed silently to Rose for forgiveness.

"Actually, I think today was more of a beginning than an ending."

"Oh?" Rose said. We both looked at her, and she shrugged off her own transparency. Sometimes the need to know was stronger than a desire for aplomb. "Has my mother fallen in love again already?" She was trying to sound playful, but her shoulders stiffened and her mouth tightened.

"The day was not without melodrama," I said.

"I see. Do you care to expand, or is it unfair of me to ask?"

"Of course it's unfair to ask," Carter said. "She's a journalist. She isn't going to break your mother's trust and tell us what happened."

I resumed my gazing at the sky. Rose was extraordinary in many ways, but I did not expect any woman to show me kindness when her husband came to my defense.

"Oh, come on, Carter. Lucy said it. Melodrama is my mother's game. She's playing with me. She's dying to tell me, and she knows I want to hear all about it, but she's going to make me wait just for dramatic effect."

"I think they've loved each other their entire lives," I said. I was still gazing out at the night sky, where I saw Edith and Anthony dancing. I heard his soliloquy and his cello, and I saw her sadness as she listened to the story of his past. "Most people romanticize the past. They romanticize romance. This is different. They didn't fall in love today. They've always loved each other."

Carter and Rose were staring at me agape, a rare expression for them.

"Wow," said Carter.

"Jesus," said Rose.

They were captivated, and I could have done with them whatever I wished. I could have told them the entire story of our day, but despite my power and their captivation, it was not mine to tell—not then, not like that. Like everyone else who wanted to know Edith's story, they would need to wait and read it in the paper.

"That's extraordinary," Carter said. "You ought to open your mouth more often." He winked at me, and I lifted my glass and took a very long drink. My reaction to red wine was a child's disgust and a choking reflex. I tried to pretend that their pinot noir was lovely. I wanted a beer.

"You think she *loves* him?" Rose said. "That raises a lot of questions. About her marriage to my father. And whether she really hasn't had contact with this man all these years."

I started to defend Edith, but Carter beat me to it.

"You can say whatever you want about your mother, but she is loyal and authentic. There's no way she would have cheated on your father, not even in her mind. She loved your dad, she loved you kids, and from everything I've ever seen, she always lived a genuine life with all of you. So, she loves Anthony, too, and maybe she always has. So what? We can love more than one person, right? That doesn't mean she wanted to be with him and not with your dad. They were high-school sweethearts. What could be more innocent? She probably forgot about him most of the time. Anyway, if she wants to spend the rest of her life with him, what's the harm?"

Rose sat up fast, and the wine sloshed around her glass and splashed onto the porch floor. "Well, you have it all figured out, I see. Christ, Carter, what are you talking about? Spend the rest of her life with him? Her life is about to end, remember? Which makes this reunion cruel, if the man actually has feelings for her. She wants to control everything, and for her, that means being alone and then being dead. Of course she loved my father. I don't need anyone to tell me that. That's why this is so disturbing. I mean, what's the point of seeing this man now? Why does she want to stir up the past?"

Then she was crying, and her head was on Carter's chest. He stroked her hair as she wept for her dead father and a mother she would never understand. I slinked off the porch and wandered into the meadow. A woman weeping in her husband's arms was no place for me, with or without a notebook and pen.

* * *

The next morning when I stepped inside the house, an eerie silence greeted me. The stillness was creepy, not peaceful. In a house with two young children, an opinionated old lady, a spirited woman, and a man who enjoyed conversation, the lack of noise disturbed me. The table top and kitchen counters showed no lingering signs of breakfast. I looked at the clock and panicked: it was after nine. Disoriented and groggy from too much sleep, I trudged into the living room and peered through the windows in a manic need for information. Carter's car was gone. Edith's car was gone. I stood still and listened. Nothing. The story was moving forward without me. My subject had run off on her own. The protagonist had ditched the narrator.

I tiptoed back to the kitchen, careful not to make a sound, as if being abandoned embarrassed me and I did not want the house to notice. I paused when I reached the kitchen, but I was too distraught to eat, so I kept moving. I walked out onto the porch. The rush of cool morning air relaxed me. I breathed and looked across the yard. Rose was crouched in the garden, her face framed by two tomato plants and her hands resting on her bare legs. Her eyes were closed, and her lips were moving. I was too far away to see the cord of her earphones or the plugs in her ears, but I knew they were there. I moved toward her and heard her singing. I walked closer, and her singing grew louder. She was trying to sing well, to provide the perfect complement and create, if only for herself, a beautiful duet, performed live in her garden with all the world and nothing at all as her witness. When she opened her eyes and saw me, the blush in her cheeks and the fidgeting of her hands told me that I had stolen something private from her. She pulled off the earphones and shoved them in her pocket. I stood outside the garden fence.

"I'm sorry to interrupt," I said.

She wiped a dirty gloved hand across her nose, and a black smudge appeared. "I've been waiting for you. I'm the one who owes you an apology."

I shrugged and shook my head a little. My mother had taught me to accept apologies by looking at the person's face and saying, "Thank you. I forgive you." I did not feel capable of that with Rose.

"I was out of line last night," she said. "I'm sorry. I shouldn't have asked you about my mother. My reaction had nothing to do with you. I have a hard time with her. I always have."

I told her it was alright. She shook her head.

"I was very close to my father. I tended to side with him. It wasn't easy growing up with a self-absorbed mother. Her eccentric ways and her big visions make her beautiful. They're who she is, but they're hard to take in one's mother."

I nodded. "She left without me."

"I'm not surprised."

"I can't write her story if I'm not there to see what happens."

Rose tossed the trowel on the ground and walked to the gate. "You're welcome to take my car."

Maybe I should have gone. That was my job, after all, my responsibility, my reason for being there. Yet, I was too annoyed with Edith to chase her and too excited by the prospect of spending time alone with Rose to miss the chance. I shook my head. "It's only one day. I haven't had a day off in a while."

"You sure? I could go with you."

That could have been interesting. I pondered and then shook my head.

"Well, then, I guess you're stuck with me. Carter took the girls to the lake for the day." She glanced at the trowel, as if weighing its importance given the change in events. "Come on." She lifted two buckets of vegetables and headed for the house. I trailed behind, like one of her children, eager to be with her, excited to know what was next, and glad to go along with whatever she proposed.

When we reached the porch, she turned to me and gestured toward the same chair where I had sat last night. "Wait here, OK?"

Edith's absence nagged at me. In fact, I was not one to sit around on a porch idling away the day. I reconsidered borrowing Rose's car. Edith and I would need to agree on some basic ground rules.

"I've never done this before." Rose reappeared holding two champagne glasses filled with something yellowish and fizzy. "They're mimosas. I thought we could re-do last night."

Maybe champagne would not make me choke. As I sipped, my lingering sense of duty to chase after Edith and get to work started to fade. Everything was vanishing: Edith, Carter, the girls, even the notion of letting yesterday end and today begin. Rose had invited me to time-travel with her and re-create a moment. She was more like her mother than she would ever admit.

"Cheers," I said.

She tapped her glass against mine and sat down across from me in the same chair as last night. Then she held up a remote control and pressed a button. "Just one song," she said. "I think you'll like him."

A few chords of guitar music traveled from the kitchen out onto the porch. Then a sad voice sang the despair of lost love, and Rose leaned her head back, closed her eyes, and sang along. I had been in love once, and I had been in a relationship once. Two different kinds of love, two very different guys. That was the extent of my personal knowledge on the subject. I may not have known about marriage, but I knew that people were very good at hurting each other whether they meant to or not. I sipped my mimosa and drifted away.

The livelier mood of the next song returned Rose to the moment and to me. She sipped her drink and raised her eyebrows at my empty glass. As she went to the kitchen to pour another round, she turned up the volume. The lyrics were poetry, and the poet was playful, wise, and a bit snide all at once. Some people knew exactly what to do with words. The more I noticed the lyrics, the more I admired the writer. Rose handed me my re-filled glass as she sang along. Calm and comfort moved through her. Whatever could do that for anyone was a blessed gift. If only for fleeting moments, our passions made us forget the loneliness of being alive and the burden of being ourselves. I knew what made me feel the way Rose looked. Nobody would ever see it, though. Writing was not performance art or spectator sport.

The song ended, and Rose finished her drink. Then she plunked her glass on the table and sighed with a hint of her mother's dramatic flair.

"I'm really sorry, Lucy, but I have to go." She looked at me as if seeking my permission. "The first line of a poem just came to me. I can't risk losing it."

I nodded to the empty space before me. The poet was already gone, headed to her desk, unable to wait a minute longer to move the words from her mind through her pen onto paper. I knew the feeling, and I missed it more than anything.

* * *

We ate lunch on the porch amidst chatter about the blossoming irises, Rose's homemade raspberry vinaigrette, and Anthony's opinion of the state capital. I was trying to show good manners, but enough was enough. Edith had some serious explaining to do.

"So, what did you two do all morning?" I asked at last with a distinct glance at Edith and her left hand.

"Let's see," she said. "We had breakfast on Anthony's patio. An asparagus frittata and fruit salad. Scrumptious. While we were eating, we saw a family of deer and the cutest little brown bunny. Then we went for a long walk in the woods. And later we stopped in town to wander around the shops and such before we came here."

Rose was smearing homemade dill hummus on the bread that she had baked earlier that morning. Her mother's "and such" had not caused a ripple on Rose's surface. Her patience and composure clashed with the news that glared at us from Edith and Anthony's fingers. My piercing glance at Anthony made him squirm. He cleared his throat, and I silently wished him good luck trying to nudge Edith in any direction for any purpose at any time. She was unnudgeable, a fact that he should have known before making a commitment of the type represented by a gold band.

Edith turned to him and raised her eyebrows. "Well, we do have some exciting news," she said. She looked with intentional emphasis first at her daughter and then at me. Only when she had our full attention with our collective eyebrows raised did she proceed with the obvious. "We got married! Anthony and I decided to fulfill our destiny. We are, at last, husband and wife."

Rose kept her eyes on her salad bowl, where her fork poked around and then stabbed with a force beyond what was necessary for even the most stubborn lettuce leaves. The tines were full, and she raised them to her mouth, stuffed and shoved, and began to chew. The three of us sat in silence and stillness as she swallowed, sipped her seltzer, and wiped her mouth.

"Congratulations," she said. "I wish you both great happiness in your coming *months* together. That's still the plan, right, Mother? I wonder whether you mentioned that detail to your new husband before you promised him forever."

Now there were two of us squirming as daughter and mother engaged in battle.

"Sarcasm is a sign of a weak mind," Edith said. "I expect better from you, Rose. You have always been the most intelligent member of the clan. That's one fact that I assume we can agree on." She paused to take Anthony's hand in hers. She held it on the table as if to reassure any doubters. "Of course I explained my plan. Anthony respects my wishes. He said anything is better than nothing."

I glanced at Anthony and cringed on his behalf. One look confirmed that he was busy with copious cringing of his own. For a man who just got married and had reportedly professed his joy at the chance for a few months with his new wife, Anthony failed to embody nuptial bliss. His face was twisted. He looked like he was going to vomit.

"That's an extraordinary attitude, Anthony," Rose said. The sarcasm was gone. "I know how important you have been to my mother for many years. She's very lucky to have found you again at last."

The job of narrating this drama fell to me, but the story did not have a chance of finding its way into ink. Only divine intervention could show me how to recreate this unfolding saga in a coherent narrative without judgment, criticism, or disdain. The journalist was supposed to stand off to the side and stay out of the way of the story. I was not capable of miracles or heroics of that magnitude. I stood from my chair and walked down the porch steps, across the yard, through the field, onto the dirt road, and as far away from Edith as my legs would take me.

* * *

Darkness fell, and Carter appeared, my knight in khaki shorts and a T-shirt. He walked through the front door of the local bar where I had landed. For hours, I had wandered along dirt roads and trails

75

through the woods until gravity pulled me downhill into town. Efforts to find missing people increased when the sun went down, as I knew from years sitting beside our police reporter. He got stuck working late more often than anyone else at the paper. I imagined the motley gang on the porch of the little red house gazing at the blaze of color across the western sky, the girls running through the yard in pajamas and bare feet, when someone, probably Rose or Anthony, proposed to look for me. I imagined Edith replying, "She'll be back when she's ready. She can figure this out herself, if she so chooses."

I had no plan when I left during lunch. In fact, I did not know that I was leaving until I was already gone. I let the fates guide me, and as it turned out, the fates were as thirsty for a beer as I was. How I would get from my bar stool back to the house and whether anyone there cared anyway had not occurred to me until I saw Carter.

"Keeping with tradition?" He was standing beside me. I could smell him.

"What tradition is that?" I did not look at him.

"You're hardly the first writer to head to a bar when the work isn't going well," he said.

I was in no mood to smile. I looked down at the paper napkin beside me and the words that I had written in an attempt to find a title for Edith's story. The copy editors would supply the headlines for each news story that I filed, but I had something else in mind now. Something new. Something big.

"That's a tricky character you're dealing with," Carter said. "You must miss your novel. At least those characters stay put. They can't run off without you and get married."

He waited for a smile or a laugh, but when I got stubborn, I was a force to be reckoned with. Edith and I had that much in common.

"Rose thinks you're angry at Edith, and Edith thinks you're grappling with existential questions."

I guzzled the last of my beer with tremendous gusto to show Carter how little I cared about what he was saying. Existential questions had nothing on the existential goodness of beer.

"I thought I knew something about life," I said. "But I don't. I don't know anything at all."

I had not intended to demand a Meaning Of Life conversation, least of all with a toothsome family man who had been sent to rescue me from myself. I did not want to be the drunk twenty-something teetering on the edge of her bar stool like a bad metaphor for the state of her life. I did not want to be the fool on the verge of her thirtieth birthday looking for answers in a pint of beer. I did not intend to play any of these roles. Yet, there I was, wobbling on a bar stool without an inkling of who I was, what to do, or what life was all about. I missed Ramona. I wanted to hold her hand and walk the cobbled streets of Bratislava.

Carter sat down on the stool beside me. "Could I get a pint of porter?"

Before us stood the bartender, my old friend who had refused for hours to dispense any insights but had smiled in silence and nodded at my efforts to climb my way out of the pit of despair that I had fallen into.

"And water and a plate of pasta for her," Carter said. The bartender nodded once and took my empty pint glass. Carter watched me watch it disappear. "You should sober up a bit."

"I'm exactly as sober as I want to be."

He laughed a little and shook his head. "If you're looking for spiritual guidance, I'm not your guy. The only big truth I can tell you is that life is filled with moments of joy, but most of the time it's pretty mundane. Sorry to break it to you."

He stopped and looked at me, maybe for approval or at least permission to keep talking, but I just sipped my water. I had no spare reassurances to hand out.

"Life is repetitive and boring, and it's very hard," he said. "I happen to believe, though, that we have a lot of control over our lives and our thoughts. Are you sick of writing about Edith? Are you disappointed that she isn't who you thought she was? Are you angry that the story has taken on a life of its own? You have two options: change what you're doing, or change how you think about it. You have a good mind, Lucy. Use it well. Keep it clear. Steer your own thinking."

I ran my finger down the side of my water glass from top to bottom, then back to the top for the next row, and around and around until I had removed every bead of sweat. Then I gulped down the water and slipped off my stool.

"Thanks for trying. I appreciate it."

Carter did not look at me. He did not seem to react. Yet, when he opened his mouth, his aim was spot on, and he hit the bull's eye.

"You expected more, right? You expected more from Edith. You expected more from your job, from life, from me, maybe. Then again, I'm just a middle-aged guy with a comfortable life, right? I chose this life, Lucy. I've walked the same road as you. I've been there. You want the world to give you something. You want something from each person you meet, and when you don't get it, you're disappointed. Edith did nothing wrong. She's just Edith, doing what she does, being who she is. What do you want, Lucy? Answer that, and the rest will follow."

I had stopped a few feet away. I stood with my back to him, in the middle of the bar. I felt his eyes on me. I turned around and looked at him.

"Do you know what you want?"

I nodded.

"You do?"

I nodded again.

"So? What's the problem?"

I shook my head. An old man with a gray ponytail and a missing front tooth was staring at me from the corner. The bartender looked up from the glass that he held beneath a tap. Carter watched my face until he understood.

"You're scared," he said quietly.

I would not admit that I was scared, but I also could not deny it. Carter patted my bar stool. I stared at it and stood still.

"We're all scared," Carter said. "Even us boring middle-age types."

He lifted his glass and drank the foamy black beer. A plate of pasta arrived. I sat down beside him and picked up a fork.

"Every year, I watch my students graduate and leave campus. The ones who don't have a plan are a mess. They have no sense of purpose. They don't know themselves. They have no ideas. They have no dream. They have no passion."

I thought of Rose's music and her poem. I thought of Edith and her list. I thought of Anthony and his cello. I thought of myself.

"Passion?" I said in a voice that was too high and too loud. "You want to talk about passion? I can tell you about passion." Carter looked at me and waited. "Passion is waking up at dawn every day so I can write fiction before I go to work. Passion is studying literature as if I were a doctoral candidate and not a deadline reporter. Passion is trying to make the day's news sound lyrical and then guarding my words against my editor's delete button. Passion is taking the time to talk to at least six sources for every story, a personal goal that I haven't missed once, even on deadline with breaking news. Passion is lying awake at night because the novelist and the reporter are always screaming at me about who's more important and which is really me. Passion is keeping a notebook in my drawer at work in case an idea comes for a novel, and keeping a reporter's notebook on my desk at home in case an idea comes for a news story. I can tell you all about passion. I have enough passion to keep writing every moment of the day, but passion won't get me published, and it won't win me the Pulitzer, and it amounts to nothing when there isn't enough talent and intelligence to write anything original or insightful or brilliant."

I was out of words and out of breath, but no sooner had I uttered my last syllable than Carter fired back.

"Bury your ego," he said.

Sympathy was not his weapon of choice, but at least I was wearing a bullet-proof vest in the form of a large beer buzz.

"Five years ago I got tenure," he said. "It was a really big deal, but I expected it. Not a modest guy at the time. I had gone to a top grad school, I defeated hundreds of candidates for the position, and my dissertation had just been published by an excellent university press. The department threw me a party. I was as puffed up as one man could be. I had passion galore. Then I started to work on a new book. The writing didn't go well, and it was hard to make time for research and writing along with my students and family. Teaching was why I chose this profession, but I started to resent it. Grading papers and meeting with students was a drain on my time and energy. Another year passed, and a nagging voice kept asking me, 'Is this all? Isn't there more?' Another year passed, and I became withdrawn.

Playing Cello for the Trees

Student evaluations got worse and worse. They said my lectures were lifeless. They said my performance in the classroom didn't match my reputation. I was called in by the department chair twice in one semester. I stopped writing, and I dreaded teaching.

"Then one day Rose took me out to the back yard. She had dug a hole, and she was standing beside it with a shovel in one hand and a piece of paper in the other. She read what she had written on the paper: 'Here lies the ego of Carter Emerson. May it rest in peace.' She dropped it in the hole and told me that I needed to get back to work. She gave me the shovel, and I filled in the hole. Then she handed me my favorite American history book, with another piece of paper taped to the cover: 'Here lies the passion of Carter Emerson. May it be his beacon.' The next day, I gave a great lecture. I really saw my students for the first time in a couple years. I felt like myself again.

"Rose saved me that day. She reminded me what mattered most, that grading papers and meeting with students is what I do and who I am. It's my choice, and I'd make the same choice today. I didn't need to change my life. I needed to change my thinking. My mind had gotten filled with disappointment and sidetracked by ego. Now I'm too busy working hard at what I really love to get distracted by any of that. I love teaching American history. I've built my life on it. It's a simple life, and it fits me well. There is no Pulitzer. There aren't any prizes. Your life is the prize. Don't let your ego turn your passion into misery. Let go of it, Lucy. Write because you want to. Write because you can't not. Write for the newspaper. Write your next novel. Stop looking for excuses and waiting for a prize or a pat on the back. Get busy. Get back to work."

I finished my pasta and put down my fork. I was done eating. I was done drinking. I was done listening, talking, and thinking. Carter was as right as anyone could have been. All I wanted was to write. I could not stop even when I tried, and I had tried. I could not stop even when the writing was so bad that I could hardly breathe when I looked at it. Maybe the fate of the pages stored in my desk did not matter as much as the fate of the person who had written them. Something new was coming into focus. It was a book, and I was the one to write it. There were stories everywhere, after all, real and imagined.

80

Carter started to laugh, and the sound jolted me back from the faraway place where I had drifted. "I know that face," he said. "I live with someone whose face does that." He reached into his pocket and handed me a notebook and a pen. "Emergency tools."

I flipped to the first page and wrote the first sentence. The news angle was easy to identify. The story of Edith's unexpected marriage to Anthony would all but write itself. Yet, there was more to the story, as was often the case, and I needed to find a way to ease the subplots and supporting characters onto the page without Cunningham hacking them out. The combination of beer bravado and Carter's speech proved an inspiring force. I had intended only to jot a few notes, but the words kept coming. There were more ideas and fully formed sentences than I had realized. I wrote and wrote until my mind was empty and the pages were full.

I clicked the pen closed and looked at Carter. "Thanks."

"My pleasure. Truly."

We stood from our stools and stepped out of the bar and into the cool night air. As we drove home, Carter asked me one last question.

"So, what's your novel about?"

"Give you one guess."

"The meaning of life?"

"Something like that."

* * *

The house was silent again the next morning. Rose's car was gone. Carter's car was gone. Edith's car was the driveway. I was in the kitchen getting breakfast when a familiar voice startled me.

"Good morning."

Edith was standing in the doorway.

"Hi," I managed without looking at her.

She stayed in the doorway. "You made it back last night."

My college psychology professor had taught us about the shadow cast by anyone we love, the underbelly of the qualities that first attracted us. If it was true that I had fallen in love with Edith when we first met, then it was also true that I was now standing in the shadow of that love. It was a cold and ugly place. I felt an urge to grip her bony shoulders and give her a fierce shove. The psychology professor said the shadow had a lot to teach us. The hardest lesson was that the beloved was not to blame. Love, with its tangled complexities, presented an opportunity to resolve the parts of ourselves that were most troubling and the parts of our past that had long been most painful. With her admirable character yet irritating personality, Edith was a mirror that showed me to myself. The unresolved problems from my past would haunt me until I stood in the shadow of someone I loved and faced the truth that I had been avoiding forever. No wonder people got divorced. Blaming the other person was an easy way out. I could not fathom why anyone would choose to face-off with oneself rather than accuse another person and make a swift exit.

I closed the refrigerator door and stared at Edith in an attempt to see the truth about myself. She had disappointed me, and she made me angry. She refused to cooperate and accommodate my needs as a reporter, as her scribe. I did not understand why she had married Anthony, and I was too befuddled to ask her. A reporter without a question did not amount to much. I longed for City Hall and the familiar, even if it was mundane, and yet I would have been a fool not to apply the wisdom of the previous night to the realities of the new day. Edith had not done anything wrong. Carter was right. She was simply being Edith. The problem, any way I sliced it, whether I believed the theories of psychology or the advice bestowed from the neighboring bar stool last night, was me.

"I'm leaving for the day," I said. "My work here is done."

"Already? My, you are fast," Edith said. "I saw the kitchen light on last night. I figured it was you, up late writing."

"Actually, I think you're the one who's fast. You're so fast that you couldn't wait for me yesterday morning. You're so fast that you married Anthony the day after you found him."

Edith sighed and nodded her head. "Life does move fast at times, dear. And I tend to move fast, too, it's true."

She was still standing in the doorway as I carried my bowl of cereal to the table and sat down to eat. "Please let me do my job," I said.

"Oh, heavens, you're angry with me," Edith said. "You were so brave to take this assignment, Lucy. You must take good care of yourself. A day alone is certainly warranted. Don't lose heart, dear."

I looked at her with sheer disbelief. Other people did not affect her. She was immune to criticism as well as praise. The temperature in her shadow dropped several degrees, and I shivered. She stood smiling before me. I looked at her but had nothing to say. I ate my cereal, and she walked away.

By the time I reached the trailhead an hour later, anger and confusion had subsided. My brain had reached maximum capacity and stopped. I was tired of trying to guide myself up figurative mountains. The time had come to climb a real one. My parents had taken me into the wilderness even before I could walk, and throughout my childhood, hikes were our way of life. In Central Oregon, a mountain meant something that extended ten-thousand feet into the sky. Vermont's miniature version made me smirk with condescension. Yet, I was not in search of conquest or triumph. Four-thousand feet would suffice. I was in desperate need of Mother Nature. I longed for the perspective offered from a mountain top and the clarity that came from looking down and out at the world below. I always traveled with my hiking boots and backpack, and before our departure to Vermont, I had researched the Green Mountains and hoped to hike a few, if time permitted.

The cool morning air still hung among the trees as I set out along the trail. A familiar sensation overcame me: a sense of home. Pine needles and moss covered the narrow path, and moist soil cushioned every step. A bird rustled through the brush to the right of the trail, and up ahead a woodpecker tapped. My senses filled with everything the place offered. My mind began to empty, and my worries vanished.

Hiking stories, like most stories, are born out of mishaps, and that day I had none. I walked, and I walked, and I walked some more. I scrambled over the rocky terrain near the top, and I huddled inside two layers of jackets on the summit. A chilly wind whipped at me, and I sat with my backpack on my bare legs. I ate a granola bar and apple that I had swiped from Rose's kitchen. There were only a few of us on the summit, and then for about twenty minutes I was alone. I turned to the next blank page in the hiking journal that my father had given me for my tenth birthday, and I described the scenery, the day, the world around me, anything but myself. I had come in search of a state of mind. The sky, sun, rocks, birds, and trees created it for me. The mountain sorted the garbage from the gems inside my muddled mind. The vast views, the sky that never ended, and the beauty of the world reminded me of my size and my place. My insignificance in the greater scheme of the planet and the universe relaxed me. I had no sense of duty or responsibility. Carter had buried his ego in his back yard. I pushed mine off the summit of a mountain. I watched it soar farther away from me and float to the ground, where it would crash, crumble, and disintegrate into oblivion.

The walk back down the mountain evoked more ideas than a writer could weave into news stories and novels in one lifetime. I jotted as many as I could remember in my notebook as soon as I reached the end of the trail.

In the afternoon, I read and swam at a nearby lake. On the drive back to Rose's house, I stopped for a long dinner to allow time to pass and night to arrive. The break from the noise of human chatter and big ideas about life had been a powerful salve. I did not want to see any of them when I returned to the little red house. I wanted to end the day without their interrogation or commentary, without a word spoken or a word heard.

When I pulled into the driveway, a single light shone in the upstairs bedroom. I stepped out of the car, and Rose stood from her desk and stepped toward the window. She raised one hand in a gesture of welcome. Her smile bore a sign of relief. I waved back. Then her light disappeared, and the house slid into darkness.

* * *

When I awoke the next morning, it was over. I had slept for ten hours and awoke to delightfully achy muscles and the sound of giggles through the porch door. My epicenter had calmed at last. The aftershocks had dissipated, and the rubble had been removed from the scene of the disaster. I recognized in myself someone that I used to spend a lot of time with, an old friend that I had been missing, someone steeped in the sort of mental clarity that Carter had touted. There was nothing like the return to normalcy after a detour through rugged emotional terrain. Time alone in nature and a night of solid sleep had restored me to my natural state. Now work beckoned.

When I stepped inside the house, happy chaos greeted me. Daisy and Sam were wearing wings and flying through the rooms with magic wands. Rose and Carter were locked in a lovers' embrace by the coffee pot. Edith was sitting on—*on*—the dining-room table, reading aloud at a hundred decibels. As if we had choreographed our entrances, I stepped into the room from the back entrance at the same moment that Anthony stepped in from the side entrance off the hallway. For a second, our eyes scanned the scene. Then our glance met, and we laughed, a little at first, then more, until we had the attention of the entire family.

"They're nuts, Anthony," I said. "Every last one of them."

He nodded. "Then we must be, too, because we've come voluntarily."

"What do you say we run off together while they're not looking?"

Edith stood up on the table. "What threat is this, invading princess, tent-dwelling lady of the pen?" she called out. The girls looked at each other, and the little one squealed. "He is mine, all mine, and I will fight you to the grave for him."

With that, Edith raised a pretend sword and called me to battle. I took up my invisible sword, too, climbed onto the table to the audible shock of all, and clashed weapons with Edith even as we both doubled over with laughter.

"Mama, what's wrong with Grandma?" Samantha asked as she ran manic laps around the table.

"Grandma's just being Grandma," Daisy said, "but what happened to Lucy? Is she OK, Mama?" She looked distressed, so I dropped my sword, bowed to my rival, and hopped off the table.

"I'm fine," I said. "We were just playing."

"You're kinda silly, Lucy," Daisy said. "Is that why you're Grandma's scribe? Because you're like her?"

"I am kinda silly sometimes," I said. "I hope we all are."

Daisy grinned as she flitted off with her fairy wings fluttering behind her.

"What does a man need to do to get some coffee around here?" Anthony asked.

"Try kissing the barista," Carter said. "It worked for me."

Anthony shot me a glance, and we both dashed at Rose and planted kisses on her cheeks. She screamed, feigned a swoon, and poured two cups of coffee.

"It's contagious, Edith," I said. Anthony and I clinked mugs and enjoyed a quiet cheers for two. "I knew it was hereditary. At least one of your three offspring has a confirmed case. Now we know it's contagious, too."

"Thank goodness," Anthony said.

"I stopped paying attention long ago to those who call me crazy," Edith said. "Now, if you please, I was reading a poem."

She gathered the papers from the floor and started to read as she moved toward the back porch with a gesture for us to follow. The fairies flew past us out the door, leapt off the end of the porch, and soared through the yard and into the meadow beyond. Anthony and I sat down at the table where Rose and Carter were eating raspberry muffins and yogurt parfaits. Edith stood off to the side at stage right and read the poem. When she finished, we applauded.

"Mother, you are a snoop and a thief," Rose said. "I've asked you a hundred times not to sneak into our room and steal my poetry."

"Ah, but this is good stealing," Edith said. "Think of me as a literary Robin Hood. You are denying the reading public your work, so I swipe fresh poems off your desk to help others, not to hurt you." Edith glanced at each of us in turn and then fluttered her eyelashes and curtsied to Rose. "It's a noble deed, my lady."

"I tend to agree," Carter said. "Music should be heard. Art should be seen. Poetry should be read, and preferably aloud."

"Some argue that a creation belongs to its creator," Anthony said. "Others think that nobody owns art, that it exists freely for anyone to enjoy."

"I think the artist decides," Rose said. "And once it's out in the world, there is nothing you can do about it. You lose control."

"Well put, dear," Edith said. "Anthony, Lucy, it's time for our morning constitutional."

This was news to us, but we followed obediently. My latest installment for *The Bend Bugle* had broken the news of Edith's marriage, but I had not been able to provide an answer to the obvious question: Why did they get married? Anthony walked between us as we made our way up the hill. He and Edith were holding hands. The obvious answer was, "Why not?" They were both alone in their old age. They liked each other and apparently loved each other—or at least the memory of each other. They despised loneliness, a truth that they both tried to conceal. Yet, "why not?" was never a satisfying answer to "why?" I had reported Edith's fairy-tale explanation that their marriage fulfilled a shared destiny begun many years ago. There was more to it, though. Anthony had signed on for a marriage with a tight deadline. His decision suggested not that he had a lifelong love for Edith but that he had nothing to lose by being married to her for a few months. Still, that did not sound like the man who played cello for his trees. Nothing that I had seen or heard suggested that he was capable of being indifferent to anything, especially Edith and her marriage proposal.

"What did you do yesterday?" As my question floated through the leaves of the birches that bordered the road, I slipped a hand into my pocket and pressed the record button on my digital recorder.

"Let's see. Oh, yes, we updated our wills," Edith said. "Now that we're married, we thought it wise to get our affairs in order."

"'We?'" I asked.

"That's right," Edith said.

I looked at Anthony's face, which was making a valiant effort to stay fixed on the scenery. "So, you're going to do it, too?"

He shrugged. I suppressed a gasp. I had never met anyone who shrugged at the prospect of choreographing his own death.

"Wow," I said. "You seem so calm."

He shrugged again. I was not fluent in shrugs. I needed words, and they were not forthcoming. The shrug could have been the manifestation of many years of loneliness and despair, a why-not and who-cares attitude after all. The silent shrug also could have been the gesture of a man who had handed his fate to his new wife, a strong-willed woman to say the least. Poking around inside Anthony's head felt like slicing open human organs for exploratory surgery. I had never been to medical school, and I felt queasy.

"You've decided to join her? To do it?" My scalpel sliced away at him, and though I cringed, I had to do it.

"Honestly, I haven't decided anything, but Edith wanted it settled, so."

"*So?*" she and I said in unison.

"So... well..." Anthony mumbled.

His wimpy words plunked to the ground like a couple of rotten acorns. There was no zest, no conviction, no gumption. His voice lacked any decisiveness, and I could surmise even without personal experience that one needed decisiveness when it came to planning this sort of event. Edith had, in fact, coerced him, a temptress with a fatal dose of sleeping pills, or whatever blood-free, no-mess plan she had concocted. I stared her down until she looked at me.

"You must not assume that this is my doing," she said.

"Oh, please!" I said.

"When Anthony finds the words, I'm sure he'll be perfectly able to explain."

"It seems reasonable," he said. "It makes sense in many ways. It's logical, for someone like me."

Aware of the recorder in my pocket, I suppressed my reaction. The news reporter was struggling to remain neutral and unbiased.

"I've, uh. Well, it's been a long and lonely haul for me," Anthony said.

"And this option appeals to you?" I asked.

"Frankly, I think I may still be a bit uncertain."

"About ending your life?"

"About all of it." He stopped walking. Then he dropped Edith's hand. "You're really serious about this? *You*, Edith? You who are so full of life? So strong and healthy? So energized and engaged with the world?"

"Anthony, sweetheart, we've been over this a dozen times. Yes, I am serious, but you are absolutely free to decide for yourself. I would never want to influence you or anyone else about this sort of thing."

"This sort of thing?" I yelled. "There is no 'this sort of thing,' Edith. We're talking about death. We're talking about choosing death. Planning it. Scheduling your own end. Killing yourself. And you're perfectly healthy. This is not normal, Edith."

"Goodness, you seem rather upset. Catch your breath, dear. Don't you have a notebook with you today? Maybe you should write some of this down."

We were standing at the top of the hill. Edith pretended to be taking in the view, carefree and careless. Anthony scratched his head and moved pebbles around on the road with the sole of his shoe. I debated the pros and cons of turning off my recorder.

"When I woke up this morning, I realized for the first time since my wife died that I have learned how to enjoy life, my small life, in my simple ways," Anthony said. "I like my home. I like my walks in the woods. I like playing my cello outside on the patio. I think the trees would miss the music. I know I'd miss playing for them. I didn't know until today how much I enjoy my simple, quiet life. Maybe this was a mistake. I have many happy memories of you, Edith, but I don't understand how you can think the way you do or possibly go through with it."

Edith intertwined her arm through his and patted his forearm with her palm. "Of course we don't know one another, dear. That's the problem with love and time. That's the problem with being a person. We can't know each other. I come with my own set of filters, and I see you through them. Maybe what I'm seeing is accurate, and maybe not. Maybe it resembles what you see in yourself, and maybe not. I spent most of my life married to a lovely man whom I shall always consider the best friend I ever had, the person to whom I was closest. Yet, in the end, I don't think I knew him either. It's impossible. So we accept the limitations, we do our best to connect in meaningful ways, and we get on with the act of living. And it *is* an act, action, the doing of it all. We can't think or even talk our way through life or through love. We must take action. So, you and I got married, and before too long, I'm going to say my goodbyes and head out. I don't need to think about it, and I don't want to talk about it. This is my choice, but it does not need to be yours."

As I listened to Edith and watched her, I wondered whether she was making it all up as she went along. People did not speak like that, at least not on the planet where I had been living my whole life. From the look on Anthony's face, the folks on his planet did not speak like that either.

"I'm not so sure about that," he said. "'Actions speak louder than words,' has never been one of my favorites. Words have power, if you mean what you say. Why should we place a higher value on our actions than on our thoughts, our emotions, our conversations with others? Here I am, standing in the middle of this beautiful country road, on the crest of this quaint little hill, and my words are all I have to offer. My words represent me. They are all that matter to me in this moment. I want to live, Edith. I want to go with you to New York City and to Greece and to California. I'd like to meet your other children and get to know them, too. I'd like to see Daisy and Samantha grow up, and I'd love to be a grandfather to them. I want to take this journey with you and see you complete your list. I want to experience the thoughts and the feelings, the sensations, the sights, the smells, and the words that come with every step of our adventure. I know now, though, that when you reach the finish line, you will be alone. I can't do it. I won't do it. Life is a gift, and I won't throw mine away or make light of it or scorn it by planning my own end. I'm greedy. I want every last minute that is mine to take. Before you appeared, I didn't know this, and I may never have learned it without you, so thank you. I'm staying to the very end, whenever that may be and whatever it may bring. I will gladly give up control over it, even if that means suffering through as my body and mind deteriorate. Call it God or fate or the powers that be or sheer chance. Call it whatever you want, but I will wait for it to come to me. I will never seek it out."

I would return to that speech—Anthony's "I Will Wait For It To Come" sermon on the hill—again and again when I lost my way, lost my will, or fell into believing that we could not know each other and were doomed to the pain of loneliness. Sometimes ordinary people saved one another. Anthony and his speeches have saved me more times that I could count. I still have the recordings and the transcripts typed out. I listen to his voice when I need it. I read his words to guide me out of darkness.

"I'm relieved that we've cleared this up," Edith said. "You're staying, I'm going, and in the meantime, we're right here, right now, together. You speak, and I'll act. We're a winning combination, I do believe."

At that moment under the birches at the top of the hill, with the Green Mountains in the distance, I saw the woman who had charmed and impressed me the first day that we had met and many times since. If Edith was infuriating at her worst, then she was extraordinary at her best. I had the answer to the marriage question now: a clear case of opposites attract, with the added comfort of mutual interests and a mutual desire for companionship. We were an odd threesome about to embark on a strange journey. Yet, our morning constitutional had resurrected my spirit of adventure and taught me what I needed to know for the coming adventures with my misguided Don Quixote and her plain-spoken Sancho.

Scribblers receive gifts from the universe at times. Like Rose and her poem, an entire story or scene of a novel could fall out of the sky and land in a writer's head. The thump of Edith and Anthony's story resounded on the hilltop that morning as it arrived in my mind fully formed. I reached inside my pocket and turned off the recorder. I did not need it anymore. In fact, I did not need them anymore, for the moment anyway.

I hurried back to the house and spent the rest of the morning writing.

* * *

Cunningham liked the story and left most of it intact. It appeared on Sunday on the front page above the fold with a color photograph that I had taken of Edith and Anthony standing on the hill crest in the early-morning sun. The shot was staged, the day after the actual moment on the hill. We just happened to be out walking again, and I just happened to pause at the top of the hill and snap a few pictures as Edith and Anthony stood under the fluttering birch leaves and gazed at the view. The photo chief called me when he received them. "Not bad for a word girl," he said. Several readers wrote letters to the editor about the story's tug-of-war between choosing life and choosing death. Already many of them aligned with Anthony and villainized Edith, and we were only one-third of the way through the list. A local right-to-die group wrote a long opinion piece that led to more letters. A state senator wrote, too, with his policymaker's take on the debate. The readers were not only reading, they were thinking and discussing, provoked and morally challenged by the stories, a word girl's dream come true.

For the first time since I met Edith, I began to doubt that she would really do it. Until then, I had assumed that she would, but after the day on the hill, I was no longer certain. I did not tell anyone. This sort of hunch was best kept to oneself.

Playing Cello for the Trees

Cunningham gave me a few days off to frolic in Vermont before my flight home. We agreed that Edith's story had reached a pause, and until she began pursuing the next item on her list, there was no legitimate work for me to do. Back home, the newsroom was in chaos. The assistant city editor had quit without warning, and too many reporters were away on vacation at the same time. They needed me, and I was glad for the chance to try editing and take a break from the high drama of Edith Small.

During my final days in Vermont, I spent long leisurely hours at the lakes and in the forest, sometimes alone and sometimes with Edith and Anthony, or with Rose and her family, or all of them. One morning, we all picked blackberries at a nearby farm. Then Carter and I worked in the kitchen with Rose, taking instructions from her for a batch of jam, while Anthony read to the girls and Edith researched Greece on the computer. I swam at the lake with Daisy and Samantha, harvested vegetables with Rose, and discussed life's big questions and amusing quirks with her and Carter on the back porch in the evening after their children went to bed. Late at night, out in my tent by lantern light, I read Carter's favorite history book, the one with Rose's note still taped to the cover. When I forgot about my official role, I would slip into the ease of family life. I felt a kindred spirit with every one of them, but least of all with Edith. Life was full of ironies, and this was a big one. I failed to understand the woman whose story I was charged with telling. I gravitated toward Anthony and his honesty; Rose and her devotion to her poetry, garden, children, and husband; Carter with his clarity about his career and his love for his family; and the children with their playfulness and spirited love of life.

We all ate dinner together on my last evening. Rose cooked a feast, and Edith baked two blackberry crisps. Anthony played bartender, and Carter played his guitar. Daisy and Samantha made me goodbye cards and sang "Leaving on a Jet Plane" with their dad. If I had lacked a loving family of my own, my heart would have broken when I left them. Yet, my heart ached for other reasons, as I pondered the intimate family story of an old woman's mission and the loved ones that she would hurt irreparably. My approaching absence at the little red house on the hill prompted me to think about Edith's approaching permanent absence and Rose's goodbye to her. I could not guess what explanation Rose would offer her children when their grandmother died, though I knew that she would one day tell them the truth.

Carter was the last to say good night. Rose and I had hugged twice already, and she was rinsing wine glasses at the kitchen sink when Carter and I stood from our chairs on the porch.

"Good luck to you," he said. "And thank you. I've learned a lot from you. There is a way to be professional and personal at the same time, to be a journalist and a human being. I had my doubts about this whole project. I still do, but I wish you all the best. I'll be reading your stories online."

He leaned forward to hug me. I was too flustered to speak. Then he kissed my cheek, and I floated off the porch and into my tent. Nestled in my sleeping bag, I was more at peace that night than any other since I had arrived. The city beat had never depleted me or taken me down in the way that covering Edith had already. I could not guess what lay ahead of us, but I was determined to find out.

And despite everything, I would not have turned back the clock for anything in the world.

HIATUS

Editing was a welcome challenge and good work, but I needed to write. With Cunningham's blessing and his gratitude for my willingness to pump out copy during the prolonged news drought that summer, I wrote about each task that Edith had completed on her list—all thirty-two of them. The interviews were already done and stored in my notebooks and my digital voice recorder. Edith had been telling me them, one at a time, here and there, since the day I had retired from the city beat.

I fact-checked the stories during my lunch break on the phone and on visits to local offices and businesses to confirm Edith's enrollment in dance classes and pottery classes, her instrument and language lessons, and her myriad fundraisers for the public library and local organizations. Most of the people who had taught or assisted Edith in the undertaking of her list were still here, still knew her, and could recall dates and facts without checking their files. Edith and her list tended to make an indelible impression on people. I made them check their files anyway. That was what reporters did, and nobody seemed to take offense, even in a small town like ours. The man who had sold Edith her bicycle for her trip across America still owned the bike shop and found his copy of the receipt for her twelve-speed tour bike. We ran a copy of it beside the photographs that Edith had given me of her with her front bike tire in the Pacific Ocean at her starting point and in the Atlantic Ocean at her destination. Folks like the bike-store owner not only enhanced the stories by adding more characters, voices, and perspectives, but the interviews, documents, and fact-checking lent greater credibility to a long serial story that otherwise could have left the more meticulous readers and the cynics wondering why they should trust what Edith said.

Cunningham gave me a limit of five-hundred words for each of the thirty-two stories. Responses from our readers confirmed that they were finding Edith's tales to be thought-provoking entertainment during a sleepy summer in Central Oregon when crime, conflict, and newsworthy weather strangely came to a standstill, leaving our pages bereft of the staples that small dailies depended on.

I sat beside Cunningham in the vacant seat of our departed assistant city editor. During those two weeks, I learned more about him than I had known for five years. I learned when and how he liked his coffee. I watched him eat the lunch he brought from home at his desk at eleven o'clock every day. I heard his murmured speeches about the serial comma, the extraneous adjectives of our crime reporter, and the pressures from his higher-ups to come up with more hard news when none existed. I knew about his love of avant-garde art, blues music, English novels, and brownies at about three in the afternoon. When our meager staff of reporters filed their stories, I helped to edit them, bouncing questions off Cunningham as they arose. More than once he told me that I had found my calling. More than once, I mumbled a non-committal, "uh-huh."

In between I wrote. I wrote in the morning before the reporters arrived. I wrote in the afternoon, when they were banging out their dailies. In my two weeks back home during my hiatus from Edith, I spent every moment possible writing the stories of her past. When I left *The Bugle* at the end of July, about one-third of the stories had run, and Cunningham had a stockpile to get him through the summer.

Halfway through my stint as substitute editor, I was blessed with an opportunity in the form of someone else's misfortune. So it goes. The environment reporter caught the chicken pox from his son the week that he had a big story slated for the Sunday front page. I pounced, and Cunningham consented. Edith's sixteenth task graced the front page, along with her color photograph of herself and Henry at the South Pole. Dear Cunningham gave me as many words as I wanted and kept his chopping to a minimum.

* * *

The Bend Bugle
"The Adventures of Edith Small, #16: Visit the South Pole"
By Lucy Hunt

The penguins ceased to interest Henry. For two days, he stood alongside the other tourists, as they waddled off the boat onto land, focused their zoom lenses, and fired off one shot after another of the penguins. The magic of observing penguins in their natural habitat had melted into a numbness from the ubiquity and volume of the flightless birds. By the morning of the third day, Henry refused to disembark.

"Frankly, my dear, if you've seen one penguin, you've seen them all," he said.

Edith gasped. Where her husband saw monotony and homogeneity, she saw variety and splendor. The Adelies and the Gentoos, the Rockhoppers and the Chinstraps, all held her attention through several rolls of film, hours of lectures from the scientists who traveled with the group, and scribbling in the pages of her travel journal. Their guide had promised them Emperor penguins the next day. Edith was breathless at the thought of them. They were, after all, the reason for the trip. The majestic and towering Emperor penguins were what had landed the trip to the South Pole on her list years ago.

"Please come," she said to Henry. "We may see an Isabelline today."

"*You* may. And you may not," Henry said. "These matters are not under the control of your emotional whims or the hovering guides and overpaid quasi-scientists."

Edith huffed. "There's no reason to be grouchy, Henry. Just you wait and see. Once you're back in your armchair, you'll think of the penguins, and you'll regret that you didn't spend more time with them when you could."

"Edith, that is the fantastical thinking of a child. If you wish to see the birds, by all means, indulge. I for one will be spending the remainder of this journey onboard with a good book."

"Henry, when you disappoint, you disappoint completely."

"I assure you, my dear, that the disappointment is not yours alone."

Edith turned her back, grabbed her camera bag with a burst of rage, and marched on deck to take her place in line at the gangplank. She was seventy-one years old and not about to waste time bickering with her cranky travel companion. In fact, when they returned home, she would fire him and hire a replacement. There was one trip remaining on her list—watch a sunrise and a sunset on a Greek Island (#19)—and she intended to enjoy it in the company of someone who shared her passion for adventure and travel.

When their boat floated into view of the great Emperor penguins the next morning, Edith sprinted from the top deck down to their cabin to stir Henry. She could barely controlled her urge to grab his hand and drag him upstairs. Although she had parted ways with Henry countless times through the years for various trips, this parting broke her heart. She left their cabin alone. She disembarked alone.

When she stood on land and at last gazed upon the legendary penguins, her anticipation fizzled into grief.

"I wanted him there with me," Edith recalled in a recent interview. "I wanted him to *want* to be there with me."

Maybe Henry was bored with the penguins and, for that matter, the whole trip, but Edith was not. This had long been a sacred tenet of their marriage: honor your spouse's passions as you honor your own, offer up your enthusiasm, and take an interest where you naturally might not, for the sake of your loved one and marital harmony. Edith believed that not many wives could have embraced Henry's unorthodox interests: the ukulele, mushroom picking, imported hard cheeses, and comic strips. Yet, Edith had supported, encouraged, and even participated through the years with a good attitude.

"To be fair, Henry had always treated my lifetime list with respect and genuine curiosity, never scorning the time or money I devoted to any pursuit," Edith said.

Neither spouse could have foretold that, after forty-six years of marriage and thirty-one years of the list, penguins would be the catalyst for the downfall of their world travels and the reason that Edith's list was put aside unfinished.

Edith was changing rolls of film when Henry appeared in her peripheral vision. The boat was empty but for the captain, on deck with binoculars, and Henry, who was making his way down the gangway.

Edith squinted to read his face but found neither the lightness of a smile nor the hardness of resentment. As she watched him descend on the walkway suspended five feet above the frigid water, the unthinkable happened. The metal handrail detached and plunged into the water below, taking with it the man whose hands remained gripped to it. Every pair of eyes shifted from the penguins on the distant rocks to the man who had careened off the plank and stood, flailing and screeching, chest-high in the ice water of the unswimmable Antarctic Ocean.

Physically, Henry was fine, but something changed, Edith said. When they returned home, her plans to replace him with another travel mate seemed wrong.

"The notion of honoring one's spouse may seem outdated, but I find it beautiful. Henry always did, too," she said.

The Smalls never made it to Greece.

"He just didn't have it in him, and I didn't want to push," Edith said.

Now it is the only trip left on her list, and she expressed sadness at the thought of going without Henry. Yet, she gained something valuable from the trip to the South Pole.

"I saw the truth, at last," Edith said.

Henry was getting old. He had arthritis, and he had gained weight. His knees, hips, and back often hurt. Travel was no longer easy for him, and so it was not enjoyable.

"I put my list away, and I stayed home," she said.

Until now. Edith and her new husband will depart in August for the Greek island of Santorini, where she intends to complete task #19, at last.

* * *

My father was an avid hiker throughout his teaching career and his retirement, but with his number-one camping partner gone for the past several years, he had not spent a night in the mountains in a long time. I arrived at his house at seven in the morning, and we headed west for the peaks of the Central Cascade Range. Our destination was Teardrop Pool, a tiny lake on the summit of South Sister. Early explorers had named the Three Sisters mountains: Faith, Hope, and Charity. Though the names were mostly out of use, my family had always called the trio of ten-thousand-foot volcanoes by their noble names. I chose Charity that day for several reasons, including that it was a manageable but long day hike to the summit with no technical climb. Although my father and I were capable of climbing anything in the Cascades, we had planned the trip on short notice and wanted to keep the ascent and our packing simple.

There was another reason that I chose Charity. Of the three virtues, Charity would serve me best when I embarked with Edith on her next adventure. Faith and hope came more easily to me. Charity I found challenging, a truth that made me aware of my shortcomings.

The sky never saw a cloud that day, and the temperature hovered in the seventies. The six-mile hike up was steady, steep, and grueling. The last mile required concentration and patience to withstand the physical and mental annoyance of taking one step forward only to slide a half-step back on the red cinder rock. We climbed in silence up the cinder field, and when we reached the summit, my father hugged me.

Mondays were the best day to hike in the summer, as the crowds were at a minimum. As we approached the perimeter of Teardrop Pool, not a soul was in sight. We dropped our packs not far from the tiny glacial lake and sat at the water's edge. Camping on the summit was forbidden, and we had never broken the rule before. My father and I were of one mind on this: You did whatever necessary to get a mountain to yourself every now and then. Also, we were inspired by my mom's favorite adage: All things in moderation, including moderation.

I pulled on a fleece jacket and a windbreaker. The summer day turned winter cold at 10,358 feet. My dad had wandered off, away from the water and the handful of hikers that had appeared. He would poke around the scrubby growth on the mountain top and identify plants as he munched on a granola bar. He would think about my mom. He would miss her up here more than he did down there, but he wanted to be here anyway. He kept his thinking and his missing to himself and seized every chance to be with the people and in the places that he loved most. He volunteered in local classrooms, coached ambitious teachers, visited Charlie in Minnesota despite his distaste for travel, read my news stories, and accepted all of my invitations, no matter what.

I sat alone and looked at the distant peaks of Mount Washington, Mount Jefferson, Mount Hood, and even Mount St. Helens across the border in Washington state. Growing up in Portland, this had been my backyard, essentially. My family spent about as much time exploring Central Oregon on the weekends, during vacations, and in the summer as we did going to work and school in the city. I stared at Mount Hood and remembered when Charlie broke his ankle on the descent. My parents carried him all the way down.

My dad appeared in the distance and waved. He was checking in on me, as fathers do. He tried to look casual, an aged father of a grown daughter who no longer needed to be checked on.

Hikers came and went all day. In the late afternoon, a group of four lingered after everyone else had departed, but they, too, soon strapped on their packs and followed the trail to lower altitudes for the night.

My father and I pitched our tent together, though both of us had done it alone more times than we could count. The temperature was dropping fast, and I set up a camp stove to warm the soup that my father brought. He pulled out of his backpack a container of rice salad with dried fruit and pine nuts, a small loaf of homemade bread, and two bottles of my favorite Oregon microbrew. This was why I did not fantasize about the man of my dreams: I already had him.

We sat side by side, facing the setting western sun as we slurped our soup and chewed the bread.

"I've befriended an interesting man," my dad said. "A professor up at the college. He launched the coaching program for teachers at the high school. The one I told you about last week."

I nodded and smiled at the familiarity of his words. My father was always befriending interesting people and relating their theories about education.

"He knew Henry Small for many years. They were more than colleagues. They were close friends."

I chewed and nodded, nodded and chewed. The world was pristine and pure from the top looking down. Nothing could pierce the serenity of camping on a summit.

"He knows Edith, too. He's been reading your stories. He was shocked by the news of her second marriage."

I raised my eyebrows and kept chewing. I knew what it meant to be shocked by the news of Edith's marriage.

"He was relieved that her new husband is refusing to join in her death pact. He's very much against it. In fact, he's written several letters to the editor. Very strong letters. He was rather upset to read that Henry had agreed to it. He says that would have been out of character for Henry. He had a hard time believing that Henry really agreed."

I swallowed some beer and ate a few bites of rice salad. I had been far away from the readers that I was writing for, and I liked hearing about this friend of Henry's and his reactions. I gave myself a figurative pat on the back for disturbing him. Disturbing the comfortable and comforting the disturbed was the mission of all serious writers.

"Frankly, Lucy, he's having a hard time believing a lot of it."

I stopped chewing.

"He says it doesn't sound like the Henry he knew. He met with your editor once already, but he didn't get what he wanted. He's planning to meet with the publisher. I thought you should know."

"I'm not sure I understand, Dad. What exactly is he accusing me of?"

"It's not an accusation, it's a concern. And he's concerned about Edith, not you."

"He thinks she's lying?"

"Not lying, no. Just not remembering accurately what happened many years ago. He thinks she's confused."

"Oh, I see. Confused. That's the word people use when they think someone is crazy or wrong or when they want to control something. 'Edith is confused.' I don't think so. Edith is many things, but confused is not one of them."

"Tom knew Henry for almost thirty years. He's known Edith that long, too."

"Who's side are you on, Dad?"

"Come on, Lucy. Let's not sink to that. My friend doesn't know that I'm telling you this."

"Why are you telling me then? Do you share your friend's *concern*, as you put it, that Edith is *confused*?"

I watched my dad glance beyond me to Teardrop Pool in the distance. We had found an ideal spot for our campsite, flat and protected from the wind by the back of the ridge. We had vast views of the other Cascade peaks and the sunset. In the morning we would see the sunrise, too.

"There's been a lot of talk around town," my dad said. "I know you read the letters to the editor, but you don't hear the talk. I had to stand between two groups of teachers last week to break up an argument that was getting very aggressive. The stories are inflammatory. People are upset."

"Good," I said. "I'm OK with inflammatory. You know I believe in the power of the press, still, despite technology and the internet and my selfish, cynical generation. I believe in what I'm doing. I may not understand Edith, and I certainly don't condone her plan, but she lives boldly and she has convictions, real convictions. If she's making people react and think about big scary questions of life and death, then I'm all for it. It's inciting in a good way, It pushes people off their lily pads and gets them wet for a change."

"That may be, but people are very upset. I thought you'd want to know."

My dad was studying the pine needles beneath his hiking boots. He was drawing circles in the ground in a way that I recognized but had seen only a few times before.

"What is this really about, Dad?"

"It's getting harder to defend you, Lucy. I'm trying, but my heart isn't in it."

"It's not your job to defend me."

"Maybe not," he said.

"Are you ashamed of me?"

His head shot up from the pine needles, and his eyes were on mine, where they usually were during our talks. This business of staring off at the distance and studying pine needles was strange and unnerving. His eyes on me came as a relief.

"No way," he said. "I'm proud of you for taking this on. Yours is the toughest position of all. It's easy for people to conflate your role as a journalist with your views as a human being, and I know you know that, but you haven't let it stop you. This is a big story, Lucy, and it's one well worth telling. I'm not concerned about you. I'm a bit worked up over the idea, to be honest. Edith's views on aging and death may be logical, but that's the problem. How can one be so coldly logical about the most emotional parts of being human? I find myself aligning with Anthony. I can't understand her. I've even gone back and reread the Stoics, but I can't accept the idea of ending your own life according to a carefully executed plan while you're still healthy and enjoying yourself and making a contribution."

I nodded, but there was nothing to say without saying everything, and saying everything was not what I did, even with my father, even in the safety and solace of a mountain top.

"I guess I do have one real concern," he said. "If I'm going to be honest with you, one-hundred-percent honest, I should tell you that I do have a concern. About you."

I looked at him and waited, giving silent permission to send anything my way.

"When the time comes, if Edith does end her life, I wonder how you'll handle it. I wonder whether this is too much for you—for anyone, but especially for a young woman who lost her mother too early."

We sat beside one another in the silence for a long time. Soon our eyes lifted to the sky, where a swath of candy-apple red striped the sky. We watched as it fused with a strip of orange and then melted into mottled pinks and purples. This was the pinnacle of all sunset varieties, with the full spectrum of fire colors and a tinge of icy purple-blue.

"Remember that time we hiked up here with Mom and Charlie, when you two were in high school?" my dad said into the long still silence.

I remembered, but I let him tell the story anyway, because telling stories is what we do when we cannot say nothing and we cannot say everything.

SIDETRIP TO NEW YORK

My suitcase contained everything that I would need for a few days in New York City, a stay of unidentified length in Greece, and a couple months in California. The strap of my leather bag was digging into my shoulder from the weight of far too many books and note-books, an incorrigible habit. I rang the doorbell and took the paper from my pocket to check again that I was in the right place.

When the door swung open, a young version of Edith stood be-fore me. Her eyes, nose, mouth, and hands were copies of her mother's. Alice led me through the entryway and into the living room. I expected to find Edith and Anthony but instead saw only the décor and antiques of a luxury apartment. Most were unidentifiable to me, including handcrafts and wares from around the world. Enormous color photographs of African children hung on the walls. Their faces were nearly two-feet tall. A few smiled, but most did not. Family pho-tographs stood among the books on the shelves, and several contained images of Edith. I followed my hostess through the living room, slow-ly, as I tried to spy on her life. There were several pictures of the same young man and of him with Alice. Edith's list of family members had included "one dead son-in-law." A black-and-white framed portrait of the man with a younger, pregnant Alice stopped me.

"That's my dead husband and our dead baby," Alice said. "I don't discuss them, especially with strangers or reporters."

She looked hard at me for emphasis. Then she left the living room and started down the hallway. The click of her short heels against the hardwood floor muffled the sound of her voice.

"This is the guestroom." She smoothed non-existent wrinkles from the cream bedspread.

109

"The bathroom is there." She motioned with a flat hand turned sideways, fingers pressed together, a gesture reminiscent of flight attendants. I started to grin, but one glance at Alice scared the humor right out of me. "There are more towels in the bathroom closet. Use whatever you need. The cleaners come every Friday. Everything will be taken care of once you've left." Translation: Alice would sanitize, if not sterilize, everything I had touched once I was gone.

The heels clicked back down the hallway. As I chased Alice through her apartment, I saw only one other bedroom and wondered where Edith and Anthony were sleeping. I did not want to be left alone with this woman at night.

"Take whatever you want from the kitchen. I brew a pot of coffee every morning at 6:15. I'll make extra. Help yourself. I leave for work at 6:30. Your key is here."

She tapped the counter. Her nails were short and neat, but the cuticles were badly gnawed. Alice looked like someone who had reasons to chew her own skin.

"My mother should have returned by now. I need to leave. I'll be home for dinner. We'll eat at six."

She pulled a denim jacket from the coat rack near the front door. Then she took a leather purse off another hook and slipped it over her shoulder.

"You know the city?" she asked with one hand on the doorknob. I shrugged and blushed. Alice made me feel about four years old. "Well, you can wait for my mother or buy a map at any newsstand. It's very straight-forward, really."

Then she opened the door and left.

I was as scared of Alice's absence as I had been of her presence. Nothing in her apartment was welcoming or warm. The faces in the living room gave me the chills. Faces were not meant to be that large, and suffering children disturbed me. I wanted to help them but at the moment could do nothing about the hunger, disease, and war that were harming them.

I stood by the front door for a long time. Visions of Rose floated through my memory. She was the flavor of sweet, old-fashioned, reliable vanilla. I had always been a chocolate lover, but my memories of Rose stirred up the creamy calm of vanilla, and I appreciated it in a new way. The contrast to her sister shocked me. Unlike most people, Alice was neither chocolate nor vanilla. She was Brussels sprouts with jalapenos: bitter with a harsh sting. I glanced down the hallway that led to the bedrooms and bathrooms. Then I looked around the corner into the kitchen and the living room. An enormous face stained with the salt of dried tears stared back at me. The girl's eyes held nothing but sorrow. I wondered about her story, her life, and her fate, but then I thought better of it. Those were the sorts of truths that none of us really wanted to know. Maybe Alice was different. Maybe she wanted to know.

As usual, Edith had told me nothing. When I parted ways with Rose, I had not known that I would be staying with Alice for three nights before our departure to Greece. I had planned to visit Charlie in Minnesota for a few days and reunite with the newlyweds in Athens. My dad's friend who knew Edith, and the teachers' fight about her stories changed my mind. I needed every opportunity to watch Edith and get to know her family. I did not accept accusations that I was an accomplice to a confused old lady who was spouting half-truths and slandering the dead. I would uncover every bit of truth. If I had asked Rose about her sister, she probably would have warned me, or rather explained, which was the kinder way to think about someone whose husband and unborn child had been stolen from her in exchange for a wicked bitterness that all the vanilla in the world would never sweeten. Edith was not likely to budge. She would make me do the work myself and refuse, again, to provide any standard background information before she sent me into the battleground of Meet The Offspring, Round Two. How far away and long ago those blissful Vermont days now seemed.

I walked into the living room. It was more of a museum than a place to relax and hang out. The sofas were the kind that most of us were afraid to sit on. One drop of coffee or wine would ruin the white leather forever. The juxtaposition of the sad faces and lavish furnishings did not make any sense. I did not know about people who commingled the faces of impoverished children with untouchable couches. I could not guess what kind of person collected art and stored it in a room where nobody would want to spend time.

Playing Cello for the Trees

I stepped closer to the bookshelves and reached for the portrait of Pregnant Alice With Dead Husband. She lacked her sister's beauty. Her dead husband was not white, and I wondered whether she had collected him, too, from a distant land. His features looked Indian or Pakistani. I returned the picture to its place and perused the shelves. Classic literature filled a few bookcases, and a few others contained row after row of history, current affairs, geography, and philosophy. The bottom shelf was poetry and theology. I could not imagine cracking the shell of Alice's spiritual beliefs, and her small religion library made her a growing enigma.

As I stepped sideways along the wall of shelves, I discovered an official United States government-issued certificate that congratulated and thanked Alice for her service in the Peace Corps. A similar certificate hung on my own wall. Unlike Alice, though, I had opted out of Africa and requested a place less demanding of one's physical stamina and psyche. I recoiled with a familiar pang of guilt over my relatively easy years in Slovakia. Alice's stint in Tanzania could have been nothing like my tour of duty in Eastern Europe a decade later. Memories of sipping coffee in old-town Bratislava on my mornings off from teaching at a rural school clashed with images of Alice working to save starving and sick children in Africa.

I stood in her living room with one more puzzle piece in my hand. I turned away from the certificate and back toward the huge framed photographs. I wondered whether Alice had taken them herself in Tanzania and whether she had gone back again since her years as a volunteer. Maybe she was a professional photographer. Maybe the portrait of herself with her dead family was taken from a tripod, a shot that Alice had set up herself. The maybes were piling up, and I felt like an investigative reporter, though the situation should not have required sleuth work. My subjects and sources back home were transparent compared to Edith's clan. I asked questions, and they gave answers. That was standard procedure until now.

There was a click followed by the bang of the front door.

"Hello? Anybody here? We're back."

The sound of Edith's voice made me edgy but oddly pleased. The excitement of being in her orbit was indisputable. I was eager to get back to work. If Alice would tell me nothing beyond cleaning day and coffee time, I would have to coerce her story out of Edith or ease it out of Anthony, dear Anthony, whom I was eager to see. His voice was music in the midst of madness.

"I'm in here," I said.

Footsteps echoed through the apartment, and Edith and Anthony appeared in the living room. Anthony smiled at me with a warmth that said he had missed me, too. Mischief flickered in Edith's eyes, and she was robed, as ever, in shades of purple.

"You've arrived safe and sound," she said. "And you've met my eldest daughter."

"Yes, I have."

"And?"

"And what?"

"How did you find her?"

"Easily," I said. "I rang the bell, and she opened the door."

"You're in a playful mood," Edith said. "Or perhaps Alice irritated you. She has a way of doing that."

"Neither." I lied. "Extremely tired."

Edith stepped closer and gave me a hug. This was a first for us, and I found that I liked it. She felt bony and even fragile under all her loose flowy clothes.

"Welcome back," she said. "We've missed you."

"Hi, Lucy," Anthony said. He reached out a hand that had aged as poorly as the rest of him. I shook it with regret. I wanted to hug him, too. "I enjoyed your stories this summer."

My flushed cheeks told me in an instant whose opinion of my writing mattered most. I had never imagined Anthony as one of my readers. He patted me on the back and left his hand there for a moment.

"I can't wait to show you the city," Edith said. "Every word you've heard about this place is one-hundred-percent true. Well, come on! Let's go."

I had expected to wander the streets of New York solo. Edith would no doubt wave her hand and disregard me, but there was no denying the truth: the bigger the experience, the more I would enjoy it alone. Then I remembered why I was in New York. I remembered my dad's friend, the teachers' fight, and my vow to glue myself to Edith.

"Take it easy, Edith," Anthony said. "She just flew across the country. What do you need, Lucy? A shower? Maybe something to eat?"

I stared at this new version of Anthony, bold and fresh. I glanced at Edith and waited for her to pounce. She looked at me and waited.

"A shower sounds good," I said. I smiled at Anthony. I wanted a long shower, a quiet afternoon, and an early bedtime. I was, after all, off duty. Cunningham did not expect me to file my next story until we reached Greece. My readers did not need to know about our stop in New York. Yet, my beat was Edith, the real Edith, not some misunderstood version that was the subject of gossip back home and a recurring source of spite in my own head. Wherever Edith went, I would follow. Whatever she did, whatever pronouncements she spoke, whatever predicaments she choreographed for herself, I was beholden to observe and record. This was no time to be off duty. I started down the hallway toward my luggage in the guestroom.

"Now? You're going to shower right now?" Edith called out.

"Notebook. Pen. Wallet," I said over my shoulder.

"Why must you be so dramatic, dear? A single sentence of clarification would suffice." Her sigh reached me at the other end of the apartment. I knew that sigh. I was usually the one to make it.

"Back off a bit, Edith," Anthony said. "She's exhausted."

"Oh, what grandfatherly instincts," Edith said. "Always so thoughtful of others, so loyal to those you adore."

Her kiss reached the guest room, too, as I rushed to get ready. We three had a long road ahead of us. Argument and contention could not be part of the baggage that we carried to Greece, but Edith rarely was the one to step into conflict. In fact, more and more evidence had piled up to the contrary, despite her strong character and stronger personality. As I walked down the hallway toward them, my shoulder bag light with a single notebook and pen and emptied of books, I saw a tenderness in Edith's face that brought me back to the beginning, the very beginning, that day on her porch, her first day as a widow. Now she was looking at Anthony and holding his hands.

"You're absolutely right," she said. "Lucy has had a long day." She turned toward me, the gentleness still in her eyes. "Are you sure you're up for a stroll, dear?"

"Positive," I said. Positive was how I was determined to feel. Edith's kindness confused me and at times caught me off guard, but I could try to meet it halfway. With a clear mind and a loving heart, one could face anything, someone had taught me.

"Well, then, away we go, into the splendor of New York City," Edith said. She skipped to the door. Anthony shook his head and waved me on.

* * *

We stepped out of Alice's apartment building and onto East 52nd Street at Third Avenue, a location that my Manhattan guidebook told me was part of the Turtle Bay neighborhood and not far from the elite Sutton Place.

"This is as good a place as any to start," Edith said.

She looked around, nodded, and took off down the sidewalk. Anthony shot me a look, and we scurried to catch up with her. Edith powered onward, as we two alternated between pulling up beside her and dropping back when passers-by rushed at us head-on. And then, right then and there, of all places and all times, Edith launched into the story of Alice's life. Barreling down the sidewalk, indifferent to our darting and retreating, she started at the very beginning with the story of Alice's birth, a natural homebirth free of drugs and medical interventions in the peace of Edith and Henry's California home. Then Edith narrated Alice's early childhood and school years, pausing to note key moments that had shaped Alice's character, in the version according to her mother, anyway. I pulled up beside her and then dropped back again, dodging briefcases and swinging arms, straining to hear Edith's voice over the conversations and telephone calls that were swooshing past me every moment. She was divulging everything, and I was catching a fraction of it. My initial relief and curiosity for the chance to hear Alice's story gave way to frustration and then anger. Then I became suspicious. This could only have been the latest of Edith's games. We were in the chaos of city streets, and I had no way to record her long monologue, the facts of which were vital to my work and our evolving story. Noise and commotion swarmed around us, and I could barely hear Edith, let alone stand a chance of remembering everything that she said. Finally, I stopped, right in the middle of the sidewalk near a park on the East River.

"Edith, enough," I said. "Please." She kept walking. Anthony stopped and looked at me. "I won't do this. I'm on strike. And I'm serious this time."

At last she stopped and turned to look at me, too. "You certainly look serious. What's the problem, dear?"

"You expect me to chase you halfway around the world like some literary slave shackled to your every word, and yet you don't even give me a chance – "

Edith raised her finger, nodded her head, and crossed the street. She entered the park, walked to the nearest bench, and sat down. She patted the empty spaces on either side of her, raised her eyebrows at me and Anthony, and tossed her head from one side to the other to beckon us to our seats. We joined her, and there we sat, the three of us, thigh to thigh to thigh on a peeling green city park bench.

Then I heard a beep.

"Handy little machines, aren't they?" Anthony said. He leaned forward and looked over at me from Edith's other side. In his hand was a digital voice recorder identical to mine.

"You're my hero," I said.

"Not this again," Edith said. "He can't be your hero, because he's already mine. Get your own."

"That's not on the agenda," I said.

"Your time will come," Edith said. She patted my leg. "Your prince, too, shall one day arrive."

"Princess, according to my mother."

"Either way," Edith said.

"No. Not either way," I said. "If *he* were to arrive, *he* would in fact be a prince, a hero, a he. But I don't believe in that nonsense."

"You don't believe in love?" Anthony asked.

I sighed. "New subject, please."

Any subject would do, any at all except that dreaded one. I watched two squirrels chase one another around a tree. This was me enforcing a boundary with Edith. I stared ahead and said nothing. I was determined to resume the discussion of Alice, but the tree was a portal into my memory. As I watched the squirrels run around the tree trunk, I slipped into a time warp. I was back home in Oregon, and my parents were standing on the edge of a trail about two-thirds of the way up Broken Top. The terrain was rough, broken by a volcanic eruption thousands of years ago. The climb was challenging, and we had stopped for a water break. My mother chose that moment and location to ask me, as casually as she could between sips of water, "Lu- "Lucy, honey, are you sure you aren't gay?" I was twenty years old and living at home for the summer. My mom's prodding about my sex life had started early in high school, when there was nothing to report, and continued into college, when there was little more to report. My reticence and privacy had led her to false conclusions. For years she assumed that I was not interested in sex or romance. Now, she thought this. A speech about sexual orientation was not necessary in a family like mine. I had been raised on free thinking, free will, and free spiritedness, invited from my earliest days to explore the world around me and examine myself intellectually, emotionally, metaphorically, metaphysically, physically, and sexually. Everything was within the realm of possibility. All options were present and available. A fear of coming out to my parents was not the issue, a fact that my mother should have known.

"My sex life is not for parental consumption," I told her. My father drank from his water bottle and gazed off the side of the mountain to the scenery beyond and below. "My love life is private, Mom."

"Well, honey, from what we can tell, there isn't a love life. I don't mean to pry, but."

"Yes, that's very clear."

"It's just that, well, a woman your age. I mean, you're already twenty, and we have yet to meet any young man—or woman—who has stirred amorous feelings in you."

"Dad, are you hearing this? Dad? SOS! Your wife wants to know if anyone has, and I quote, 'stirred amorous feelings' in me."

My father screwed the top back on the bottle and sighed. He looked first at me and then at my mother. "Lucy has been visibly happy, presumably single, and possibly celibate through the ripe age of twenty," he said. "Let's leave parental worrying for something more deserving, shall we?" Then he turned back to me. "Good?"

I nodded. "More or less."

"More *more* or more *less*?" he inquired.

Every girl should have had a father like this. "Mostly more *more*."

"And the less part? That, I would imagine, is merely the youthful angst of 'what am I doing with my life' and 'I'm already twenty, and I don't have everything figured out yet.'"

"Exactly. Mom, are you getting this?"

She had walked on ahead, and she brushed us off with a flap of her hand. "Go ahead. Mock me. All I do is care about you and show an interest in your life, and you ridicule me and belittle me."

I ran up the trail and patted her rear end. We almost never argued, even though my teenage years, and this was a rare moment that I did not like one bit. She swatted my hand away. I patted again. Her flesh was firm at the age of fifty.

"I have only good intentions," she said. "I want you to be happy. Marriage and family have been the source of so much joy for me. How could I not want the same for you?"

"I'm twenty, Mom."

"I know. I don't mean now. It's just that I get the sense that you've already decided this, that you've already eliminated it from the list of possibilities. I don't want you to be lonely."

"Show me a married person who doesn't get lonely," I said.

She said nothing. We walked in silence for so long that I had nearly forgotten the conversation and even her presence behind me on the rocky trail.

"We're social beings," she said into the thick silence. "We're meant to find mates, to live with others, to be in community, to make families, to connect."

"Then I'm an aberration," I said. "I'm a loner by nature, Mom. That doesn't mean there's anything wrong with me. The trees and the rivers and the sky are my community. Books are the connection I want. Plus I have you two and Charlie. You don't need to worry about me." I turned around to smile at her for reassurance. She did not look convinced, so I gave in. "OK. Here it is. I hope you're happy that you've pushed me to this. I will tell you, and then we'll be done with this." I turned and faced her with my arms at my sides, my face void of expression, and my voice flat. "I've been in love once. Last year. And I had sex for the first time the summer before I left for college.

118

Right here in my sweet little hometown, under a juniper tree out east. And to a *boy*, just to be crystal clear. Right now, I want to be alone. I'm in *college*, remember? I'm supposed to be studying, not planning my wedding." I reached for her hand and squeezed it. "I'm not cynical, Mom. I'm afraid. That kind of love scares me."

She did not say anything. The way she looked at me was her best effort to take every ounce of mother love, put it on her face, and give it to me. Everything was there: her respect for my honesty, her reassurance that it was alright to be afraid, and her faith that love would come to me when the time was right. She was quiet. She may have been wondering which hometown boy had done the deed. I softened my face and kissed her cheek to let her know that telling her had been my choice, in fact, with no grudge held. I was glad that I told her. Now that she was gone, that moment was a piece of her that I could take out and look at any time I needed to.

Nothing had changed since then, except that I had amazing and unforgettable sex followed by amazing and unforgettable heartbreak with a guy in Bratislava that I loved but who did not love me back. That did not help me overcome my fear. It left me staring at tree trunks and watching squirrels instead of examining myself with anything akin to courage.

"Back to Alice?" Edith said.

"Yes," I said. "And may I please borrow that?" I asked Anthony. He winked and reached across Edith to give me his recorder.

"Alice will tell you nothing," Edith said, "and I do mean nothing. She will reveal nothing of herself to you or anyone else. I'll tell you anything you want to know about her."

"Isn't that a gross breach of her privacy?"

"Yes."

"So why would you betray your own daughter like that?"

"I have my reasons," Edith said. "The only one you need to know right now is that I've asked you to record the final chapters of my story, and my children are an integral part of it."

"Whether they like it or not?"

Edith patted my leg again. "Precisely. Ready?"

I nodded.

"And we are fine, at last, are we not?" she asked.

119

Edith had turned her head and was looking at me. This was not a question for Anthony. In my absence, they had already done the work of arriving at their version of fine. I looked at her for a moment. Something emitted sparks through the top of her head. The gem at the center of her, the mind inside her skull that was like no other, glowed more brightly than ever. I nodded, despite everything and in honor of everything.

"Very well then," Edith said.

The sense of finality bode well. In our remaining time together, the subject was never revisited. We were, in fact, fine at last. I, it seemed, would perhaps be fine, too.

We sat on the bench and let the rushing city pass us by as Edith told a long story without a happy ending.

* * *

From the age of three, Alice had uttered pleas to the world to change its wicked ways: "It just isn't right." "There must be a better way." "But that's not fair."

She was a soldier in the battle for justice, and not only for herself. She wanted to make the world a better place for all, especially those who needed it most. As she grew older, accusations that Alice was naïve and idealistic flew at her like bullets from more enemies than she could count. Yet, she stood on the side of justice and repelled the attacks with determination and a sense of self that nothing could shatter.

In first grade, Alice and her classmates wrote books at the end of the year to show off their skills as new writers. Their task was to write about what mattered to them most. Fifteen children wrote about their families, their pets, and their favorite toys. Alice wrote about human rights.

In second grade, at the age of eight, it was none other than Alice who stood between the notorious school bully and the class nerd. She received a black eye in exchange for her refusal to yield.

In third grade, Alice persuaded the girls in her class to cut their hair short in solidarity to show that prettiness was in fact pettiness in the eyes of some nine-year-old girls. She went on to lead the girls to victory over the boys not only in the school-wide spelling bee but also in the championship kickball game.

In fourth grade, Alice converted half her class and one lunch lady to vegetarianism and nagged the principal until he agreed to an assembly on animal rights. Thursdays in the cafeteria became meat-free. That, however, was not enough. Alice attended school-board meetings and spoke at the podium during the public-concerns portion each month until the board adopted a policy of one vegetarian meal each week at the other schools in the district, too.

In fifth grade, she demanded a feminist curriculum on March 8 for International Women's Day. The teacher's response to Alice's demand was a homework assignment for each student to make an oral presentation on a famous woman in American history. Alice watched her social status plummet among her peers.

In sixth grade, she established a sister-city partnership with the former hometown of a Mexican immigrant boy who joined her class halfway through the year. He knew no English, so Alice tutored him after school and taught his parents English on the weekends.

And so it went, year after year, until Alice graduated valedictorian with half the school in awe of her brain and her moral rigor and the other half celebrating the end of the torment known as Alice. She cared little about doing well; she wanted only to do good. Edith and Henry insisted that she apply to the best private schools in the nation. Every college application led to an acceptance, yet Alice declined the best, earning her father's consternation and her mother's respect. Off she went to the state university. "Real education for real people," she said. She studied history and anthropology in a double-major mission to learn the story of human society. Her concentration was social justice, and she wrote her senior thesis on the history of U.S. aid in certain regions of Africa. Of all the places in the world that needed her attention, Africa in general and Tanzania in particular won for the simple reason that Alice's roommate during her sophomore year, and her closest friend forever thereafter, was from Tanzania. That was how life worked, pivoting on coincidence and circumstance. A girl from the other side of the world walked into Alice's dorm room, plunked a suitcase on the second bed, and changed the course of Alice's life, pushed and pulled forevermore by the prevailing African wind.

"I'm Zalira." The girl thrust out a hand for shaking, as she had learned from her book about etiquette in America. She had tried it for the first time on the admissions officer who picked her up at the airport. It worked then, and it did with Alice, too. "I am from the land of Tanzania, and I have come to study agriculture. I want to grow the apple trees. For me, the apple is most exotic fruit in all this world and most beautiful food. This is my dream—to help the Earth make apples."

Alice loved her that instant. They ate three meals together every day. The fact of Zalira spending her time in science classes and on the university farm while Alice made her academic home in the humanities created no obstacle. On the weekends when Alice drove two hours across the mountains to visit her parents and indulge in home-cooked meals, Zalira went, too. During winter break, the roommates shared Alice's old bedroom back home for a month, and Alice taught Zalira how to ski. Holidays with the entire Small clan cemented Zalira's status as an honorary member of the family. Edith and Henry adored her as their own. Rose accepted her as another sister. Zalira's crush on Billy went unnoticed by nobody, except Billy. For more than twenty years, her every phone call and letter to Alice mentioned her best friend's younger brother.

Commencement Day arrived. The friends collected their diplomas, boarded an airplane, and traveled halfway around the world to visit Zalira's family and village. Upon arrival, Alice did not speak for two days, stunned into silence by the impoverished conditions that had—impossibly, to an American mind—produced her intelligent, funny, life-loving friend. On day three, Alice emerged from her silence with an announcement, a practice which she had no doubt learned from her mother: "I love you, Zalira. I love your family. I love your people. I love your country. You go back to America and grow apples. I'll stay here and grow healthcare and nutrition." They bid farewell at summer's end. The African returned to America, and the American remained in Africa.

For a year, they were pen pals, the old-fashioned way via international post. Zalira worked at an apple orchard in Washington state, and Alice worked in Zalira's village of three-hundred souls, using every connection and resource that she could cultivate to start new farms and growing practices, import vaccines, build a regional clinic, and spread the word of birth control for women and vitamins for all. She accepted her victories and her defeats. Then she kissed her adopted family goodbye to take a two-year post farther north under the of-official auspices of the United States government. Despite her free will and her free spirit, Alice learned after a year on her own that government programs would be the only way for her to make a dent in the suffering.

After three years in Tanzania without a single trip home, she departed for the States and graduate school, where she collected a piece of paper that would tell those in charge that she knew about public policy, too. With her save-the-world vision and a plan to chart the course for the rest of her work life, Alice stepped into the enormity that was the United Nations. She would leave only to make trips to Africa. Back and forth she ricocheted, from her office in New York to the villages of Tanzania and other African nations. She would spend her life feeding hungry children. She would work seventy hours each week and travel thousands of miles each year to decrease the rate of childhood starvation in Africa.

Her friends worried about her. Her family worried about her. Alice did not worry about herself. She claimed that the children brought her more joy than a normal American life ever could. Her work did not even feel like work. It felt like her being who she was here to be. She did not want a marriage. She did not want a family. She already had thousands of children to love. "And their love is the best kind anyway," Alice said.

Her mother remembered those words. Certain key moments in Alice's life came with lines of dialogue that Edith had memorized years earlier and could recite on demand. Nobody would think to question her accuracy, but if anyone did, Edith could produce the journal with dated entries where she had written Alice's words at the time when they had been spoken.

One summer day, as Alice walked from her office building to the corner deli for lunch, cupid's arrow struck the bull's eye of her heart. His name was Surat, born and raised in upper Manhattan of Indian immigrant parents who poked and prodded him to succeed in the American dream of professional achievement and the income that came with it. Along the way, however, Surat spent a semester in his ancestral land. The poverty and the hunger changed him in a way that his parents would never accept. He followed their plans for law school, and then parted ways with them to use his degree for non-profit work to help his native country. His parents' shame of him created his shame of them, a loop that destroyed any chance for a relationship. As Surat stood in line behind Alice at the salad bar, spooning lettuce and tomatoes into a plastic container, the sticker on her water bottle that dangled from her shoulder bag caught his attention: "Hungry children need to eat."

Surat laughed. "That makes it sound so simple."

Alice gave him the look that she reserved for everyone who was not an African child or a person working to end world hunger. "Excuse me?"

"Your sticker. It's so simple. Just feed the starving children. No controversy, no obstacles, just 'Hungry children need to eat.' Huh."

"The reality of hunger is actually extremely complex," Alice said. She was drizzling raspberry vinaigrette over her salad and did not look at Surat. "Sometimes it is literally impossible to get food to starving people."

"You sound like you know what you're talking about," he said.

Alice was disarmed by his soft voice, a concession that she would not make fully even to herself. She stood still for a moment as the salad container lid flapped up and down.

"I work with groups that are trying to feed children in India," Surat said. "Sometimes it's impossible. " He paused while his lid flapped, too. "I'm a staff attorney. The more impossible it gets, the more it becomes my problem to solve. You'd be amazed how many intelligent adults spend their time trying to keep food away from starving children."

Alice snapped her plastic lid shut. "I'm not amazed. I'm disgusted. I detest them all."

She paid for her salad and tea and left. She was walking along the sidewalk back to her office when Surat appeared at her side out of breath.

"Hello again."

"Hi."

"You're still frowning. This is not good."

"Do you generally concern yourself with the well-being of strangers?" Alice moved swiftly along the crowded sidewalk, eyes ahead, heels clicking against the cement in a rhythm that made no space for rests.

"No," Surat said. "People tend to disappoint me and annoy me. In fact, I try my best to avoid them. Which brings me to my point."

"You have a point?" The heels clicked along in steady rhythm.

"I have no friends," Surat said. "I have no life. All I do is work. I care more about children in India that I'll never meet than I do about anything else. Wow. It sounds insane when I say it out loud like that. I'm not, though. Insane, I mean. Oh, god, am I really saying this out loud to you?"

"Unfortunately, you are," Alice said.

Alice walked quickly, but Surat kept up. "Here's the situation," he said. "I have one friend at work. We used to hang out a lot. We were always each other's date at weddings and for work events—dinners, concerts, cocktail parties, the whole dreaded bit. There is an event tonight, a benefit dinner at the Indian Embassy. And yes, I mean the embassy, in D.C. A bunch of us are flying down in a chartered jet. My friend just got married, so now she brings her husband to all the work events. I'm stranded, and I'm in really big trouble this time, because my boss said I can't show up alone tonight. The ambassador is very suspicious of single Indian-American men my age. I've been warned that he may try to arrange a marriage for me. Please don't laugh. I don't want an arranged marriage, as you may imagine. So I was wondering—oh, God, help me—would you please kindly consider coming with me to Washington this evening? I know it sounds crazy, but it could be fun. I've never flown in a private plane before. Have you?"

Alice nodded. Surat caught his breath and wiped his forehead. "The dinner should be easy, and the food is always excellent. Plus, they've promised to return us to New York by midnight, so there shouldn't be any problems of the glass-slipper and pumpkin-carriage sort."

"Yes."

Surat stopped walking. "You said yes?"

"Yes, because you said 'please' and 'kindly.'"

"You're flying to another city for dinner with a stranger because I said please and kindly?"

"Yes."

"Wow. That's weird. What if I said, 'Please kindly start a local chapter of the Taliban with me.' Or, 'Please kindly marry me at sunset.' Or, 'Please kindly donate a kidney to save my life.'?"

Alice stopped, too. When Surat looked at her face, it was smiling. Then she was laughing.

"I like you," she said. "And I never like anyone."

"I know the feeling," Surat said, though he did not specify which of the two sentiments he knew.

Alice kept cocktail dresses, shoes, jackets, and purses in her closet at work for the events that she, too, was expected to attend on a regular basis. Most were fundraisers. Some were for networking. A few here and there were for "consciousness raising." She drank too much at those. On purpose. With Surat's business card tucked in her pocket, she entered her building and then her eighth-floor office with its coveted window. She ate her salad and sipped her iced tea through the afternoon while she finished writing a report on her latest trip to Africa. She watched the clock and assured herself that she was not watching the clock. She narrowed her wardrobe selection to the two top contenders: the standard little black dress that looked perfect, though perfectly ordinary, and a wine-colored silk shift. She locked her office door and tried on the dresses. There was nobody to turn to for advice. She had no friends to get her through the rough moments at work. Like Surat, she had no life. She, too, cared more about the children on whose behalf she worked than she did about anything else.

Alice had made no progress with her dress dilemma by 4:45. Surat would be waiting in a taxi outside her building in fifteen minutes. She contemplated calling her mother. She told her mother everything, after all. Then she pulled his card from her pocket and dialed the number.

"This is Alice, from the deli. Alice of tonight."

"Oh, no. You're calling to cancel. You've come to your senses."

"No. Wardrobe crisis."

"Oh."

"Option #1 is the little black dress. Option #2 is a wine-colored silk shift."

"#2 sounds better."

"But I look perfect in my little black dress."

"Of course you do. Every professional woman does, so that's what they all wear, every time. They're like invisibility cloaks. You don't even notice the person. They all blend together like a mass of black nothing. Distinguish yourself. Come in polka dots."

"Polka dots aren't professional."

"Well, then, anything but black. Surprise me."

When Surat arrived, Alive stepped onto the sidewalk in a navy-blue cocktail dress with dime-size white polka dots.

She wore it a week later when he asked her out to dinner, just the two of them, no work event.

And she was wearing it the night they celebrated their one-month anniversary. If an Alice and Surat museum were ever to open, the polka-dot dress would have been hanging in the central exhibition room on a satin hanger inside a well-lighted glass case with a security alarm.

Alice was twenty-eight years old when she fell in love for the first and only time. A year later, she took Surat with her to Africa to introduce him to the continent and the person that were the other loves of her life. Zalira had satisfied her apple dream and returned home to run a local farm and the food programs that Alice had established in her village years earlier. For one blissful month, Alice was in the place that she loved most with the two people whom she loved most.

For her thirtieth birthday, Alice asked Surat for a trip to India. Off they trotted for her to meet the other love of his life. The poverty of India looked different from the poverty of Africa, and yet something in the children's eyes looked remarkably similar. Surat had not been to his motherland for almost ten years, but he had assumed that his memories of the place and its people had remained vivid. The return trip blew his mind and his heart. For the first time since they met, Alice saw her lover cry.

The next summer, they were married in Alice's backyard, the little haven with the goldfish pond and the canopy of birches. There were twenty people at the wedding. Edith walked Alice down the gravel pathway as Surat's parents looked on in shock. Henry was her Man of Honor, and Rose, Billy, and Zalira were her attendants. Surat's parents watched with escalating horror.

The newlyweds had many happy times and adventures of the international and New York City types. At the age of thirty-two, Alice became pregnant, a fact that made her giggle like nothing before and nothing since. Life and love had led her to a destination that she could not have imagined herself arriving at: domestic bliss.

The baby was growing. Names were pondered. Grandparents-to-be celebrated, shopped, and bestowed upon the young couple the usual heaps of unwanted advice and baby equipment, clothing, and furniture.

One day about six months into the pregnancy, Surat and Alice both had work events. They kissed goodbye at home that morning. They expected to reunite at home late that night when their fundraiser dinners ended. They were sad to be attending work functions alone, and yet it was the first scheduling conflict that had kept them apart when they wished to be together. Oh well, they shrugged as they parted for the day. After all, it was only one night.

Alice arrived home first. She changed into the red satin pajamas that Surat had given her for her birthday a few years back. The elastic waistband was loose enough to allow for her growing belly. She poured herself a glass of seltzer with a wedge of lime. She began to read.

Ten o'clock came and went, followed by eleven o'clock. Soon it was midnight, and Alice grew puzzled. Then it was one o'clock in the morning, and Alice was worried.

At 1:17 a.m., the doorbell buzzed.

She opened the door and saw two New York City police officers. The police officers saw the city's newest widow. A single bullet shot by a fleeing armed robber had passed through her husband's chest as he walked from a taxi to the front door of their apartment building.

At her next prenatal appointment, Alice's midwife could not find the baby's heartbeat. Call it stress. Call it a loss of will to live. Call it the mystery of life.

Alice found herself alone once again. This time, however, was different. This time was not by choice.

* * *

When Edith came to the end of Alice's story, Anthony was sobbing, and I was watching a squirrel nibble at an acorn gripped in its tiny paws.

"That was ten years ago," Anthony said. "Has she dated anyone? Has she even tried to recover? Her whole life is still ahead of her."

"Oh, no," Edith said. "She works twelve hours a day, six days a week. Work owns her. Work is her. She planned it that way. Half her salary every month goes to the organization that Surat worked for. She takes care of his children and her own. When she isn't working, she looks at art. Every Sunday afternoon, she goes to a museum or gallery. She goes alone. When she's traveling, she looks at any art she can find. Once when she was in a place too remote and too hungry for art, she gave some of the children crayons and paper and asked them to draw. Their pictures are hanging in her office. I asked her once about her Sunday ritual, about art. She said it's the only thing that makes her feel good. When she looks at art, she feels something that isn't pain."

Anthony took a handkerchief from his back pocket and blew his nose. "For me it's the cello. For her it's art." He looked at Edith, his unexpected wife. "Or it was the cello. There's no replacement for human connection. I know that now."

I thought of Rose. For her it was poetry and her favorite musician. For Carter it was the outdoors and American history. They had much more than that, though. They had each other and their children as a foundation for everything and a haven in rough times. Alice had art and Africa. She did not have much else, but at least she had that. Anthony had his cello, his trees, and his love for Edith. And Edith— well, she had everything. For her, life's salve was everything everywhere. That was her beauty and her magic. It was what each of us could come back to whenever she pushed us too hard and made us brush up against a part of life or something in ourselves that we preferred to avoid. Edith's passion was life itself. She found joy in anything anywhere. She had something that I believed we all wanted but did not know how to get.

"Not everyone wants to connect," I said.

"Nonsense," Edith said. "Every last person on the planet wants to be loved. The whole damn lot of us is lonely and scared. Most are too afraid to admit it, though. They're too scared to let themselves say they're scared. They're too scared to say that they need love. And rightly so, because it is a terrifying risk to love another person."

I snickered a bit, despite my best effort at good behavior and meeting Edith halfway with kindness. "What could be more ordinary than love?"

Then it was their turn to snicker, a duet of cackles directed at me. "That's an odd comment from a woman who denies any interest in finding a man," Anthony said.

I stuck my tongue out at him. Edith kicked my foot with hers.

"Shall we walk?" she said.

"Yes," we said.

"Big overpriced sweet slushy coffee drinks?" Edith asked.

Anthony raised his eyebrows. I gave up and raised mine, too. Then, in a move I had not seen coming, I threw an arm around Edith.

"You always seem to know what the moment calls for," I said.

Then she looked at me in the same way that my mom had looked at me that day on Broken Top, the way that made the loneliness and the fear diminish for a time, the way that everyone wanted to be looked at. Like my mom, Edith did not say anything. She did not need to.

* * *

When we returned to the apartment a few hours later, Alice was carrying food to the dining table. It was two minutes before six. When she called us to the table, I glanced at her kitchen clock again: six o'clock exactly. Each of us sat alone on one side of a rectangular table. Alice and her mother were at the ends, and Anthony and I sat opposite one another on the long sides. I wondered where Alice sat when she ate alone.

"Blessings on this beautiful food that we so gratefully receive," Alice said. Her eyes were closed, and her hands hovered above her plate. "Thank you, Mother Earth, for the bounty that has reached us at a time when so many are suffering and food is controlled by the powerful and the greedy as our brothers and sisters around the world starve. Thanks to Mom, Anthony, and Lucy for enjoying this food with me tonight."

Our hostess then lifted the lids off a bowl of brown rice and a casserole dish containing a plethora of fresh vegetables in every color nature offered. The aroma was unfamiliar but tantalizing, and I waited for further instructions, semi-paralyzed by guilt.

"Mom, please." Alice gestured toward the serving dishes, and the clanging began as we filled our plates. The combination of spices and flavors was unlike anything I had ever eaten.

"I can taste half the world in your cooking, sweetheart," Edith said.

"Not quite half," Alice said. "Just parts of Africa and a touch of India."

Anthony and I looked up as Alice looked down. The evening passed without incident, a miracle. Alice and her home kept my nerves primed for something awful. Edith and Anthony cleaned up dinner while Alice read on the couch. Then they watched a documentary about the fast-food industry. I was in the guest room, pretending to write. In fact, I was staring out the window at the apartment building next door as I tried to make sense of Alice's life. She had carried on like this for ten years. Nothing would stop her from continuing for the next ten, twenty, thirty years with long days at the office, trips to Africa, and weekly viewings of art. She had not mentioned her sister or brother, though Edith told me they were all very close. There was nobody else in Alice's life other than her mother, her sister, and her brother. I picked up my pen and scribbled some unaskable questions about how often they visited one another, talked on the phone, and wrote letters. Beneath that I wrote Zalira's name, followed by a string of question marks. Cunningham would never let me wander that far off, but I could not control my curiosity. Edith was on pause. New York City was her waiting room. Her action would not resume until we landed in Greece. In the meantime, here was Alice, an enigma. As everyone knows, the inquisitive mind of a journalist and would-be novelist cannot resist an enigma in the form of a human subject.

* * *

The next day, the three of us took a tour of the United Nations. Edith had visited her daughter's work place several times but wanted to see it again. Anthony looked spellbound and asked the tour-guide several earnest questions. When the tour ended, we met Alice in the employees' cafeteria for coffee. She and Edith talked about Rose and Billy. Anthony and I smiled politely.

Then Alice escorted us to her building, her floor, and finally her office. Enormous framed photographs like the ones in her apartment covered the walls. The village children's crayon drawings were framed and hanging on her office walls, too, just as Edith had said. I heard some murmuring behind me about restrooms. Edith was calling my name, and I shook my head and waved her off as I continued to look, drawn into the children's sometimes vacant and sometimes piercing eyes. What I sought in their faces was not an explanation of who they were but a clue about who Alice was.

"I know the media write about whatever they want."

The voice startled me, and I swung around to face her. We were alone, and I had never wanted Edith so badly.

"You don't care about privacy," Alice said. "Even 'no comment' doesn't work. You always win in the end. You'll dig up something. You get others to speak about us if we refuse to speak for ourselves. I find your profession hideous."

Alice paused, but she did not look away. I did, though. I was desperate to look anywhere but at her face, even if that meant staring at the floor in defeat, like a child.

"I will not be a character in your sick story about my mother's so-called final adventures and her deranged plan to end her own life. Then again, you're too busy trying to untangle the pathos of your poor tragic heroine to pay much attention to me. I want to make myself absolutely clear, though. I don't condone my mother's plan. I oppose it for every reason you could think of—personal, ethical, political, spiritual, familial, everything. I expect that you'll write all sorts of detestable things about my mother and her plan, but if you dare to print one word about me, my life, my past, my job, or my thoughts on this subject, I will make you miserable. I will make you suffer. If you mention me in any way, especially in regard to my mother's planned

132

suicide, I will go after you every way I know how. And trust me, I know how."

When Alice finished, I heard something behind me and turned toward the doorway. Edith and Anthony had returned and were smiling. I excused myself to use the restroom and then proceeded past the door, into the elevator, and out onto the street. I started to walk, and I did not stop. I found my way to Central Park, and I walked every square foot of it. I stopped a few times to sit on a park bench and listen to how people talked to one another. I needed to hear one person say one kind word to another person. One kind word would have saved me. It would have rekindled my faith. What I heard instead were lovers' quarrels, parents hurling criticism at their children, and men and women of all ages, sizes, and colors in suits, dresses, jeans, shorts, and athletic attire whining and barking at one another and into cell phones. I gave up. I gave up on the people of New York and then the people of American and then, when I reached the very bottom of the pit of despair, the people of our planet. I walked and walked until my stomach was knotted with hunger, my feet were blistered, and my bladder was so full it stung and leaked.

The sky over Manhattan was growing dark. I found a pizza place with a public bathroom. I sat on the toilet to relieve myself in more ways than I had expected. Tears fell off my chin and mixed into my pee in the stench of a germy toilet that could very likely have given me an incurable disease that I was sure I deserved.

* * *

In the morning, I hid in the guest room and read *Don Quixote* until Alice, Edith, and Anthony were gone. I spent the day alone, despite my vow to glue myself to Edith for professional reasons. My profession had created an identity crisis and an ethical dilemma that I was in no hurry to face. I turned the other cheek, ignorant and blissful enough, and spent the day sightseeing. The city was more interesting than my own dark state of affairs, and by nightfall I had recovered from the doldrums.

I returned late, and they were already asleep. Tip-toeing in the dark past Alice on the living-room couch was the second most terrifying moment of my visit to New York. Her "I Will Go After You" speech stood at number one and also ranked high in my personal all-time top-ten moments of terror list. With all the variations of danger and disaster available in a city the size of New York, the one that had hunted me down was a petite international bureaucrat with venom in her tongue and fury that could cast a shadow on the Empire State Building.

When I emerged from the guest room the next morning for our departure from New York, Anthony greeted me.

"You just missed Alice," he said. "She took Edith out to breakfast. Then she had to get to a meeting."

He looked sorry for me. He had no inkling that Alice was my personal monster. We ate breakfast together at the counter in Alice's kitchen and swapped stories from yesterday's sightseeing adventures. He and Edith had visited the New York Public Library, too, and Anthony described the main reading room with poetry and precision that I could not have matched. We packed our suitcases and called for a taxi. Edith returned right on time, and together the three of us left Alice's apartment.

As we crossed the bridge and left Manhattan, I swiveled my head for one last look through the back window of the cab. Among the towering buildings, I saw one woman. I saw her at her desk in an office plastered with the faces and the art of a mission that saved her. I saw her eating alone at her dining table and sleeping alone in her big empty bed. I saw her at the deli when Surat appeared. I saw the photograph of her pregnant belly. I saw her love for her mother and her crushing fear of losing another loved one. I saw her devotion to hungry children half a world away. I saw her selflessness alongside her bitterness. I saw her victories in Africa and her grief in New York. I saw the parts that made up the whole truth about one human life, complicated, layered, miraculous, malicious, forgivable, and infinitely beautiful in its fragility.

I saw Alice all alone in that enormous city, and I missed her already.

TASK TWO:
SUNRISE AND SUNSET IN GREECE

A thousand feet above the Aegean Sea, the village of Imerovigli boasted the highest altitude of all the towns on the island of Santorini. The air was hot, but not too hot, and moist, but not too moist. The clicking and clunking of our suitcase wheels on the cobblestones announced to the local children a fresh batch of foreign tourists. I smiled at them. A boy smiled back and waved, and a girl stuck out her tongue. The others examined my clothing, my face, and my luggage.

Out of nowhere appeared a man. "Where will you stay?"

In unison, Edith, Anthony, and I said the name of our hotel. The man gestured down a narrow stone path. Through swinging wooden gates painted blue and across courtyards with stone and cement surfaces, we followed the man. He turned sharp corners faster than we could with our suitcases. He darted through narrow passageways that separated neighboring buildings by a mere two feet or so. At last, he stopped, nodded once, and pointed at a building with a sign bearing the name of our hotel. Then he was gone.

We were staying in one of the many family-owned and family-run inns known as cliff houses. Built on ledges and into the rocky hillside, our white inn with cobalt and turquoise accents was simple outside and elegant inside. Edith had researched the Greek Islands years ago and selected Santorini, the southern-most isle, north of Crete. When I signed on as her scribe, she had reserved a room for the month of August. We figured that I would stay for about a week, since my job of recording Edith as she witnessed a sunrise and a sunset could only be dragged out so long. We planned to share a room with a kitchenette, bathroom, and two-tiered private patio, one tier for each of us. Then Edith went and got herself a husband. With a few phone calls and his natural finesse, Anthony had managed to book a second room in the same inn and insisted on paying for it. As he saw it, he was the reason that I lost my status as Edith's roommate. *The Bugle* should have paid all my expenses, though that would have meant staying at a cheap hotel twenty minutes away in the island's sole city.

Edith and Anthony went to check in, and I walked to the edge of the courtyard to check out. Within moments, I was gone. Everything that I recognized as myself disappeared: worries, confusion, distractions, brain chatter, identity crisis, ethical dilemma, lingering memories from my recent visit to the pit of despair. As I looked down the jagged slope of the volcanic-rock cliff and out upon the bluest blue sea, I felt a metaphysical shift. Nothing happened, really. I just stood and looked. Yet, the looking, the gazing outward at beauty, was not nothing, it turned out.

"It's so beautiful," I said to nobody.

"It's so beautiful," I said to Edith when she handed me my room key.

"It's so beautiful," I said to Anthony when he suggested a walk into town for lunch.

"It's so beautiful," I said to the woman who emerged from the office and took the handle of my suitcase.

"Yes," she said. "Is beauty. This is our home, our life. This beauty."

* * *

I skipped lunch even though I was famished. The time I spent stowing my bags in my room and washing my hands and face were all that I could spare. The sea was calling me. I sat on a wooden chaise lounge on my courtyard patio, and I looked. Throughout the afternoon, I sat and looked. Looking at the natural beauty of the world was familiar. I had looked many times at lakes and streams, mountains and meadows, forests and wildflowers, full views from the top of the world. I had looked at the ocean before, too. Yet, I had never before felt so satisfied for so long from mere looking. I had never been spellbound from one hour to the next by any natural setting. I could not believe that there were people who got to live their lives, every single day, on Santorini. New York City was a distant and all but forgotten memory.

The sky was saturated with the blue of eternal summer and gave symmetry to the sea below. Large cloud clusters dotted the sky and zipped through the air on an afternoon breeze. They moved past the sun one at a time and changed the shade of blue on the surface of the water. One cloud cast shadows that darkened the sea to sapphire. When the sun reappeared, the water turned cobalt, and then turquoise. The nuances in the shades of blue above and below filled me with a hope that made anything seem possible. Before long, the hope morphed into something more active, and I began to sense anticipation.

Time passed. Minutes turned into hours. I looked at the beauty around me long enough that the truth came into focus. Sitting alone by the edge of the sea for an entire afternoon, nothing happened. Nothing at all. Yet, I would never be the same.

* * *

We walked single-file along a narrow stone path into town, winding our way toward a restaurant that Edith and Anthony had scouted out for our first dinner. This was the night when Edith at last would witness a sunset on a Greek island, one-half of task #19. At tomorrow's sunrise, #19 would be complete. Only one item would remain on her lifetime list.

"I don't want to leave," I said. "Now that I've seen this, now that I know this place exists, I don't want to be anywhere else."

"It is indeed stunning, dear," Edith said as she led us down the path. "Yet, life goes on."

"No," I said. "Life should not just go on. This place is amazing. All I need to do is look, and I'm fine. I'm at peace. It's as if the looking alone tells me what I need to know. The beauty of this place reorders everything."

"Goodness, that's some view you have from your patio," Edith said. She glanced back at Anthony. "We must have a partial view. I could not quite glimpse what I need to know from our patio."

"Well, I'm with Lucy," Anthony said. "Beauty has a way of clearing the garbage from your head."

"I'm delighted that you two are enjoying your stay," Edith said. "Just beware of an addiction to beauty. It's not to be found everywhere, and one must not depend on it."

An idea that I had been circling for a long time was finally in my grip. That was what the three hours of looking had done. It seemed obvious now.

"I want to quit my job," I said. "This story is too big for a newspaper. I want to tell it properly."

Edith stopped, then Anthony stopped at her heels, and I braked in time to prevent a pile-up. "You're quitting?" she said.

"Not exactly."

"Good."

"But I called my editor this afternoon, and he agreed to let me use my vacation time to stay here longer."

"I see," Edith said.

"I won't get in your way," I said.

"Goodness, Lucy, when will you stop assuming that I'm thinking the worst of you?" Edith said. "You will have a marvelous time, I'm sure. Maybe you'll meet a young man. Just a friend, of course. Enjoy yourself, by all means, but don't be late for our final stop on September first."

"Edith, there is nowhere on the planet that I want to be on September first except with you at your final stop," I said.

"Not even here?" She smiled and patted me on the back.

I could have stayed forever. There was an American couple that ran a cafe in the village, and from the taxi on the way through the main town I had spotted an English-language bookstore that was probably run by ex-pats. There must have been a monthly travel guide or a publication in English for tourists that needed a writer. I had never worked in a restaurant or a bar, but I had a secret fantasy of writing by day and bartending by night. I could have found a way to stay, if I really wanted to. I had a hunch, though, that trouble eventually surfaced for those who tried to turn a dreamy vacation into a permanent life. Or maybe trouble did not surface, and then maybe that was not much of a life.

We followed Edith into the restaurant and to a table by a wall of open windows on a porch with vast views straight down the steep cliff and out over the sea. Edith recited a poem about sunsets, and Anthony delivered a speech on our theme du jour of beauty. We told one another our reading lists for our stay on the island: the Greeks for me, American history for Anthony, and the autobiography of Amelia Earhart and *The Spirit of St. Louis* by Charles Lindbergh for Edith. She was gearing up for the cockpit already.

When our meal was over and Anthony had paid the bill, he stood and gazed through the open windows at the sea. "On the darkest days of winter, when the wall of gray is thick and the cold gets into the very marrow of my bones, I still crack open the window and play for the trees," he said. "And then I read the day away and listen to music. It won't be so bad, really, as long as I have my cello and my books."

The ticking of Edith's clock was growing louder. Already Anthony was charting his survival course, and he was counting on books and music to guide the way.

After dinner, we walked back to the inn and watched the sunset from the front patio where breakfast would be served each morning. After a few minutes, I wandered off to allow the romance of the moment to flourish. When I turned back for one last peek, Anthony's hand was silhouetted on Edith's shoulder as he held his arm around her. Her head lay in the crook of his neck. Their voices were soft and then silent, drifting out over the sea to blend with the red of the falling sun.

* * *

In the morning, we met at dawn and walked through the village to the hillside overlooking the other side of the island toward the east. In the afterglow of the Mediterranean sunrise, my new truth remained present. It had withstood the test of night and sleep. I returned to my room, wrote my next installment of Edith's story, and wandered into town after breakfast in search of an internet connection to send the article to Cunningham.

Item #19 was done. Two down and one to go. One to go.

* * *

Plato, Aristotle, Herodotus, Sophocles, and Homer, plus the Stoics Zeno and Epictetus, became my steady companions during our first week in Greece. Some days I ventured no farther than the seaside courtyard patio with my book, a notebook and pen, and the accoutrements of a modern Oregonian in the Mediterranean: sunscreen, baseball hat, and water bottle. The classics of ancient Greece did to me what they were meant to do. They drilled a hole straight to my brain and deposited big ideas about life while extracting petty obsessions, self-absorption, and the remnants of other nonsense that had been plaguing me of late. The Greeks boiled human life down to its essence, and upon this lean essence I feasted mentally for hours and days and weeks.

Nothing happened, really. I was on vacation, a woman of leisure. I had traded in my hiking boots for flip-flops, and I gazed down at the sea from a rocky cliff rather than down at the trees from the top of a mountain. I read. I pondered. I looked. I saw the sirens and the Cyclops. I heard a harp song and the flapping of Odysseus's sail. The gray-eyed Athena soared by en route to Olympus. Every now and then, I wondered about the future and an income, but not much. Time passed with ease. The three of us together and I on my own accumulated many fine days that would before long fade into a single blended memory of a happy time in a beautiful place.

Then one day I met a boy.

* * *

The clicking and clunking of suitcase wheels on ancient cobblestones announced a fresh batch of foreign tourists. I was sitting on my patio with a book and a bottle of wine. I no longer used clocks but measured the day by the sun and my state of mind. The line of demarcation between morning and afternoon was a slow transition from coffee to wine by way of a few intermediary glasses of ice water. The local white wine was light and refreshing. I sipped it throughout the afternoon, and the mild inebriation lulled a dreamer alone by the sea yet did not interfere with a mind set on reading.

My bare feet rested on the stone wall. The scalloped edge of my sundress flapped in the sea breeze in harmony to the flapping pages of the book that lay open on my lap. Sundresses by the sea could make even a gal like me feel pretty. Socrates and his boys were drunk again and delivering speeches about the origin of love. My favorite was the two halves theory. If only the modern world would produce for me a man like Aristophanes, with an oversized intellect, a yearning for romance, and a search for truth.

The clicking and clunking grew louder. Two male voices speaking American English penetrated the dream that had carried me off. Nobody new had arrived for days. I reached for my wine, tipped back my head, and sucked down the last drop as my hair brushed against my bare shoulders and back. The approaching travelers were probably recent graduates touring Europe with backpacks, goatees, and Daddy's credit card, or maybe they were middle-aged men recently divorced and looking for love with their travel books and wilted manhood to guide them. One young and one old voice passed behind me. The clicking and clunking grew louder and then faded into silence.

The next day at sunrise, I made my way down to the terrace where I ate breakfast each morning. The inn's cook was the only other person awake. I sat at my table by the front wall at the cliff's edge and placed Aristotle on the second placemat. The sea was everywhere. The day's new sunshine poured upward from the imaginary place where ocean met sky. The innkeeper's daughter who served as chef and server poured my coffee and left a basket of toast and jams. I was smearing raspberry preserves when I heard someone approach from behind me.

"Jet lag?"

I kept my eyes on the toast. "Early riser."

"Ambitious for a woman of leisure."

I glanced at the book that lay in front of me and took a bite of toast.

"Actually, I'm here for work."

"I saw you yesterday. A bottle of wine and a stack of books. A woman of leisure if ever I saw one."

He was gazing out at the sea, speaking as if to nobody, as if I were not sitting a few feet away receiving his words

"The sun is lighting you from behind. You look like a modern-day sun goddess. The auburn specks in your hair are glowing."

He still was not looking at me, though apparently he had stolen a glance or two.

"I'd like to join you, but you look content," he said.

He started to walk away, but I invited him to sit down.

"Are you sure?" he asked.

When he turned, I saw his face at last. It was not much better than my own. He stretched out a hand.

"I'm Tuck."

We shook hands, and he sat down across from me.

"I'm Lucy."

"Short for Lucille?"

"No, actually. Just Lucy. Tuck short for Tucker?"

"No, actually. My real name is Plato. Plato Zielinski. My dad's a Polish Jew, and my mom's a Yankee with a passion for the Greeks."

"Your parents named you Plato?"

"Preposterous, huh? Could have been worse. At least I'm not Zeus."

"My brother's name is Charlie. Charlie and Lucy."

"Your parents are a bit different, too, I guess. No dog by the name of Snoopy, I hope."

While we ate, he elicited basic facts from me, including my hometown, my job, and why I was in Santorini, as well as the story of my assignment covering Edith and her list, minus the part about her plans for the grand finale. I preferred to be the one who asked the questions, yet that morning I enjoyed the role of interviewee. When our omelets were gone and the fruit bowl was empty, we wiped our mouths and stared at the sea. I had about four seconds to come up with something before he would stand to leave, and yet I hesitated. Not once had he smiled, and I did not really want to know why. He slid his chair back and stood. I did the same.

"Are you here with your dad?" I asked.

"He's my uncle. My aunt just died of cancer. I thought the sun-shine and the sea would make him feel better, but he hasn't left our room."

He stood with his arms dangling at his sides, which made him look vulnerable, more vulnerable than most people would allow.

"They were married for forty years," he said. "She was every-thing to my uncle. They had two children, but one died from leukemia at age ten and the other was killed in a car crash in high school. My aunt and uncle managed to live, though, even after all that. Then my aunt got stomach cancer a few months ago, and now she's dead."

We were quiet for a long time. I did not say that I was sorry or how horrible it was or anything. I could not figure out where to put my hands. In the end, I let them drop to my sides.

"I wanted to help him, but now bringing him here seems like a mistake."

He sniffed a few times. I thought maybe he was crying, but sneaking a glance was too risky. We were standing beside one another, arms dangling, eyes set on a distant point out on the sea.

"He once said that he considered himself lucky because of the years he got to spend with his daughters. He said anyone who pitied him didn't understand. He was grateful to have had them as long as he did."

Tuck turned away from the sea and looked at me, and of all the moments to pick, that was when he showed me his smile.

"Can you believe there are people like that?" he said.

The smile changed his entire face and made me a little shaky.

"No."

"Me neither."

"If that's who your uncle is, he'll be OK," I said. "It can take a while, though."

"You know this?" he asked.

"My mom died in a car crash seven years ago."

"That's very sad. I'm sorry."

"Thank you."

He looked at me for a while. Then he turned back toward the water. I waited, but he did not move or speak, so I climbed the stairs to my room. I was halfway up when I heard his voice.

"I'm in Room 5, if you're looking for something to do."

* * *

I sat on my patio and pretended to read. I stared at each page, and every so often I would turn to the next page, ready or not. Concentration was one of my best skills, and with the exception of my mother's death, nothing had stopped me from reading. That morning, though, my mind would not focus on Aristotle or *The Iliad*. I tried gazing at the sea, but the view that had sustained me for days had lost its magic.

Room 5 was next to Room 4, where Edith and Anthony were staying. I sneaked past their room on bare feet, noisy flip-flops in hand. I knocked quietly at Room 5 and waited. If he was in there, he probably could not hear the knock. If I knocked more loudly, though, Edith would appear and ruin everything. I climbed the stairs to my room and put my books on the shelf. I had explored the island's big town once, but there was more to see. I threw a travel guide, my wallet, and a notebook and pen into my backpack and headed toward the door. I stepped outside, pulled the door closed, and locked it.

I turned to look at the sea, desperate for an anchor to which I could attach myself. All I saw was water. I had seen it a million times before. Back home, a team of reporters were scouring the town for election news, interviewing candidates for the city-council seats up for grabs in early November, sniffing out campaign fraud, and surveying local residents about the issues that mattered most in the election that I would miss. I had not filed a story since our second day on the island. I was writing, sort of. I was taking notes. I had an idea, the one that had been born in Vermont and followed me to Oregon and New York and now Greece. I was not giving it my full attention. I scratched at it from the sides, scribbled lists and outlines, and wrote a few lines here and there.

"Are you OK?

Tuck was standing on my patio, about three feet away, staring at my face.

"Why couldn't you read?" he asked.

I frowned at him.

"I saw you from our patio," he said. "Something looked wrong."

"I'm not good at vacation. I need to work."

Tuck nodded. "When you knocked on my door, I couldn't come. My uncle was crying."

"Oh. Is he OK?"

"He started talking. A whole month of silence, and then suddenly it all comes out. On me."

"Are you OK?"

He shrugged. "I'm tougher than I look. Kinder, too."

"You look both to me."

He did not bother to smile, and I did not bother to worry.

"What did you want?" he asked. "At the door?"

"You," I said.

"Oh."

"Will you go into town with me? We could walk around and have lunch somewhere. There's an archeology museum that looks interesting. We could rent a scooter, and I'll show you the beaches down south."

"OK." He did not move.

"Do you need to get your stuff?"

"I don't have stuff."

"So, you're ready?"

"After you."

We walked along the path that led to the village center, where we rented a scooter for the day. I had driven one to the southern beaches, and there was little to learn and nothing to worry about, except traffic. The traffic on the island was not heavy, but drivers did not seem concerned with following rules or staying inside lines.

"I'm scared," Tuck said.

We were wearing our helmets as we stood on the sidewalk outside RENT MOTO. I pulled the straps of my backpack onto my shoulders. I had filled out the rental form, since I had done it before and knew the routine. I wrote down both our names, and we both signed the form. I figured we would take turns driving.

"Why didn't you tell me before?" I asked him.

"I'm scared to drive it."

"Oh."

"But I'm the guy."

"So?"

"In case you hadn't noticed, feminism hasn't reached the shores of Santorini. They'll laugh me off the island."

"I'll laugh you off the island if you don't trust me and get on."

We cruised down the long hill out of the village toward the capital city of Fira. We parked the scooter and walked along the narrow streets. The main road through town zigged and zagged to accommodate old churches and buildings. Traffic was a mess. Tuck pointed out a bookstore, and we went in. I liked to look at the Greek letters but lost interest after a few minutes. He browsed on and on, which seemed strange since there was not an English-language book in sight. Then I remembered his mother's love of everything Greek and wondered whether he knew the language. He bought two books and thanked me for my patience as we left the store.

We discovered a café overlooking the sea and ordered iced coffee and pastries at a table on the back terrace. I eased Tuck's biographical sketch from him, one question at a time. He was born and raised in a small town in northern Minnesota, where his parents were dentists with their own practice. The youngest of three children, he had grown up on nature, books, and world travel. He liked languages, especially old ones, and had studied Latin and Greek from the age of seven with private tutors. His parents did not believe in competitive sports, though ice hockey was the center of the local culture and community. They went to the big games and cheered for both teams. His entire family still lived in Minnesota, including his parents and two siblings as well as aunts, uncles, cousins, and both sets of grandparents. He was the only one who left. After seven years in New England for college and graduate school, he took a job in California. He did not care about the warm weather, but he loved being near the mountains and the ocean.

"I'm out there every weekend," he said. "I'm not much of an athlete, and I'm not one of those guys who need to conquer nature to prove themselves."

He looked away for a minute.

"I'm sure you know the type. That's probably the kind of guy you grew up around, the sort you hang out with."

He was right, but the only two mountain men in my life shared my genetic coding.

"Mostly, I walk," Tuck said. "I walk on the beaches for miles, and I walk in the mountains for miles. I love it, but I can't imagine living there forever. Sometimes I think going back home would be nice."

Our similar interests and background were a coincidence, a comfort, and an instant bond, though Oregon had nothing on the north of Minnesota. The winters that Tuck described were brutal, and a small-town childhood was far from what I knew. Our work was different, too. I was out in the world learning about and from other people, on whom I relied for information and insights. Tuck sat alone at a desk, where his only interaction day after day was with the screen in front of him. He was a computer programmer.

"You know, one of those guys who work a ton of hours and earn lots of money that they never spend because all they do is work," Tuck said. "I like to travel. I guess I could plan some exotic trips. This is my first vacation in two years."

He looked at me, and I nodded and smiled because he needed me to.

"It's not as bad as it sounds," he said. "I never work on the weekends. That's when I go to the mountains or the coast. And I really like my job. It makes all the parts of my brain work together in the best way they know how."

I watched his face change, and I knew what he was probably feeling, because I knew how I felt when my face looked like that.

"I love my job, too," I said. "And I don't have many friends, either. In fact, none, really."

He kept looking at me. "I've never told anyone this."

"It's OK. Please don't worry."

He was shaking his head. "I don't mean that. I mean what I'm about to say."

"You don't have to tell me anything you don't want to."

This was the problem with connecting with a fellow human. He told you his truth, then you had to tell him yours, and before long, someone got hurt or disappointed or wound up dead.

"I want to," Tuck said.

His face looked calm. He was not nervous. He actually seemed excited to tell me his secret.

"I take a long lunch break every day, but not to eat lunch," he said. "I go to a building in our complex that has a daycare center."

He had moved to the front edge of his seat, and his elbows were on the table with his hands clasped together as if in prayer. He was leaning toward me, and his face had come alive.

"My boss doesn't know. Nobody knows. They think I'm at meetings or working out or whatever. A lot of my co-workers exercise at lunchtime. Not me. Do you know what the human brain needs in order to develop well? Do you know what we need most from the second we're born?"

I shook my head. His face was getting red and looked hot.

"Love. The human brain needs love to develop to its full potential. And the most essential form of love for a newborn baby is physical contact. Touch. Right after I first started my job, I went to the daycare center, and I found the baby room. There were two women and twelve babies. The parents work eight to twelve hours each day, five days in a row. All parents love their children. I believe that, but the reality is that if you're at work, you aren't holding your baby. And if two adults are caring for a dozen babies, well, do the math. Not enough holding. As a culture, we don't hold our babies nearly enough. So, I asked if I could hold them. One of the women was skeptical and asked if I was a father. Then she wanted to see my employee ID. The other woman was really warm and gentle, and she said of course I could hold a baby, because that's what babies wanted, to be held. She handed me one, and it was magic. Its skin was so soft, and it smelled good. Nothing smells like a baby. It looked at my face, and just as it was about to cry, I started to walk around and sing a little, and the baby got quiet and stared at my face. It was magical and beautiful. So I went back the next day, and the suspicious woman didn't say anything. I went every day for a week, and then I went the next week, too, and now it's been almost two years. I spend an hour with the babies every day. The women who work there told me they could get fired if anyone found out. They told me not to tell anyone. We could probably all go to prison. They probably put you in prison if you hold someone's baby without their permission. Some of the mothers come on their lunch breaks to breastfeed. Talk about beautiful. God, it still blows my mind. They probably figure I'm a dad. Most of them are so rushed and stressed out that they don't even notice me. I bet they need to be held, too, the nursing mothers. Anyway, I go every day, and I've seen a lot of the babies grow up. It happens so fast. One year. They go into a different room when they start walking. I stick to the baby room, though. I like the little ones."

He did not look away from me once. Eye contact for Tuck was as effortless as good manners and honesty. When he reached the end of his story, he was pink and calm again. A smile covered his whole face. He looked peaceful and content. Most people wanted validation or approval after a confession like that. Not Tuck.

"That's your passion," I said.

"Not really. It's just something I do. Like a funny hobby."

I shook my head. "It's not funny. It's wonderful," I said. "And it is your passion. It gets at a part of you that nothing else can. It brings you to life. It makes your face turn red and hot, because it brings your blood to the surface and makes you feel more alive than anything else."

Tuck gave me an odd look, which was unfair, because I had not given him one single odd look during his entire speech. He must have seen my face get sad, because he started to nod.

"I never thought of that before," he said. "You're probably right. What about you? Is your passion discovering other people's passions?"

I thought he was teasing me, but when I looked at him, I saw only sincerity and joy. I half-shrugged, unwilling to agree or disagree. He may have been right.

"You collect life stories," he said. "An ancient tradition. You're like Homer and his characters all wrapped up in one, traveling the world, gathering tales of human lives along the way, and writing them down for others to read."

I was pondering his theory when who should appear at the front door of the café but Edith, with Anthony three paces behind.

"Oh, no."

"What's wrong?"

"We need to get out of here."

"You have enemies in Fira?"

"Worse. I have friends." I slid down in my chair. "We need to leave. Now."

"This must be a record. We've spent something like three hours together, and already you're embarrassed of me."

"It's not you. It's her. Please don't make me explain. We need to get out of here."

I glanced around the cafe and spotted a back door. Edith and Anthony were being led to a table.

"Follow me," I said.

I fled to the back door and out into an alley. I followed the alley past several stores and restaurants until I reached a street, which I walked along until I reached a park, which I ran through until I had put enough distance between myself and her. I collapsed on a bench. A split second later, my sightseeing partner plopped down next to me. We stared straight ahead through the dangling tree branches at the church across the street.

"How can you write about someone you hate?" Tuck asked.

"I don't hate Edith."

"Doesn't look that way."

"It's complicated."

"Always is with people."

I looked at him. "Are you social?"

He sighed. "If I say no, you might think I'm a loner or a weirdo or even a misanthrope. If I say yes, you might think I'm lying."

"Misanthrope?"

"Yes. Lovely word. From the Greek, coincidentally."

"It is a lovely word," I said. "Ironically."

"I haven't answered your question," Tuck said.

"Yes, you have," I said. "I'm a loner, too."

"Except that you knock on strangers' doors before you go into town, rather than going alone," Tuck said.

I did not look at him, but I heard a distinct kind of teasing in his voice that was commonly known as flirting. "I've been here for more than two weeks," I said. "I needed a change. And anyway, it's not habitual. It's not 'strangers' doors' in the plural. One stranger. One door."

"I think it's possible to be a contented loner but also to get lonely," he said.

"I think that, too," I said.

"Good," Tuck said. "So, right now we're just taking a break from being lonely loners."

We decided to go to the archaeology museum. Tuck walked close beside me as we meandered through the park. I felt his hand brush against my skirt, and I withdrew my hand before he tried to hold it. As we waited on the sidewalk to cross the street, the hum of a scooter caught my attention. I turned to look at it, and a fast car crossed my peripheral vision. The driver on the scooter was leaning forward to check for traffic, but a tour bus was parked in the way. My brain did the calculations a split second before my eyes saw what happened. The scooter lurched forward to cross the road.

"NO!" I yelled.

Tuck and I watched the speeding car smash into the scooter. He sprinted down the street, and I followed. He knelt down beside the scooter driver who had been thrown across the road and was wedged against the curb.

"Can you speak? Can you hear me?" Tuck said.

A pair of eyes blinked inside the helmet. I knelt beside Tuck.

"She's trying to speak," I said.

"Americans," she said. "Hi."

We nodded. Her breathing was loud and rattly. She closed her eyes, and I gasped. Then she opened them again.

"It's OK," she said. "I loved my life. I used it well."

She breathed more loudly, and then she said, "Tell my children I love them forever. Tell my husband to—"

Her breathing rattled one last time. Then she was gone. Tuck had his ear to her face, and then he started CPR. "Go get help," he said.

I stood up, but a crowd was pushing in around me. Then the police were there, and someone shoved me out of the way. The sirens and the crowd and her words and her rattling breath moved in and out of my ears, louder and louder, until all of a sudden there was nothing.

* * *

When I opened my eyes, two men were lifting me onto a stretcher.

"Hello. I'm fine. Stop, please."

I tried to sit up, but one of them pushed me down. "No moving," he said. "You hurt head."

I gave up and lay still. All I had wanted was to see was a Greek sunrise and sunset, but now I was seeing the inside of a Greek ambulance, soon to be followed by a Greek hospital. I wanted Edith, which confirmed my level of desperation.

"Lucy, I'm right here."

I lifted my head to find him.

"No moving, girl!"

A hand on my ankle gave a gentle squeeze.

"I'll go with you," Tuck said. "Don't worry."

We boarded the ambulance, and with a medic beside me and Tuck at my feet, we zipped through the streets of Fira. Tuck's hand did not leave my ankle. He squeezed again. The medic shined a light into my eyeballs. Then he took my wrist and checked my pulse.

"You went down pretty hard," Tuck said. "They're worried about a concussion."

"She died," I said.

He squeezed my ankle.

"She died," I said again.

"Yes," Tuck said.

I wanted to see him, but all I had was his voice.

"Is it my fault?" I asked. "Because I didn't run for help right away?"

"No," he said. "She must have had massive internal injuries. There was nothing anyone could have done."

"Did you hear her?"

"Yes."

"Do you remember what she said?"

"Vaguely."

"I remember every word. I have all of it exactly. That's what I do. I remember people's words. I can remember every word exactly right for about an hour."

The squeeze left my ankle. I felt something on my hand. Tuck was beside me now, and he held my hand and rubbed the top of it with his thumb. It was working. It was soothing me, and apparently I needed to be soothed, because the medic came at me with a tissue in his hand and wiped my eyes.

"I dreamed about her when I blacked out. I saw her. I heard her voice. I need to know who she is. I have to tell her family what she said."

Tuck nodded. "Edith was there," he said. "She appeared out of nowhere right before you passed out. We agreed to split up. I came with you, and she's trying to track down the woman's name and address in the States."

"Edith?"

"She was really worried about you,' Tuck said. "I had to fight her to be the one to come with you. From what you said about her earlier, I thought you'd be upset to see her when you woke up."

I felt pain on the back of my head, and a wave of nausea moved through me and then away. "What time is it?"

Tuck looked at his watch. "About one o'clock."

"I met you at breakfast."

"Yes."

"That was six o'clock."

"Yes."

"Today."

"Yes."

"You're sure it was today?"

"Yes."

"So, we just met, and we've spent maybe four or five hours together."

"That sounds about right."

"And you know these things about me? And you did this for me?"

Tuck nodded and tried to smile a little. The pain in my head throbbed more, and the wave of nausea came and went again. I closed my eyes and waited for blackness or vomit or both. My symptoms were consistent with a fall and head injury, but the truth was that something else entirely was happening to me. I was not suffering from a concussion. I was about to swoon for the oldest reason in human history.

* * *

I did swoon, but the cause was in fact a mild concussion and dehydration, according to the emergency-room physician. I did not drink any water all day. That was true, but the reason for my not remembering to drink water pointed at the actual underlying problem. Coffee at dawn followed by more coffee with my sightseeing partner, eyewitness to death and dramatic final words, and intense sun exposure without sunscreen or a hat had landed me skull-to-pavement and in the local hospital. Those were the facts, but no doctor would find what truly ailed me.

Playing Cello for the Trees

They would not let me leave. For an hour, and then another hour, and then another, I waited in a recovery room. Tuck stayed with me the entire time as a saline drip rehydrated me. He told me more of his life story, and I told him more of mine. We played entertaining getting-to-know-you games, such as describing the highlights and low points of our youth, and listing our favorite books, music, mountains, beer, cities, college courses, and reasons we still liked our parents. We overlapped in places—Mozart, dark beers, Greek philosophy, Eastern Europe—and parted ways in others. He liked opera, which I could tolerate for no more than a few minutes. He liked cross-country skiing and called downhill skiing an "unsport." I forgave him, since he was from an essentially mountainless place and because I was in a foreign hospital having fun rather than in a foreign hospital alone and scared. He listened to my tales of hiking and camping in the Cascades as a child with my family. He could not believe that I had slept alone in the mountains on several occasions.

"I am man enough to tell you in no uncertain terms that I am not man enough to sleep alone in the mountains."

A nurse came in to check me one last time. Then I signed my discharge papers, and we left. In the taxi, I told Tuck the entire story of how I met Ramona in Bratislava. He had a best friend from childhood that he still saw often, and he looked genuinely happy for me. He was the first person that I ever told about Ramona, other than my dad and Charlie, and it felt like giving him a piece of myself. I was glad to give it.

When we got back to the inn, the sun was going down, and we went straight to my room. We slept together, but not in that way. The emergency-room doctor said I needed full surveillance for twenty-four hours because of the concussion. Tuck set an alarm to go off in two hours. He would wake me every two hours all night to be sure that I would wake up and was alright. When the lights were out, and I was in bed, he lay down on the couch. I was still trying to think of something to say when Tuck started to snore. I lay awake for a long time, as the dying woman's final words repeated in my mind again and again.

* * *

When I woke up the next morning, Edith and Anthony were eating breakfast with Tuck's Uncle Lewis. As it turned out, I was not the only one who had been busy making new friends and gathering life stories. While Tuck and I had been at the hospital, the others were having a grand time of their own. There was a chummy spirit to the threesome's conversation and a familiarity in their shared laughter that stirred my curiosity and envy. Edith's charm had no limit, and if anyone could preach a love of life back into a recent widower, she was the best candidate for the job.

I had a wicked headache but no amnesia, no coma, and no permanent paralysis. Yesterday was over, and today was ahead of us, though I was under doctor's orders to rest for two days. I shooed off the newlyweds and the Minnesotans and settled in for a day with my book, my water bottle, and a slew of pain relievers.

An hour later, Tuck was back. "I put them on a sightseeing boat to a nearby island for the day," he said. Then he disappeared into his room.

A few minutes later, he pulled up a chair beside me at my favorite seaside wall and opened a book. We passed the day side by side, each of us lost in our own books and thoughts. We chatted once in a while, too, about nothing in particular.

Later that afternoon, I wrote a letter to the dead woman's family. Writing was my way over, around, and through human emotion, but the letter also seemed like a moral obligation, given what I knew and they did not. I expressed my condolences, conveyed her final words, and assured her family of their accuracy and my qualifications for remembering and reporting. The letter fit on one side of the crisp white stationary that I had found in my room. Tuck walked into the village center to mail it.

He was gone for seventeen minutes, and I missed him at minute four.

* * *

The night before their early-morning departure, Tuck and his uncle said their official goodbyes to us. The five of us ate dinner together on the patio, thanks to a special arrangement that Edith made with the innkeeper. Hugs and exchanges of contact information ended the night. When Tuck and Uncle Lewis turned toward their room for

an early bedtime, I started up the stairs to my room. My own departure was a few days away. I would have time alone now to finish the
final book on my Greek reading list. The sense of accomplishment
would satisfy me. Reading would occupy me. Time would move
along at a fine clip, to be sure. And anyway, a loner like me would be
relieved to be alone again.

When the door closed behind me, the darkness looked emptier
and the silence was quieter than any night since we had arrived. A
voice inside my head pleaded with me not to despair. The voice was
gentle, a kinder narrator than usually showed up for me. I thought of
my mom and her concern that I had turned my back on love. I thought
of my dad and his concern that I would arrive alone for our weekly
dinners every Sunday for the rest of his life. Tuck lived about an hour
away from Edith's son in California. We planned to call each other
when I arrived. The last of Edith's three tasks would take much longer
than the other two. Soon I would be occupied with my notebook and
pen again, observing and following her through every step of her last
adventure. My days as a woman of leisure would drift into my own
history and into the shared past of an adventurer, her husband, a ta-
galong scribe, a sightseeing partner, and a grieving uncle. I pulled a
scrap of paper from the pocket of my skirt and placed it on the table.
Tuck had written down his address and phone number in advance and
brought it to dinner. I had done the same. Our hug goodbye had been
our first hug ever. He smelled like his scooter helmet, the Aegean Sea,
and laundry detergent. He felt like a teddy bear without much stuff-
ing, safe and cozy but perhaps in need of a little comfort himself.

I shuffled on bare feet into the bathroom and brushed my teeth.
The narrator in my head had changed tactics and was using logic to
remind me that I had no interest in or time for entanglements, and that
literary ambition and my role as a reporter were the truth, the whole
truth, and nothing but the truth, so help me Edith. The voice grew
more aggressive and insisted that we were doomed from the start on
the morning that Tuck appeared at my breakfast table, looking anywhere but at me and making smileless jokes. The narrator droned on
and on, eager to draw me in, but nothing worked. The voice of doom
had failed. I was not listening. I had forgotten my first impression of
his face. I knew only his appeal, which started in his eyes and his oc-

casional smile, continued in his mind, and moved down into his heart, the heart of a protector who had battled Edith to win a seat by my side in a Greek ambulance, the heart of a devoted nephew who led his grieving uncle to an island paradise to recover, the heart of a computer genius who loved his work and loved babies, too. I spit my toothpaste into the sink, rinsed my mouth, and dashed out the door.

A full moon was rising up from the water as I flew across my patio and darted down the stairs toward Tuck's room. I was a bold if not confused Cinderella, reversing my untimely exit to return to the scene of aborted romance, sprinting barefooted to the place where we had recently parted. I reached the bottom of the stairs still moving at top speed despite a stone wall that was quickly coming closer. My stomach hit the top of the wall, and my toes jammed hard into the bottom. I nearly flipped over onto the terrace below but somehow managed to steady myself despite the searing pain in my hip bones and big toes.

"Lucy."

I rubbed my hips as I looked to my right and then to my left. Tuck was sitting on a wall on the lower terrace. He was facing the sea and the moon with his legs dangling out over a long drop down. I had never thought of him as dangerous, but sitting like that seemed insane. I hobbled over.

"Why were you running so fast?"

"Oh. That." My hips were throbbing, and my toes were bleeding. "I, uh."

He looked out over the sea. "The moon?"

"Yes," I lied. "I caught a glimpse of it from my room and wanted a closer look."

He looked back at me. "The sea isn't visible from your room."

No lie or excuse in the world could save me from what was about to happen, because I did not want to be saved. The narrator had been wrong, and Tuck was right. The moon was not my destination, it was a prop on the stage that the gods had set for me. I sat beside him on the wall with my back to the sea and my bloody feet on the terrace. I was looking at his face, and it was a fine face to look at—a face that had earned my trust through hours of listening, a face that had offered the best smile it knew at the least expected moments, a face that seemed like the perfect match for my own face. I put my hand on his leg, opened my mouth slightly, and leaned forward. My lips ran into his cheek bone. He had seen me coming and turned his head. I leaned back, pulled my hand off his leg, and stood up.

Then I was gone, flying on the staircase again, a failed Cinderella with blood-stained feet and tear-stained cheeks. I heard him call after me, just once, as I closed the door behind me and cursed the gods, the Greeks, and the goddamn narrator who reminded me that my face was no better than his and no good for wooing a prince under the moonlight.

TASK THREE:
IN THE COCKPIT

Billy Small lived in a bungalow three blocks from the beach. By day, he read on his roof-top sun deck and surfed the waves of Half Moon Bay, shaggy-haired and reckless as a teenage boy. By night, he worked at an animal clinic, where he provided after-hours emergency care for local pets, the pampered dogs and cats—plus the occasional rabbit, peacock, or monkey—of the wealthy professionals who commuted into San Francisco. After he graduated from college with a degree in biology, Billy had flown to Alaska and worked for a year on a fishing boat. With the money he saved from one of the most dangerous jobs in America, he made the down payment and got a mortgage for a 1,200-square-foot cottage that was now was worth millions. The zip code that once belonged to a quintessential sleepy beach town now was a status symbol for a quintessential overpriced yuppie paradise. Billy shrugged if anyone mentioned the value of his property. He was not looking to make a fortune or make a move. He wanted to enjoy life, and by all indications, he was succeeding. During his first few years in California, he had commuted into the city for classes. Once his training as a veterinarian was complete, he had no use for the city. His little slice of the coast was all he needed.

He picked us up at the San Francisco airport wearing faded board shorts, a T-shirt with a hole in one armpit, and flip-flops. At the age of forty, this was Billy's uniform at home. For work, he traded the shorts for jeans and the flip-flops for running shoes, not because the clinic was air-conditioned but because too much bare skin seemed unprofessional, even to a man like Billy.

Edith sat in the front seat of his jeep, and Anthony and I squished into the backseat. We had woken up that morning in Santorini, flown through Athens and London, and landed at last in San Francisco. Exhaustion made us indifferent to a bad back seat. We were glad not to be on an airplane, and we were less than an hour from our final destination.

"You guys OK back there?" Bill asked every so often. He stretched his neck to peer at us in the rearview mirror. He winked at me once, and I spent the rest of the drive trying to get a glimpse of his left hand. When he pulled into the driveway, I finally got a clear shot of his ringless hand when he opened the back door for me.

The house was nondescript from the outside: one-story, beige with white trim, grass with no landscaping, and a short gravel driveway. Inside, though, it was a marvel. The kitchen had the trimmings of a modern chef, including marble counters, copper pots hanging from the ceiling, an island with a built-in mini sink, and unstained wood-and-glass cabinets that showcased the handmade glassware and hand-thrown pottery of a man who lived alone but spent hours cooking and entertaining for his own and others' pleasure. I was still gawking at the kitchen when Edith called my name. I followed her voice to the back of the house, where identical bedrooms stood side by side, each with its own private bathroom. One was Billy's. The other was the guest room.

"Anthony and I will stay here," Edith said. "And you'll be staying—"

"Let me show her, Ma."

Billy was standing at a door in the back of his bedroom. He tossed his head to one side and smiled in a gesture that meant I should follow him. He walked outside, leaving me free to snoop my way through his room. There was a desk with neat piles of magazines, books, and notebooks, and I managed to catch one title as I passed: *Frankenstein*. There was a king-size bed that the housekeeping manager of any five-star hotel would have approved: top sheet peeled back and folded over the bedspread, extra pillows with olive damask shams resting at the head of the bed, extra blanket folded accordion-style across the foot of the bed. There was no television or computer anywhere in the room. There was also no dirty laundry strewn on the floor or the upholstered chair. I wondered whether Billy had a cleaning service, a dominant tidy gene, or both. As I took a final look around, I scolded myself for my sexist assumptions and began compiling a list of unaskable questions for Edith's only son, including whether *Frankenstein* was representative of his literary taste, how often the other side of his bed had an occupant, and how an animal doc-doctor, surfer, reader, chef, and meticulous maid could fit into one human being.

I stepped outside and took my first look around. A knack for creating backyard havens apparently was genetic. Billy's yard boasted the same tranquility and wonder of his mother's, yet with his own flair. His bedroom door led out to a tiled patio. There was a long teak table with eight chairs, and several cushioned chairs, benches, and chaise lounges placed among potted plants, flowering trees, and lanterns on short metal posts. A hot tub stood in the corner, nestled against the back of the house. Opposite it, along the back fence, was a building akin to a shed. Billy stood at the door of the little hut and beckoned to me. He opened the door and invited me into the smallest and most appealing room I had ever seen. There was a sink with a mirror against the back wall, a double bed beside it, and an open closet with a hanging rod and shelves. At the front of the room, beneath a large window, was a simple yet elegant writing desk with a single drawer. The entire ceiling of the room—every square inch—was glass.

"I built it for my sisters," Billy said. "I thought maybe they'd come visit more often if they had a place of their own. So far it's worked." He looked around. "Rose says she writes more here in one week than the rest of the year at home. I made the desk for her, but Alice has been using it, too, lately, now that she's working on her memoir."

"Alice is writing a memoir?"

"I probably wasn't supposed to tell you that. You know Alice." He smiled sadly, the way anyone who loved Alice would.

"I'm really only writing about your mother," I said.

"Right," Billy said.

"Alice made it quite clear that I'm not to mention her."

"Yeah, well."

"It's a beautiful room. The perfect room for your sisters."

"I love it when they come," Billy said. "They're the only ones who have ever stayed here. Everyone else uses the guest room in the house. I thought you'd like it, though. Rose told me a lot about you." He looked at me and winked. "After the tent, I figure you'll be OK out here."

"Of course. Thank you. Are you sure your mom wouldn't rather sleep here?"

"She wants a bathroom nearby, which is lucky for me, because I wouldn't have been able to stand up to her if she asked to stay out here," Billy said. "It has nothing to do with her, really. This place is sacred—sister sacred, writer sacred. It's not for everyone, and I get to choose. This little cottage means something to me. Who stays in it means something to me." He gazed at the glass ceiling, as if remembering or anticipating. "I guess you'll have to share my mom's bathroom. Or if that's weird, you can use mine." He laughed and looked at me. "And if that's weird, too, well, I guess you'll have to pick which kind of weird you're more willing to deal with." He laughed again, and I tried to laugh with him. "When I remodeled the house, I wanted two master bedrooms with bathrooms. There wasn't room for another bathroom anywhere in the house, and when I built the cottage for Al and Rose, I wanted to keep it simple." He shrugged again. "There are worse things than sharing a bathroom, right?"

Voices on the patio pulled Billy's attention away from me. I stepped further into the one-room hideaway. Photographs of the Small siblings hung from the front wall and had not been visible from the doorway. Billy was always in the middle. In a few of the photos, they were children with knobby knees and more holes than teeth in their smile, but most of the photos were recent. Then I noticed a photo hanging on the back of the door, this one much larger than the others. It was an oversized portrait like the ones in Alice's apartment and office, but it had two faces pressed together, side by side. One was Billy, and the other was a young woman with the bright-colored fabrics of Africa showing around her neckline. I had seen the face before, in Alice's apartment and in her office, though I had not known at the time who it belonged to.

"You still in here?" Billy appeared from behind the half-closed door. "Oh, yeah. The portrait. Surat was an amazing photographer. An amazing person. And Zalira, well, she's a beauty, isn't she? God, I had a great time with those three. That week in Africa was the best time of my life. Everyone was so happy. Hope was everywhere. Now look at us. Surat dead. No baby. Alice all alone. Zalira and me... Anyway, you probably already know all this. I'll tell you anything, but there isn't much to tell."

He squeezed through the door, careful not to move it, and stood beside me facing the front wall. "I talk to Rosie and Al pretty much every day, so I know about your visits out there. Rosie must've told you about our reunions." I shook my head. "Every year they both come for a week, no matter what. Pretty fantastic. The three of us together for a whole week. Even now, with Rose's family and Alice's job and traveling, they come every year. Ma doesn't know. We figure she'd feel left out and pout or insist on coming. It's not like that, though. We're not excluding her, we're just including us. There's a difference."

Billy walked closer to the wall and looked at each picture, one at a time. "My sisters are everything to me. I wouldn't have made it without them." Although he was speaking aloud, he was not talking to me. I just happened to be there to hear it. He looked at the portrait of himself with Zalira. "I haven't seen her in one hell of a long time. She's married now. I blew it. Missed my chance." He reached out one hand and moved his fingertips across her face. Then he stepped back from the door and looked up at the wall again. "Al comes for Thanksgiving and Christmas. She would never admit it, but she hates being alone for the holidays. She misses him most then. Then she and Rosie come together every February. They like the break from the cold back East. Lucky for me. Sometimes I think I wound up in California just so I'd have a magnet to pull my sisters to me. They love the ocean. Who doesn't, right? I don't mind if that's what does it. I mean, if I lived in Kansas, I might never see them, but I don't spend time wondering about that. I'm just happy that they come. We started it right after Surat died. Rosie and I thought it would help Alice. We're still waiting to see what in this world will ever help her." He brushed a hand through his hair and looked at me. "You already know all of this, right? I mean, I know you and Rose hit it off. Carter, too. The two of you on your bar stools, sorting it all out. Kinda funny, huh?

Life is elusive, and being a person is pretty much impossible, don't you think? I don't envy your youth. It's one hell of a confusing mess. The twenties are just one identity crisis after another with a lot of bad relationships and miserable loneliness mixed in. The loneliness never ends, by the way. Nobody ever says so, but it's true. Eventually you grow into it and learn how to ride it out. I loved the story about Daisy and Sam and the pancakes. Priceless. God, I love those little girls. I go out every summer. Rosie's been asking me and Al to spend Christmas there so her girls will have family around for the holiday. We finally said yes, so this year it'll be a White Christmas in Vermont. I don't know what I'll wear. I haven't owned a pair of socks in years, let alone a parka or any of that business. We still haven't told Ma. She loved our Christmas here last year, after Dad died." He turned around and pointed at a photograph over the bed. There they were: Edith, Alice, Billy, Rose, Carter, Daisy, and Samantha. I started across the room to take a closer look, and Billy jumped back in alarm. "Oh, shoot. Your bags. Sorry about that."

He disappeared across the patio and through his bedroom to unload our luggage from his car. I stared at the picture of Edith and her family for awhile. Edith had been a blurry background object during our time in Santorini. After she had seen a Greek sunset and sunrise and checked it off her list, I had checked her off my list. The time that I had spent reading, lounging, and sightseeing—alone and with a now-former platonic friend—now seemed wasted. I could read anytime. I could lounge later. Greece would still be there, but Edith was right here, right now, perhaps soon to be gone. My blurred vision began to clear, and the wallowing of the previous few days started to subside. More than sixteen hours on multiple airplanes plus hours of waiting in airports was more time than any defeated lover needed to contemplate her failed attempt to consummate amorous feelings. One-way love was the oldest kind of broken heart. I had a window seat and no neighbor all the way from London to San Francisco. I pouted away the hours, my face glued to the window and songs of gloom and despair playing in my headphones. Halfway through the flight, Edith sat beside me, placed her hand on mine, and left it there for a minute. She rubbed my palm for a moment before she stood and left. Anthony must have given her a stern lecture, because she did not say one word to me—no unsolicited words of wisdom, no pep talk, no one-line zingers about doomed love or parted lovers.

Our time was shrinking. The date was September first, as Edith had planned. She would turn seventy-six in less than two months, if she was not careful and committed. Yet, she was careful and committed. One task remained on her list. She intended to obtain a private pilot's license within six to eight weeks, an accelerated though feasible timeline. Her flight lessons would start in three days and end before her birthday. If she had her way, she would earn her pilot's license before her deadline, too.

I stared at the family photograph and thought of Rose's complex relationship with her mother and Alice's dependence on her mother. I heard the voices of two small girls who delighted in their grandmother's playfulness. Edith had spent hours walking and talking with her granddaughters, reading and laughing with them, splashing in the brook and working in the garden. I knew without asking that she had always given them her full attention, not only then, during her last visit to their house, her last time with them, but always. That was who she was and how she lived.

I fell onto the bed under the weight of disbelief. I had missed it. I had failed to see it as it was unfolding, and now all I could do was try to glance back at the memories. Absorbed in my own nonsense, shackled by self-created fiascos of writerly identity crisis and girl-boy drama, I had placed my attention on the universal default character: myself. I traveled back through my memories to my last day in Vermont, a day steeped in a sense of relief to be returning home and sorrow to be leaving new friends. I could barely find Edith in the video footage of that day. I was enamored of Rose and Carter, and my stored images featured them, with Edith again a mere blur in the background. Maybe Edith had planned it that way. She planned everything else, after all. She had probably expected me to return to my default setting again and again, me me me, my favorite character. This was not the sort of reliability to which I aspired, sleepwalking through life with the switch set on self-absorption to the exclusion of all else.

As I lay on Rose and Alice's bed, a small truth began to revive me. I had worked hard on my summer stories about the early years of

Edith's list. Those five-hundred-word dispatches from Edith's past represented some of my best writing to date. The challenge was to do it again and again for the rest of the assignment. This was my duty and my chance to resist my default setting. Although my wilting ego and my deep sense of regret were far from healed, I stood up from the bed, demanded better from myself, and set out with renewed determination, though also with lingering ennui that I hoped was a symptom of jet lag. The impossible lesson that we all must learn is how to stay awake as our lives unfold and the world swirls all around us. I had fallen asleep under the lull of self-interest and selfishness, but the photograph of Edith and her family woke me up. And awake now— sooner rather than later, despite the time that I had lost in Greece, New York, and Vermont—would have to be sufficient. It would have to be good enough.

When I left the guest house and stepped outside, there was Edith, soaking in the hot tub. Anthony was beside her. The jets were spewing water and humming at a hundred decibels.

"You should come in!" Edith yelled. "It feels great after sitting on the airplane!"

Anthony beamed a rare grin my way. "She's right for once. It does feel terrific after that long flight. Come on in!"

He looked peaceful beside Edith, until she jabbed him in the side with her elbow. "What do you mean, 'right for once?'"

Anthony chuckled. I thanked them and started to mumble something about the bathroom and the suitcases, but then I remembered to stay awake.

"Be right back," I yelled. I grabbed my suitcase, made a quick wardrobe change, and climbed into the hot tub.

Billy appeared on the patio with my backpack. "Right on. Good for you guys." He kept walking to the cottage, and after placing my bag on the floor, he reappeared. "I'll grab some towels." Off he went again, at home in the role of host. A few minutes later, he returned with a stack of towels under one arm, a pitcher, and glasses. He dropped the towels on a chair and placed the glasses beside them. Then he poured four margaritas, handed one to each of us and climbed into the hot tub with us.

I agreed to every refill that Billy offered, I listened to every story Edith that told about our trip, and I smiled at every observation that Anthony offered about the Greeks, the airlines, and our friends from Minnesota. He and Lewis had made plans to go fishing in Alaska, a lifelong dream for them both. Perhaps Edith's flair for lifelong dreams had inspired them. My vow to myself was working, and I listened, stored away lines of dialog to jot down later, and outlined my next installment for *The Bugle*. Billy regaled us with stories from the clinic, including the sad struggles of a monkey named Mr. Nilsson, after the monkey from *Pippi Longstocking*.

"I loved those books," I said.

"Me, too," Billy said. "I own all of them. You're welcome to borrow anything from my shelves."

Then, with no use of a transition, Edith, master of non sequiturs, asked whether there was a woman in his life.

"Aw, come on, Ma."

After he climbed out of the hot tub and wrapped a towel around his waist, Billy turned to me and said, "Oh, Lucy, there was a letter for you in the mail today. I put it on your bed."

Minutes later, at about seven o'clock in the evening, I was sound asleep in my cozy little hut. It was a calculated decision. I set the letter aside until morning to give myself one night off from thinking about Tuck and facing whatever he wrote to me.

* * *

Dear Lucy,

I've started this letter seven times. That's a fact, not an exaggeration. I'm going to put the most important part first, in case I lose you and this winds up shredded and snowing down through a recycling bin full of cans and bottles.

I wish that I had kissed you back. I wanted to, but I couldn't. I was afraid, and everything in me froze up. I'm sorry. Please consider trying again. (Not likely.) Or perhaps consider allowing me to try. (Also unlikely, but just in case, let's agree that all you need to do is stand still and flutter your eyelashes, and I'll know that's my cue to lay one on you.)

Maybe at the very least you'll agree to meet me as we planned, in two days, at any location of your choice, preferably within the borders of California, but I do mean *any location*. I will go anywhere and do anything for the chance to see you again and to try to correct my mistake.

OK. That's the end of the most important part.

There is more, though, if you want to keep reading. Please keep reading. I know that I have no right to ask anything of you after what I've done. Forgive me, Lucy. Please forgive me. I can still feel how your lips parted and opened to invite me into your kiss. I can still feel my own mouth petrified into a full lock-down, closed more tightly than it ever has been before. Full oral paralysis. Why oh why oh why? For days I've been asking myself. The truth will make you squirm. I squirmed over it for three days, but now I am still and ready to present it as mere fact, true autobiographical information, squirm-free:

I've never kissed a girl. (Or a boy, in case you're wondering if that's the problem here.) I tried once in sixth grade, before anyone had explained to me that physical attraction had to move in both directions for a kiss to succeed and that I was lacking a face that could inspire physical attraction in a girl. When I leaned forward to kiss Stephanie Kanopolous, she moved away from me. She recoiled and leaned back, way back, so far back that she fell off the playground wall that she was sitting on and got a concussion. This story, as you surely see, is critical to our mutual understanding of our tragic failed kiss, because 1) it reveals the emotional scar from my first-ever attempt at intimacy, and 2) it identifies a bizarre similarity between that kiss and our/your kiss, namely the location of the kiss recipient (offerer, in your case) perched dangerously upon a wall. Stephanie told everyone who asked, including the playground aides, our teacher, the entire sixth grade, the principal, her parents, the school board, and the emergency-room personnel, exactly what happened, why, and who was to blame.

I waited a full ten years before attempting my second kiss. Throughout high school and college, I suffered the torment of seeing others paired off and connected at the lips (and elsewhere, I am sorry to report, having walked in on three different college roommates through the years. Doesn't anybody believe in privacy anymore—or at least blankets?). The summer after I graduated from college, I met and fell madly in lust with a young woman at the software company

172

where I worked. I had ample evidence this time that physical attraction moved in both directions: 1) her skirts got shorter each week, 2) she asked me whether I liked her skirts, 3) she cut her hair short exactly four days after I had revealed to her that I loved short hair on women, 4) she invited me out to dinner and a movie, and 5) she held my hand during the movie. This was, as our sports-obsessed culture would surely proclaim, a slam dunk in the making. After the movie, when I walked her back to her apartment and we were intertwined in a goodbye hug, I leaned forward to kiss her, and sure enough, she leaned away. You aren't the only one with a talent for recording and storing lines of dialog verbatim. I recorded this one more than six years ago, and I can still recite it perfectly: "Way to go, Tuck. Thanks for ruining one of the best friendships I've ever had, with your god-damn hard-on and some ridiculous notion that I would actually want to be your girlfriend." That's verbatim, Lucy.

I'm twenty-eight years old, and I've never kissed a woman. If you're still reading, thank you. We're almost done. I have only two more critical facts to confess: 1) I am physically attracted to you. 2) I am, as you must clearly see, a virgin. This is terrifying for a man my age, and yes, it is more than potentially embarrassing (for everyone involved).

Finally, you may be wondering—you, who cannot help but wonder about so much and so many—why I've chosen to confess. I have nothing to lose, Lucy. I've waited so many years to feel this—all of what you inspire in me that I have not even described yet—and to have someone else feel it, too, for me. But here's the thing. This is not just about kissing or physical attraction. It's about finding the courage to ride our scooter, because when I'm with you anything seems possible and nothing seems as scary. It's about undertaking a fierce verbal battle with the bold and intimidating Edith Small to win a seat beside you in the ambulance and watch over you while you were being treated by our friends the Greek medics. It's about sleeping on your couch and how that was the best night of my life, because every two hours when the alarm went off, you didn't hear it, and I got to sit beside you and touch your face and tell you everything I was thinking without you actually hearing it or responding. It's about knowing the vital pieces of your personal history after only two weeks with you. It's

173

about reading your news stories on-line the second I got home and confirming that you are in fact even smarter and more talented than I thought. It's about wondering how you find the courage and strength to follow Edith and meet her family and write her story, knowing how it will end. It's about admiring the way that you don't make yourself the main character and always keep your eyes and ears and mind cued to everything and everyone around you. It's about knowing that you take the tomatoes off your salad and save them for last. It's about settling into a sort of daily life with you in a faraway place that can never happen again, with coffee until noon and wine in the afternoon and water all the time because now we know that dehydration is real and must be avoided at all costs. It's about wondering whether I hurt you in a way that means I will never see you again and believing that isn't possible because I think I know you, and the Lucy I know will give me one more chance.

I'll meet you anywhere. I'll drive to the coast if you want. We could walk on the beach, like old times. (Old from last week. That's kind of funny. Please laugh with me, Lucy.) Or you could come here, and I'll introduce you to the babies.

I hope your flights went OK. I hope Billy is nice and more like Rose than Alice but mostly like neither so you'll get a chance to write a new character. I hope Edith is treating you well. I hope Anthony isn't too sad that the end is approaching. Uncle Lewis talks about their trip to Alaska non-stop. Edith and Anthony revived him in a way that I couldn't, and for that I am grateful. Finally, I hope the flying lessons prove exciting but not too exciting. May all of Edith's landings occur on certified runways.

Goodbye, dear Lucy. Adieu. Ciao. Farewell… only for a while, I hope…

Yours,

Tuck

P.S. In case you're wondering how it is that I turned out to be a scaredy cat in the romance department when I appeared suave and self-possessed that first morning on the breakfast terrace, here's my explanation: I fell in love with you the minute I saw you reading on the patio the day before—bare feet on the stone wall, hair tucked under a baseball hat, skirt flickering in the sea breeze, glass of wine defiantly in one hand, book in the other—and I figured I didn't have a chance of capturing your heart in the traditional way (i.e. physical attraction that moves in both directions), so I pulled out my linguistic bravado in the hope of reaching you, a women of words, through your mind. You were reading Plato that afternoon and Aristotle at breakfast. I saw the reaction on your face when I turned around that morning. I sounded great until you saw what I looked like. I know there's hope, though, because you kissed me. Perhaps because of everything, and maybe despite everything, you did it. You ran full-speed down the steps in your bare feet in search of me. Me. And that's something, Lucy. That's something I can hold onto.

   * **

I read Tuck's letter at three in the morning, when I woke up with a jolt and instant awareness that it awaited me. I read it a second time, and then I slipped into the hot tub in the darkness and the silence. I sat in the hot still water and thought about Tuck. Then I went back inside, read his long letter again, and fell sleep.

The next time I woke up, it was seven in the morning, and the sun was awake, too. A new day had arrived, and for the first time in what felt like eternity but was in fact the four days since the failed kiss, I had a childlike sense that anything was possible. I looked out at the day like a blank piece of paper, and I wanted to write the next page of the story. When I stepped onto the patio in my T-shirt, shorts, and bare feet, the sunshine stung my eyes and warmed my face and arms.

"Good morning, sleepyhead," Billy called down to me from the roof. "Come on up. It's just me. Ma and Anthony went for a walk."

"How?"

"How what?"

"How do I get up there?"

Billy laughed. "Didn't you see the spiral staircase in the living room? You're supposed to be observant, Luce."

I stared hard at him. "Jet lag. Margaritas. No house tour."

He nodded. "Right. We'll fix it all today. Coffee?"

"Yes, please."

I walked through Billy's bedroom, where the bed was unmade, a bunch of magazines and *Frankenstein* lay near the pillows, and yesterday's neatly stacked piles were strewn about his desk, evidence that

175

hired help had almost certainly cleaned the house before our arrival. I stepped over a pair of shorts and entered the living room. Its simplicity made for a fast tour. I stood in the middle of the room and looked around: blue couch, twin brown leather chairs, coffee table with more magazines and books, bookcases lining the walls, and a stereo cabinet in the corner.

"You coming?" came a voice through the hole in the ceiling where a metal staircase swirled upward into the sky. I climbed the narrow stairs and emerged on Billy's rooftop retreat.

"Oh, wow," I said. "Holy…"

The ocean was everywhere, and so was the sky. The three-hundred-and-sixty-degree view captured the Pacific to the west, the mountains to the east, and infinite blue sky above, free of clouds in every square inch.

"You can guess how often I use the living room," Billy said.

I turned my gaze to the rooftop deck, which had the same contents as the back patio, minus the hot tub, plus a small kitchen. There was a long teak table identical to the one below, several more of the cushioned chairs, and one chaise lounge. Nestled in the back corner was a tiled kitchenette with a partial roof over a small refrigerator, stove, sink, and counter. Potted trees and plants made me forget that I was on a roof, and music was being piped in somehow from somewhere. The sleepy melody of a guitar matched my mood, as I stood taking inventory of Billy's penchant for material comfort and his appreciation of pleasure.

"I lugged a tree up here when everyone came for Christmas," Billy said as he handed me a mug of steaming coffee. He sat down on a cushioned chair, so I did, too, across from him and facing westward at the ocean in the distance.

"I decorated it myself before they got here, lights and glass balls and everything. We had champagne up here on Christmas Eve, and I turned on the tree lights for the first time. Rosie and Al both gasped like little girls."

The memory of his sisters made him smile in a way that perhaps explained why he was not married. With that much love already devoted to two women, maybe there was none left for a third.

"On Christmas morning, we were eating brunch up here when a hot-air balloon came up over the mountains and headed straight out over the water. It was red, orange, and yellow, like the sun. I'll never forget that. Rosie wrote a poem about it. It's one of her best." Billy sipped his coffee and then smiled up at me. "You have to interrupt me or I go on and on. I don't mean to be a talker. It just happens. How are you feeling? You sleep OK out there?"

I nodded. "It's so quiet and peaceful. I can see why your sisters love it here."

"Yeah, well, don't get me started on them, or I really won't shut up."

Getting him started on them was precisely what I wanted to do, but not until my mind was awake and my notebook and pen were in hand.

"So, was the letter a good one? Ma told me about Tuck."

The Smalls were masters in the art of candor. They got away with comments and questions that the rest of us would not dare. In the case of three out of four Smalls, their charm combined with frankness to obtain answers to questions that should have been unaskable. I participated knowingly for reasons that I did not understand.

"I have nothing to compare it to, because it's the only one I've ever gotten," I said. "It was shocking and beautiful and strange and sad."

"Wow," Billy said. "The high romantic drama of a Jane Austen novel, right down to the letters. I should have brought it to you on a silver tray."

I checked his face for sarcasm and farce, since there was not any in his voice, but I found none.

"So, is he coming over today?" Billy asked. "You must be eager to see him. And just so you know, there aren't any rules here. You do as you please." He winked and made me laugh.

"I think you may be more outrageous than your mother."

"Nah. Not outrageous. Just me, living the good life, the real thing. I'm not into bullshit, that's all. Your boy's welcome anytime. You two will have a nice time around here. You have your own room, the hot tub, the beach just up the road, and a bunch of decent places to eat and drink. It's only about a ten-minute walk into town. So, dive in, Luce. What's your plan?"

"I don't have a plan."

"Call him."

"It's not that easy."

"Oh, no. You sound like me."

"It's too complicated. I'd rather be alone."

"Trust me: Call him," Billy said. "If you start making excuses now, the next thing you'll know, you'll be forty and alone. And that is not what you want, no matter what you think now. Don't get me wrong. I love my life. I have great friends and a great family, but most of them have spouses and kids of their own. They're all I have, they're my everything, but I'm second for them. That's how it goes when you're single. And believe me, hanging out with other single people isn't the solution. Then all you do is tell lies about how much you love being single and recite the same old lame excuses about why none of your relationships worked out. Anyway, I'm not saying you need to marry old Tuck tomorrow or anything. I'm just saying you ought to call the guy. He's been home for days waiting for you. Don't break his heart, Luce. Call him."

"He's the heart-breaker," I said. "He rejected me." I stopped and closed my eyes. "Why am I telling you this?"

Billy winked and gave me a thumbs-up.

"I made the first move," I said. "On our last night. And he rejected me. Flat out refused to kiss me back."

"Oh, come on. You're not going to let a little thing like that get in the way, are you? I mean, this is love, right? If it's love, you have to keep going, you have to try again."

"That's what the letter said. He apologized. And explained everything. And I do mean everything."

"Well, good for him. A real Mr. Darcy. So, get moving. What more do you want? You and I both know you spent the whole trip back from Greece sulking over that kiss. Now he's apologized, and he wants to see you, right?"

I nodded.

"Take it from me, you need to move on it. *Now*. Don't start plotting to make him wait it out. That's baloney, and it's not you. Hell, even Elizabeth Bennett figured that out in the end, after all the self-righteous judgments. Don't get me wrong. Darcy had problems of his own, no doubt, but Elizabeth could have shown a little more compassion a little sooner, don't you think? Choose forgiveness, Luce. Love. A little humility. It takes guts to write a letter like that. You have to match him now. You have to be brave. You need a car? You got it. I know without asking that you can drive a stick and that you're not afraid of a jeep." He stood up. "I'm going to cook you some breakfast. You eat eggs?" I nodded. "Good. We'll get some protein into that jet-lagged body of yours and a whole bunch of fresh fruit, too. We got all the fresh fruit you want in this place, every month of the year. My head spins at what people eat in this country. At my house, we eat real food. I guess I lied. I do have one rule: Nobody eats crap at my house. We eat food that grows out of the ground. Let's do this thing, Lucy. There's no time to waste. I'll have breakfast ready in ten minutes. Go call Tuck and tell him you'll be there in half an hour. Forty-five minutes tops. Then shower and hurry back to eat."

I nodded and stood. Billy reached out and took my empty mug.

"You need a hug, kiddo?"

I nodded first and frowned second, disoriented by the offer and my own transparent needs. Billy was the mom everyone dreamed of. He was my mom reincarnated. Love oozed out of him in every direction, including mine. He stepped forward to hug me, but it was more of a hold than a hug, a taking in and reassuring, pulling me in and closing me up in his sun-drenched skin, hairy arms, and oversized heart. He did not try to let go. He taught me what a real hug was made of: standing still for so long that the other person got to decide when it was over. I took my time.

"You OK?" Billy asked.

"I guess so," I said. "You may be right about this."

"Do you need to cry? You might feel better if you cry now and get it out before you see him."

"I don't cry." At least I never used to, until the plane trip from Greece. "Much."

"You scared?"

"Yup."

"Good. That's keeping it real, Luce. That's love right there."

179

I finally stepped back. I stood there on the roof and looked at Billy. He looked right back, no squirming, no fear, no evidence on his face or in his body that there was anything wrong with two people taking a good long look at one another, even if they had known each other only for a day.

"You're better than a superhero," I said.

"Nah," Billy said. "You're the superhero, globetrotting with my ma, talking with Rosie about her writing, being nice to Al even though I bet she was nasty to you. You're out there trying to understand people and then stick it into words. Those are beautiful stories you've written about Ma. Not many people can do that. Anyway, this Tuck character better be good. I'll crush him with my own hands if he isn't good enough for you. Now go."

Billy swished me away and turned toward the rooftop kitchen. I navigated the winding stairs down to the living room and wandered into the bathroom off his bedroom. I peeked behind the shower curtain to assess the supply of shampoo, conditioner, and soap. His fruity and flowery selection suggested that he was ready to host females at any moment. I wondered how many got an offer and why he was alone. I pulled off my shorts and shirt, and as soon as the hot water hit my shoulders, tears dropped down my cheeks, off my chin, and into the drain. Crying was not too bad, especially if you did it alone. In fact, there were benefits. I felt clean in all ways, inside and out, when I finished my shower.

After breakfast on the roof with Billy and a long goodbye hug, I pulled out of his driveway in his jeep. I waved, and he yelled, "Good luck!" He had printed directions for me while I was in the shower, and the paper was beside me on the seat, anchored in the wind by the edge of my backpack. Some handwritten words caught my attention, and I lifted the paper to read them: "Crying is good, not bad. It's brave, not weak. Good luck!"

When I got to the stop sign at the end of his street, Billy came running up behind me. "Do you have a bottle of water?" he shouted. I gave him a thumbs-up through the open top of his jeep. "Good. We don't want another trip to the ER, huh?"

When I arrived thirty minutes later, three facts became clear as I parked outside Tuck's apartment building. The first was that I should have taken Billy's advice and called Tuck first. The second was that I had not used my driving time to prepare for my reunion-slash-showdown with Tuck. And the third was that I had yet again broken my vow to stick to Edith. I glanced at the clock: 8:10. If I was brave and efficient and everything went well, then I would be done by the time Tuck needed to leave for work in twenty minutes. I had no agenda, no goal, and no method in mind, but that did not figure into my calculations. I could be back in Billy's driveway at nine o'clock, on the job, ready to go, notebook and pen in hand, switch flipped back to an external focus: Edith.

I made my way through the entrance of the apartment building and up the elevator to Tuck's apartment on the top floor. I pressed the doorbell and waited. Symptoms were erupting inside me: churning stomach, light-headedness, heavy perspiration. This was why reading the paper alone on Sunday mornings was a better option. This was why Billy was alone, despite his ability to love, an ability that apparently included any and all people that were not eligible mates.

The door opened, and there was Tuck.

"Hey," he said.

"Bathroom," I said. "Now."

"Oh. OK. Down the hall and on the right."

If only it were a full water bottle's worth of urine that I needed to expel. I shut the door and turned on the exhaust fan and the faucet to dull the noise of me barfing into Tuck's toilet. There was a first time for everything, and as I stood staring at the remains of Billy's natural-whole-foods breakfast, the fact that I had vomited from fear impressed me. The human body was a mighty mystery. When I lost interest in watching the egg and melon mush float in the toilet water, I flushed. Then I moved to the mirror to assess the damage. I was white as notebook paper. I pinched my cheeks and splashed cold water on my face. Then I squirted some of Tuck's toothpaste on my index finger and rubbed it over my gums, the roof of my mouth, and my tongue. After copious spitting, rinsing, and fluffing of hair, I breathed for a few moments and then exited.

Tuck was standing in the middle of his kitchen.

"Hello," I said. "Sorry about that."

"Are you OK?"

"I'm fine. Too much coffee before I hit the road."

He nodded, but I sensed that the fan and the faucet had not done their job.

"Would you like some water?" he asked.

I nodded. Tuck invited me to sit with him at the kitchen table.

"It's my responsibility to start this conversation," he said. I would have laughed at his formality if I were not so scared. "I don't wish to repeat what I've already written in my letter. I do want to thank you for coming. I of course don't know your intentions, but that you came to see me is beyond what someone in my position should expect from someone in your position."

And then I did laugh, loudly, at his funny list of do's and don'ts, and at his choice of words. Before he could take offense, I reached my hands across the table and placed them on top of his.

"Tuck. It's OK. Please. It's just me."

He started to nod a lot, and he was breathing too loudly. Then his face crumpled, and his eyes pinched closed. He looked like he was imploding. I steadied my own breathing and rooted for him, to no avail. All I could do was watch as he broke down into a hyperventilating fit of sobs and a repetition of, "I'm sorry. I'm sorry. I'm sorry." There was no time to ponder the meaning of so many unexpected tears in one morning. As my guardian angel would surely have said, it was time to move.

"Tuck, it's OK. I forgive you. I'm fine."

My words failed to penetrate the dread that had engulfed him. He kept muttering "I'm sorry," and he started to shake, a little at first, and then violently. I squeezed his hands to remind him that I was there. He was far away, weeping and shaking and suffering at the invisible hand of his own self-inflicted doom. There I was, right in front of him, but he could not see me and he could not hear me.

"Hey, come on," I said. "It's alright. It was just one kiss. We'll try again. In fact, we could try right now. Do you feel like kissing me? Right here in your kitchen? I know it's early and people don't normally feel romantic at eight in the morning before work, but you only live once, right? I mean, why not?"

He looked at me through glassy eyes. Then everything stopped. The noise of his weeping, the dripping of tears, the shaking torso, the muttering apologies—it all stopped.

"I didn't cry when my aunt died."

I nodded for reassurance.

"I didn't cry when I left home for college, even though my whole family was crying, even my dad."

I kept nodding, even as I puzzled over the theme du jour. I tried to make my face look grave to match his and non-judgmental so he would keep talking. He was trying to get to the bottom of something, and it was my job not to stand in the way. I needed to let him fill the room with himself and stay in the room with him. That was all listening ever was, really, yet most of us botched the job every time.

"I didn't even cry the time my mom left us for a whole night after a fight with my dad."

I kept up with my nodding and my grave face, because I sensed he was getting closer.

"I didn't cry when Stephanie fell off the fence, and there were two reasons to cry then: because she didn't kiss me back, and because she blacked out and I thought I had killed her. I didn't cry when I tried to kiss my co-worker Joanna after the movie. There were two reasons then, too: because she didn't kiss me back, and because she said the cruelest words that anyone has ever said to me. The truth is that until now, I've only cried once in my entire life, and compared to all the other bad stuff that's ever happened to me, it was a ridiculous reason to cry. When I was eight years old, my dog got hit by a car in front of the school. My entire second-grade class ran to the windows when we heard the screech of brakes and a crash. The car hit a telephone pole, but the driver was fine. She was standing in the road staring at my dead dog. He died right before my eyes while my whole class looked at me. I was crying more from shame and hatred than sadness. I didn't want my whole class looking at me when I was feeling scared and sad. I hate it when people look at my face, and crying makes any face uglier."

We had reached the end, and I needed to do something. I searched around for something to say and found this: "I think crying might be good. I'm not sure yet. I'm still new at it myself. But I think it's part of our beauty. It's something we're supposed to do."

Tuck lifted his eyes and was trying to look at me, but he was too upset to see anything but himself. "I've been terribly distraught about what happened," he said. "And then writing that letter only made it worse." I started to smile, but when he looked at me, I stopped. "I'm not embarrassed, Lucy. That's not what I mean. I'm not sorry that I told you everything. I was glad to. I don't feel embarrassed of who I am around you. What makes me sad is how this whole part of life has been ruined for me. Falling in love is supposed to be a joy. It's supposed to be one of the greatest parts of life."

"Only in fairy tales," I said. "And Jane Austen novels. Not in real life."

He shook his head. "No. In real life. Not because of romance and lust and promises of forever, but because of this, right here, right now. Two people looking at each other and talking to each other. Two people who have spent time together and want to spend more time together. That's all it is, and that's everything. The wanting to be together, the talking and the listening, the way two minds can speak to each other directly, every once in a while, if you're really lucky and you really try, it's a miracle. I felt like my brain was plugged into yours when we walked on the beach and sat on the terrace by the sea. I felt for the first time in my life that it may be possible to know another person, that there may in fact be a cure to loneliness. Setting an alarm every two hours to keep watch over you was my favorite part of the whole trip. I got to look at you while you slept. I talked to you then, when it was safe, when you couldn't hear me."

I was smiling for real now. "You sound like your letter." I stared at the table. Then I whispered, "I can't believe you wrote that to me." Then my whisper got even softer. "Thank you."

Tuck did not look away from me, but he got quiet for a while, too.

"So, why did you come?" he asked at last. Then he studied the table with me.

I almost said it right away without stopping to think first, because I was worried that I would talk myself out of it. I counted to five, and I decided along the way that if I got to five and he had not said anything—if he had not botched the job of matching my face and letting me get to the end—then I would say it.

I made it to five.

"Because I love you."

That was the easy part, because next I had to find a way to unsquint my eyes and lift my head and look at him, at the face that he hated people looking at. I tried counting to five again, but when I got to three he said:

"I'm really really lucky then, because I love you, too."

Then all of a sudden there was a huge supply of oxygen in the room, as if a truck had pulled up outside Tuck's apartment and was shooting it in through the vents and windows. We both did a lot of breathing, because we needed to after puking and crying and confessing our love, and because nobody knew what was next. We were still sitting at his kitchen table. A set of salt and pepper shakers stood between us, and I could not understand how I had avoided knocking them over when I had reached for his hands earlier. I started to wonder what Tuck was thinking about, and I was glad that he did not know that I was thinking about his salt and pepper shakers. Technically it was my turn to speak, because he had spoken last. I felt like a superhero for saying those three famous words. All he had to do was repeat them and add a "too," so I was not feeling generous about coming up with the next line in our tragi-comic script of salvaged love. Then I remembered his letter. We would not have arrived there at that moment if it were not for his letter, so that made him a superhero, too. Then again, we would not have needed his letter if he had kissed me in Greece that night.

In the end, it was Billy who saved me: *If you start making excuses now, the next thing you'll know, you'll be forty and alone.*

And: *If it's love, you have to keep going, you have to try again.*

I stood from my chair, walked around to Tuck's side of the table, offered my hand, and invited him to stand, too. Then I stepped forward to hug him, but it was more of a hold than a hug, a taking in and reassuring, pulling him in and closing him up in my freckled skin, thin arms, and undersized heart that was trying to grow. I did not try to let go. I stood still for so long that he got to decide when it was over. He took his time.

When he was done, he pulled away, looked right at my face, and kissed me with his mouth open and his tongue busy the right amount and his lips strong yet gentle the right amount. Nobody had ever kissed me like that. I felt it in my scalp, my toenails, and the winkles on my elbows. We took our time, and we stood still for so long that nobody had to decide when it was over. It ended on its own when it was complete and perfect.

We looked at each other—or tried to anyway. Tuck was better at it. I glanced down at the floor twice. He let me, and his letting me told me that he trusted me to learn whenever I was ready, even if that was never. As I was looking at his face, I thought again about how beauty came from the inside. Tuck had become so beautiful to me that there was not a way to see ugly in his face, especially when he was crying or crumpling and letting me glimpse all that lived inside him. Within the history of any love, there was a continual story that accumulated through the minutes and hours and days spent looking at a single face. Couples that have been married for decades know one face in a way that they know nothing else in this world. I wondered whether Edith still looked at Henry's face inside her mind. There could be no doubt that Billy was the master of Rose and Alice's faces, his two true loves. One look at my dad's face could convey my entire existence in a single moment, as if his face contained some fact of my being, a sense of my own me-ness stored within the person that I had been looking at forever. Looking at my brother's face could make me feel better even when I did not know anything was wrong. I took one last look at Tuck's face to store in my brain the green flecks in his irises, the creases near his mouth, the lips that were red from recent exertion, and the feeling of calm that he brought me. I saw that he knew something about life that I could learn from him. Looking at him helped me to know it just a little, because his eyes sent it out to me, a gift to be received without words and even without my own understanding.

And then, because we were in fact two adults in modern America and not characters in a Jane Austen novel, we parted ways to go to work. Tuck accepted my invitation to join us for dinner that evening at Billy's. I needed to work an eight-hour day like the rest of the world to regain my grip of the story, my focus on Edith, and a sense of integrity, all of which I explained to Tuck, because I liked telling him my truths even when he already knew them.

I pulled on the seatbelt and looked at him standing on the sidewalk.

"Do you think it's possible to regain a sense of integrity?" I asked. "Or is it gone forever once you've lost it?"

"Anyone who cares about regaining her sense of integrity probably never lost it in the first place."

"I hope you're right," I said. "Enjoy your babies."

"Enjoy your Smalls."

* * *

I parked the jeep in Billy's driveway and walked through the house and up the spiral staircase to the roof. Edith, Anthony, and Billy were sitting at the table with empty plates before them. Their idleness clashed with my exuberance. My sense of accomplishment and the vivacity of love made me feel invincible. I urged my face not to advertise this, however, lest Edith detect it.

"Welcome back," Billy said. "Did you find the right contact-lens solution?"

I did not think it was possible to love Billy even more, but it was. "Your directions were perfect," I said. "I found exactly what I needed."

"Excellent. There's nothing worse than blurry vision. You must be relieved." Billy dared to wink and give me a quick thumbs-up while Edith and Anthony had their eyes on me.

"Relieved in more ways than one," I said. "And very hungry."

"Gotcha," Billy said, as he stood from the table. "We need more plates up here. Could you give me a hand down in the big kitchen?"

I did not need another wink to get it. Down we went, through the opening in the roof, like Alice chasing the White Rabbit. Billy gestured for me to follow him, and we stepped into his bedroom.

"Are you OK?" he whispered.

"I'm fine. Better than fine."

"You did it?"

"Yes."

Billy squeezed my shoulders and kissed me on the cheek. "I'm proud of you. You really told him, huh? Good for you. That's fantastic."

"I've never said it to anyone other than my family."

"Wow. That's heavy-duty. Are you OK?"

"I am now. I threw up when I got there." There was no way for me to understand this newfound urge to divulge my secrets to Billy, so I stopped trying and plowed ahead. "I've never done that before."

"Yeah, well, you've never done this before, right? This is the real thing. I can tell. Wow, Luce. This is huge. I have a friend who's a therapist in town. I could call her and try to get you in. You know, just to talk with someone who's good at that sort of thing."

I laughed. "I'm fine. Thank you, though. Thank you for everything."

"Well, we all need a little nudge now and then. I'm glad to help. I figured you don't want Ma to know."

I shook my head. "Not yet. He's coming for dinner, though. You said it was OK, so I invited him. I want you two to meet." Then I grinned. "And I really want to see him."

"Of course," Billy said. "I can't wait to meet him, but what about Ma? She'll know right away when she sees you two together. That is, if you manage to hide it from her all day. You are, as they say, glowing."

I laughed again and shrugged. "Oh, well. What's a girl to do?"

"I figured there's some sort of professional boundary. It's your job to pry into her business, but it doesn't go the other way, right?"

"Well, I suppose if I'm allowed to eat pancakes, maybe I'm allowed to fall in love, too—*and* tell Edith about it."

"Reporters are people, too?"

"As it turns out, yes. Especially on a 'special assignment' like this one."

"Yeah, well, we need to talk about that. My mom has some wacky ideas."

Billy was not smiling anymore, and there was nothing to laugh about. I felt it, too, the weight of her number-one wackiest idea. I wanted to ask him what he thought about it, but his face told me not to. Not yet, anyway.

"Plates?" I said.

"Plates," he said. Then he looked at me again. "You're something else, Lucy. I'm glad you're here. If anyone can usher this to the end, it's you."

He tousled my hair and walked to the kitchen, leaving me to sort through a pronouncement that he intended as a compliment but that felt like a burden that I was not qualified to fulfill.

* * *

An hour later, Edith and I were alone on the back patio. We had our usual props: pitcher of herbal iced tea, two glasses, voice recorder, notebook, pen.

"Tomorrow is your first flying lesson," I said. "What have you done to prepare?"

"I've read the textbooks used for private pilot training and for ground school. Over the summer I spoke with my instructor several times on the phone. The schedule is intense, but others have done it in six to eight weeks, too. I'm not mechanically inclined, so this will be challenging for me, perhaps even insurmountable. That's the truth. I may not be able to do it. That's just the way of it. It's a matter of what kind of brain is inside your skull. Mine is not built for mechanics, and flying an airplane is about mechanics, technical expertise, and precision in operating a machine that is constantly reacting to its environment. It may prove too much for me."

"Did you ever doubt your ability to complete any of the other items on your list?"

"No. I have a strong mind and a strong body. I made the list accordingly. My hands would learn to make pottery on a wheel, even if it was thick and unoriginal. Anyone can learn to paint, however poorly. My body could learn how to do ballet positions, even if they were ungraceful and imprecise. The travel was a matter of stamina and patience. The volunteer projects required time, generosity, and an ability to work with others. And anyone who can pedal a bicycle would eventually make her way across the country, if she had the will to do it. Although the ultimate goal was to finish each item and cross it off the list, it was the process that fascinated me and inspired me, not the final product or the quality of my performance. I wanted to master each skill. That was my wish. And yet, I never managed to become an expert in anything. I knew I would do all of it, even finding Anthony. If he'd turned out to be dead, I planned to visit his grave, cross him off my list, and move on. So the answer is no. I never doubted my ability to complete any of them, except this. I knew from the beginning that this might be the one. That's why I saved it for last. I'm bothered by the notion of failing. What a pity it would be to complete all but one."

"Why did you put it on your list then?"

"Because I love magic, and flying is a form of magic. We invented it. We humans wanted to fly like the birds so badly that we didn't give up until we figured it out. Aviation was born in America, and I want to be a part of the tradition of flight, even if my brain limits me."

"Are you afraid?"

"No."

I lowered my pen and cocked my head. "Edith."

"I'm not scared to fly an airplane. I'm concerned that as the lessons and maneuvers become more complex, I won't be capable of doing what's required of me. I may be wrong. I've accomplished a good bit in my life, and I've overcome many obstacles, so I think it's reasonable for me to hope for the best and, as you kids say, go for it."

"To say that you've accomplished a good bit is a gross understatement."

"Perhaps, but if every person at the age of seventy-five were to review her life and make a list of her thirty-five greatest accomplishments, I'm certain that many of the lists would resemble mine."

I laughed out loud. "And I'm certain that you're wrong. That's absurd, Edith. People don't just wind up achieving what you have over the course of a lifetime."

"I challenge you to prove me wrong."

I laughed again, from nerves, not humor. Edith did not issue challenges as a joke. "How would I do that?"

"Goodness, dear, you're the reporter. How would a reporter go about this? I'd imagine that you'd need to interview as many people as you can who are seventy-five or older and ask for their lists."

I stared at Edith as my own mechanics, the machinery of a writer's brain, seized on her idea. I could pitch it to Cunningham as a way to bring a broader context to Edith's story and to keep readers interested in the concept of a lifetime list while the pilot made her way through weeks of lessons.

"That's actually a pretty good idea. Thank you."

"You're quite welcome," Edith said. "And not the faintest note of sarcasm, either. Lovely."

"I don't like sarcasm either, you know," I said. "We're not as different as you might think."

"That's a novel observation from you, dear," she said. I forgave her for laughing at her own pun. "I'm glad to hear that you're seeing more clearly. That must have been a very productive trip to the pharmacy this morning." Her eyebrows went up and down.

"Let's focus on the interview, please."

"Only if I get to interview you when you're done with me."

"That's bribery."

"Perhaps."

"We've made it this far fair and clean, bribe-free."

"That may well be, dear, but I've been following your story, too, even if it doesn't appear in a newspaper."

"We are getting profoundly sidetracked, and I have work to do, Edith. I need to file a story within the next twenty-four hours."

"Ask away, but you aren't playing nicely. I'm rooting for you, Lucy dear. I just want an update on the score."

"There is no score, Edith. It's not a game."

"Goodness. So serious. It must be true love."

"You sound like Billy."

"Isn't he extraordinary? If only he could find love."

"Edith, you are so far out on a limb that you're about to break the branch and fall to the ground."

"Oh, but this is so exciting. It's almost enough to make me stick around and add item #36 to my list: Become a newspaper reporter, and investigate the secret love story of Lucy Hunt."

"Edith, enough," I said. "We were discussing your preparations for your flight lessons. Do you feel ready for tomorrow?"

"My goodness, I begin tomorrow. Mercy."

I put down my pen and stared hard at her. "You are scared, aren't you?"

"The truth, dear, is that I am a little scared," she said. "Tomorrow is the beginning of the end. I've been enjoying myself immensely these past few months."

"It doesn't have to end."

"I don't expect you to understand. Few do. You've been reading the Greeks. Read the Stoics. They understood the choice to die well. It matters how one dies—and when. It matters to be prepared and to accept the end of life. At some point, it has to be enough to have had a good life and lived well. Enough is so much more than most people ever get."

"I have read the Stoics, Edith. Philosophy isn't life. Theory isn't reality. You're in excellent health, and you're enjoying your life."

"What better time to bid farewell."

We had agreed at the beginning that I would not try to persuade her to change her plan. The point was not whether Edith was beyond my powers of persuasion—of course she was—but rather that she found efforts to influence her irritating. Nobody wanted to be lectured on how to live or die.

"You must admit that the order of events is strange," I said. "You're going to face the greatest challenge of your entire list and then make your exit, as you say."

"Perfect planning," Edith said. "What brilliant foresight to leave flying for last, if I do say so myself. I will be prouder than ever if I manage to accomplish this, because I have anticipated it for so long. I really am not sure whether I'm capable of this. Flying means more to me than any of the others."

"And if you succeed, then you'll celebrate by killing yourself."

"Goodness, Lucy, that was not delicate."

"It's a little late for delicacy."

Edith laughed and put her hand on my knee. "Perhaps you're right. Our candor and honesty have been great assets. I thank you for that."

"All I do is listen and watch."

"That's more than enough," Edith said.

"Will you show me the airport? I'd like to get to know my way around before your lesson tomorrow."

"I'd be delighted. We can meet my instructor together in person for the first time. His name is Spencer. He goes by 'Spence.' He's not like most of the others. Instructors tend to be—"

"Young guys who want to log hours so they can get their next rating and become commercial pilots, or old guys who are retired and have nothing better to do."

"Yes," Edith said. "You've done your homework. You always do."

"Spence has been teaching people how to fly for more than thirty years," I said.

Edith nodded. "It's all he's ever done. They say he's one of the best. And his rates are very reasonable."

"Speaking of which, flying is expensive."

Edith grinned. "I'm worth it."

"The last hurrah."

"Indeed, dear."

We sat together in the silence for a while. Then Edith stood and took the pitcher and glasses in her hands. "Billy has two bikes. Shall we pedal to the airport?"

"That sounds lovely."

"Many of my ideas are, you may find."

"I have found."

Edith sighed in a way that I would hear more now. She may not have been suffering from a fear of flying, but her fear of failure and her awareness that the end was near had dulled the shine in her eyes. I walked through the house and out the front door. She stood in the driveway between two bicycles.

"Red or yellow?" she asked.

"Oh, no. After you," I said.

"I'll take yellow," she said. "Like the sun. What pilot hasn't dreamed of touching the sun?"

That left red for me. Red like the blood that would soon stop flowing through Edith's veins. I had never let myself wonder how she would do it. There would be no mess and no witness. That was an inherent truth about Edith—her awareness of others and her desire to treat them with respect. Unfortunately, her bigger inherent truth cast shadows over everything else. She loved her family, but she loved her ultimate idea more. As I climbed aboard the red bike, I saw an inherent truth about myself, too: Setting emotions aside was no longer possible. We were moving toward the endpoint, a destination over which I had no control. I could focus my mind externally, I could ask every question and monitor Edith's progress as a pilot, but nothing could stop me from wondering what would happen and from hoping that she would change her mind.

* * *

The stretch of coast south of San Francisco was home to the wealthy, and the aircraft in the hangars at the local airport reflected that. There were several six- and eight-seat airplanes, and Spence pointed out retractable landing gear on some. He showed us several airplanes by an innovative manufacturer who made a glass cockpit, rather than the traditional instrument panel, and an emergency parachute that eased the plane down to the ground in the most dire of situations. Then he walked us past the experimental planes and the kit airplanes that the most adventurous pilots assembled themselves.

"Which one is mine?" Edith asked.

"That's the fleet of trainers that belongs to the flight school," Spence said. He pointed to four airplanes on the other side of the airfield and walked toward them. "We'll use mainly the new two-seater. You'll like it."

"Two-seater?" I said.

We were standing next to the newest model, white with red detail, call number N1205. December fifth was my birthday, and though I did not believe in signs, fate, or messages from the gods, the call number got my attention.

They turned to look at me. "Right. It's a two-seater," Spence said.

"There are three of us," I said.

"In fact, there are two of us," Edith said.

"Edith, come on. You must be kidding."

Spence began to study the asphalt.

"Kidding how?" she said. "I don't know what we're talking about."

"I'm coming with you," I said. "Flying. How else am I supposed to watch you?"

"Oh, no," Edith said. "Not this. No way."

"This is absurd, Edith. 'Full access at all times.' That was our agreement from the beginning. Those were *your* words. I have them on record, if you'd like proof."

"But I didn't mean this," Edith said.

"It's the most important part of the entire list," I said. "I have to be there."

Edith walked around the little airplane and approached its big sister, the four-seat version. She looked through the windows and inspected the instrument panel, the cockpit, and then the back seat.

"Let me go up alone tomorrow," she said. "After that, you can come anytime."

Her offer was reasonable, even generous, and yet there was no way I could concede the first flight. Firsts happened only once. I shook my head.

"What I want is the exact opposite. If you let me go tomorrow for the first flight, then I'll leave you alone for the rest of your training."

Edith shook her head. "I can't."

Spence standing before us. "Ladies, if you'll allow me."

I looked at Edith, and she nodded. Then I nodded, too.

"The three of us can go up together tomorrow morning," Spence said. "I'll be flying, of course, and we can put Lucy up front beside me and Edith in the back." He looked at me. "Your goal is to experience what it's like to learn to fly an airplane, right?"

I nodded despite the gut-level "no" that was shouting inside me. Pilots believed that driving a metal machine thousands of feet above the earth was normal. For me, flying was not a pastime pursuit or the means to experience a thrill or freedom. It was a method for moving efficiently from point A to a distant point B. I was not a nervous flyer. I was calm in my seat on any commercial flight, which was where I had planned to spend the entirety of my flying career. The front seat in a four-seat airplane was not an option that I had ever entertained. The difference between the front and the back was gigantic. Nobody expected a person in the back to do anything. The back seat was for passengers. In the front, you were inches from the controls and could wind up touching them whether you wanted to or not. You could even be forced to try to use them if the pilot had a heart attack mid-flight or her door opened unexpectedly and she fell out.

And yet, my head was nodding against my will.

"Great," Spence said. "You'll sit up front, and when you're ready, you can take the yoke and see what it feels like."

Oh, no. No no no.

"You'll get a pretty good sense in a few minutes of what Edith will be facing. It should give you some good material for your articles."

He was smiling. Edith was nodding. I could not get the word "no" out.

"Then I'll land the plane, and you can get out so Edith can concentrate on her first lesson without an audience. After she's logged a few hours, we'll invite you into the back seat and take you up again. How does that sound?"

It sounded logical and smart, well-intentioned and thoughtful, a good compromise, except that it denied me of what I wanted most and thrust me into a situation that I did not want. At all.

"Well done, Spence. Thank you," Edith said.

"Yeah, thanks," I said. Spence nodded once and started across the tarmac. "Sometimes I hate you." I meant to say it inside my head, but when Edith looked at me, I knew that it had slipped out, accidentally on purpose.

"For shame, Lucy," she said. "You have a job to do."

"Exactly," I said. "For shame, Edith. Let me do my job."

She squeezed my hand to soften the blow. I pulled it away and walked off.

Spence was walking toward the building near the edge of the runway. Edith trotted up alongside her teacher.

"There are a bunch of forms you need to sign, and you should pick out a logbook and a headset," Spencer said.

I followed at my own pace toward the FBO, or fixed base operation, the building that housed the flight school and rental desk. A glass case contained a variety of headsets and pilot's logbooks, and there was a display of aviation maps, called sectionals. As I unfolded one, the monumentally complex process that Edith was undertaking also unfolded before me. In addition to learning how to fly the plane,

196

land it on a runway, and manage emergencies such as engine failure, she also had to learn how to read the sectionals, navigate alone during flight using a GPS, file a flight plan before take-off, communicate with the control tower and other pilots via the radio, and complete the pre-flight check of the mechanical parts of the airplane. Cramming all that and more into six to eight weeks seemed not only impossible but foolish. The minimum requirement for a license was forty hours of flight time, but most student pilots flew sixty to eighty hours before obtaining their license. Edith was not average. She would be living, breathing, and dreaming aviation most hours of most days until she earned her license. If she succeeded, she would be licensed and instructor-free terrifyingly soon. I glanced across the room to where she was trying on headsets with Spence's help. Her face was sheer delight, yet there could be no doubt that she knew the work before her would prove rigorous. If she earned her license, she would be among the oldest first-time pilots ever, and she would be among the oldest female pilots in the history of aviation. She had already been examined by an FAA-approved physician, who claimed that she was in excellent health and cleared for lessons.

"Ready, dear?"

She was standing before me with a messenger bag that bore the name of the flight school and a pair of wings on the front.

"My headset and logbook are right here in my trusty new flight bag." She patted it. "Take-off is nine o'clock sharp. Spence says the cloud cover usually lifts by then. We need to be here by 8:40 to watch him do the flight check."

We walked out to the bike rack and got on our bikes, hers yellow as the sun, and mine blood red. This is how it would be for the next month or two. Edith coasted down the sidewalk and onto the street.

"This is the perfect bag for my bike commute," she yelled.

She pedaled down the road, giddy over the new bag and the contents that accessorized her as a pilot, in the full bloom of life, robust in mind and body, intoxicated with the thrill of embarking on a new endeavor. Her joyful exterior was a façade, behind which she heard the call of death, a call that she alone heard beckoning. All I heard was joy and an exuberance that promised years of good living still ahead for her.

* * *

For the rest of the day, I kept my vow to stick to Edith. We sat at the table on the patio for hours as she showed me her manuals, log-book, headset, and the GPS that Rose and Carter had sent as a good-luck present. Anthony came and went, and with each return his raised eyebrows asked me, "Are you still listening?" Edith's command of aviation terminology and aeronautical concepts revealed no gap where her self-proclaimed mechanical inabilities could fit. She lent me the ground-school book. I looked across the table to Anthony and offered it to him.

"You're her co-pilot," I said. "Don't you want to know this stuff?"

He looked at Edith and then at me. "Theoretically," he said.

Billy made us lunch on the roof, and then the four of us walked into town, where he pointed out each restaurant, café, and store. A bigger town up the coastal highway a few minutes by car had much more to offer, including the animal clinic where Billy worked. As we started back toward the house, I suggested a walk on the beach, but Billy declined.

"I need to shop for dinner," he said. Then he whispered to me, "I don't want to let you down, love bug."

Anthony mumbled about a bad night's sleep and a nap. More and more, he had been slipping away to be alone. Maybe he wanted to give me and Edith time together. Maybe, though, there was another reason, of which a bad night's sleep, extended silences, and serial dis-appearances throughout the day were symptoms. I resolved to poke around and inquire about his whereabouts, physical, spiritual, psycho-logical, and emotional.

As Edith and I walked on the beach, she talked and talked as if suddenly everything needed to get out at once. I had no notebook or pen but did not need or want them. Our talk that day, and similar con-versations in the days that followed, was not an interview. Edith wanted to talk, and I wanted to listen. She told me the stories of her children's births. She described how they looked the first time she held them. She narrated their school years, described their first boy-friends and girlfriend, and told the tale of Billy and Zalira. She recalled family trips, holiday traditions, and her favorite memories of

Henry, whose name she had not uttered for months. I had to stop and count backward to correct my own confused sense of time. From the day that I had sat in Cunningham's office and received the assignment to that first walk on the beach with Edith, I had traveled farther than from Oregon to Vermont to New York to Greece to California, and I had lived more life than what could fit into a mere three months.

"This would have been useful background before we started," I said.

We took the last step off the sand and onto the pavement back to Billy's house. The sun was moving downward, soon to slip into the ocean for the night.

"You say that now, but really it would have crippled you," Edith said. "It would have been a crutch, a disruption from the real story as you saw it unfolding."

"Why do you trust me to tell your story? You could do it yourself. You have all those journals. I know you still write every day."

I had waited forever to ask her this. I had feared that it was an unaskable question. Like most fears, however, this one had existed only in my mind. From the beginning, Edith had said and done everything possible to encourage me to ask questions and assure me that nothing was off limits. Then she had watched as I enforced my own limits and erected walls. She turned to face me.

"Henry's obituary."

She said nothing more. I waited and waited, but that was all. We walked home to Billy's, side by side, two caterpillars who had busted out of our cocoons and become free-flying butterflies. When we turned the corner onto Billy's street, there was a second car in his driveway. Edith elbowed me hard in the ribs.

"Ow!"

"Hee hee." She put her hand over her mouth and giggled in imitation of the person whose car was parked a hundred paces from us. "He's here," she whispered.

I kept walking and looked straight ahead. "Yes, Edith. He's here. My love. My knight in shining sunscreen from the shores of Santorini. The man who captured my mind and my heart as the sun rose and I ate my breakfast on a day that I wrongly assumed was like any other. The man who wrote the most stunning love letter that any woman has

199

ever received and who chose me as the woman to receive it. The man with whom I intend to share my bed and my thoughts and travels and books and toothpaste as long as he will allow me. Plato Zielinski, a man as rare and unique as his name. Tuck, beautiful Tuck, the love of my life."

"Oh, Lucy, that's not fair," Edith said. "You left nothing for me to add."

"Precisely my intention."

"Love?"

"Love, Edith. The real deal. Travel buddy, ambulance angel, moto driver, love-letter writer, proclaimer of true love for little ol' me, holder of babies, creator of cutting-edge computer programs, devoted son and brother and nephew, and more that I don't even know yet."

"Babies?"

"Yes. Babies."

"That sounds very intriguing, dear."

"It most certainly is."

I had spread my wings wide enough to show my secret to Edith. Fears were vanishing left and right. The prospect of crossing the threshold and beholding my Tuck stirred in me a wondrous anticipation. This was what every lover wanted: to be with her beloved, gaze upon him, hold him in her arms, feel his eyes upon her. The longer I waited to get him alone, the sweeter the moment would be.

Something tickled my hand. It was Edith's wing, spread open wide enough to touch mine. "You've chosen well, Lucy. He's lovely."

"Thank you," I said. "I don't think we choose whom we love, though. I think we choose whether to love."

In we went, and there they were, the three men in a row, standing in Billy's living room, chatting and laughing like old friends.

"Welcome home," Billy said. "Ma, Anthony, come on up and give me a hand. Lucy, I'll let you give Tuck the tour, if that's OK. There's food on the grill that needs me."

Billy made his way up the spiral staircase, and Edith and Anthony followed. I took Tuck's hand and led him through Billy's room and out onto the patio. We paused to admire the flowers, the hot tub, and the solace of the backyard haven. Then I crossed the patio and opened the door to the guest cottage.

"This is where I get to stay," I said.

I held the door open, and he walked through. Then I closed the door and went to where Tuck stood in the middle of the room, staring at the framed photographs on the walls. I wrapped my arms around him and dove in for a world-class kiss that lasted long enough that we were late for dinner but greeted with three grins that forgave us as we clinked glasses. We ate seafood and vegetable kabobs and drank white wine from a vineyard up the road as the sun set and evening chilled the air. Tuck asked Edith about flying, Billy asked Tuck about work, and Anthony and I listened and tried to forget that our meals, laughs, and conversations together were numbered. Over fruit salad for dessert, we agreed on a tour of Billy's clinic the next afternoon, followed by dinner in town to celebrate Edith's debut flight. Then she and Anthony thanked our host and retired for a good night's sleep before her big day. I searched her for nerves but found only serenity and a smile that showed she could hardly wait to pull on her headset and get her hands on the controls.

Billy refused to let us help with the dishes and insisted that Tuck try the hot tub.

"This is the perfect time for it. The temperature will drop ten degrees in the next hour. Shoo! Go. I mean it, you two." He grabbed a stack of dirty plates, turned his back to us, and walked toward the open-air kitchen. "I put extra towels on your bed, Luce," he called over his shoulder.

Tuck looked at me and shook his head. "He's like a mom."

"The feminist in me wants to punch you, but the child in me totally agrees."

We walked to the staircase and began to wind our way downward.

"He's much nicer than his sisters, huh?" Tuck stood at the bottom and waited for me. I led the way through Billy's bedroom and across the patio.

"Nice is hard to define," I said when we were inside the cozy cottage. I sat on the bed, and Tuck sat beside me. "Rose has a kind soul and an easy way of moving between her own world and her family.

She leaves a quiet trail of goodness wherever she goes. Alice has a broken soul, so it doesn't seem fair to condemn her, but she is bitter and angry to the core. There is something else inside her, too, though, a fierce commitment to real problems in the world that need our attention. She treats pretty much everyone outside of Africa with disdain and contempt, but she also has sacrificed everything—every basic human happiness—to devote herself to making the world a better place. I don't know what nice is. I don't know which is better—to treat people terribly while doing valuable work for the world, or to treat people kindly while doing work that serves nobody but yourself."

"I thought writers weren't supposed to judge their characters."

"They're not, but this is my life right now. This is what I do. I follow these people around, I listen to them, I watch them, and I try to make sense of their lives. Isn't that different from judging? I want to understand Rose and Alice and Billy—and especially Edith."

"Edith saved my uncle Lewis."

"You saved your uncle Lewis."

Tuck shook his head. "Edith saved him with her stories. She told him about her list. She told him one story after another in a way that seemed light and casual, just the ordinary conversations of people getting to know each other. She knew exactly what she was doing, though, infusing him with hope and a love of life. Before we left, she gave him a scrapbook that she made of all your newspaper stories about the list. Well, all but the first two."

"What?"

"They were photocopied on fancy paper and bound with a beautiful cover. She said newsprint fades in time. They were in the order that she did the tasks, so he could read it like the story of her list, the chronological story of her life."

"When did she do that? Make them into a book?"

Tuck shrugged. "She said she made it for herself, but then she gave it to Uncle Lewis. She said he needed it more than she did."

"She never told me. She never says a word about my writing."

"Well, she picked you. She chose you to do this. That seems like approval to me."

I looked up through the glass ceiling at the sky and watched long enough to see the last tinge of twilight-blue darken into black. The blue of early night marked a beginning and an end, bittersweet yet not absent of hope.

"She didn't tell him about the end, did she?" I asked.

"No," Tuck said.

"That's the problem with suicide. You're not around to clean up the mess you've made for everyone else. I can't imagine what your uncle will think of her when he finds out."

"She won't do it," Tuck said. Then he was quiet, very quiet. "Will she?"

"With Edith anything is possible."

"It's sort of funny that she mapped out her life with this long and demanding list and then actually did it all, and meanwhile her son just wants have a good time."

"She values the process, not the final product or performance. She loved doing it. She loved tackling something unknown and making it familiar, adding it to her skills, absorbing it into who she is. She still has hundreds of lines of Shakespeare memorized, and her kitchen is filled with pottery that she made herself more than thirty years ago. She can play two string instruments, speak five languages, paint, dance, and persuade city officials to pass ordinances that she wants. She is the quintessential renaissance woman. She wasn't trying to prove anything. She didn't need attention or accolades. She loved the doing, the act of learning everything she could, the process of engaging and participating. She taught her children everything that she was learning. They lived the list with her, and there was a trickle-down effect. When she was studying Spanish, there was Spanish in the air, and they all wound up learning some. When she was making pottery, she would talk about it at home—how to mix clay and how to glaze a pot and how the kiln works and why some artists work with terra cotta and others with porcelain. Everything fascinates her. She wants to do and go and create and learn and see and hear. She invented the ideal job for herself, and with it she made the ideal life for herself and her children."

Tuck was watching my face, as if studying me would help him decide whether to believe me. I was not sure whether to believe me.

Playing Cello for the Trees

There were three ways to get at the truth: through Edith's words, my interpretation of them, and my own observations. Yet, that simple equation in fact had countless variables that could yield an infinite number of conclusions. I had to choose one—only one—write it into a concise story, and send it to Cunningham for public consumption while the disjointed remainders stayed in my head forever. Journalism was a flawed means for capturing a human life. It required summaries and approximations. It left out far too much. Yet, at the very least, when done well, it was an authentic attempt to combine those three ways for getting at the truth and blend them into some version of a person. That version may not have had any practical application in the end, though, other than perhaps entertainment. The readers of *The Bend Bugle* knew one version of Edith, the one that I was creating, and they gobbled it up like candy, a tasty but perhaps meaningless substitute for the real person. They were still—as always—left with the same question: Who was Edith Small, really? Who were any of us, really?

Yet, what kept me going and what kept me writing was a hope for more. Enlightenment through truth was my noble yet futile goal. Teaching through journalism. Observing a human life, translating it into language, and offering it up to others for their own consideration. That was what good writing did for us, after all. That was the purpose of stories: to show us another human being, real or imagined, and allow us to watch from a closer proximity than we could in real life. We all are voyeurs at heart, and we watch one another out of curiosity and out of fear that we are different, or strange, or inferior. On the pages of written stories, we get the closest and most intimate glimpse of all.

"What is it like to be an expert on another person?" Tuck said.

I looked at him. He had been watching me think for a long time, long enough for me to forget that he was there beside me. We were still standing in the middle of the room. The time for sitting had passed long ago, and now we were stuck in a moment and in a place, standing with our arms dangling at our sides and the stars above our heads.

"It feels like failure, because it's not possible to know another person."

"That's grim. It's not like you to take a defeatist attitude."

"I never asked Edith's children what it was like growing up with her as their mother."

"And still you know."

"I never asked. I didn't think to."

"You didn't need to ask," Tuck said. "You know. You know because you watched and you listened. That's who you are and what you do. You understand who Rose is and who Alice is and who Billy is."

"I'm a fool. I never asked."

"Lucy, you're a fool if you think the only way the find an answer is to ask a question." Tuck shook his head and took my hands. "Do you need me to tell you? Do you need someone to look you in the eye and tell you that you're a good writer and you're doing a good job with Edith's story? I can do that. I can tell you that, but here's the problem. I'll have to tell you again tomorrow and the next day and the day after that. And when I'm done telling you, you'll need your editor to tell you and your dad to tell you and your brother to tell you. It never stops. There's no end, Lucy, because the only one who can do this for you is yourself. You're a writer. You know it, I know it, Edith knows it, your readers know it. You work for a newspaper, and you carry a reporter's notebook, and you are a real writer. If you can't know that in your own mind and you can't feel that in your own bones, then there is nothing anyone can do to make it real for you. We have to validate ourselves. We can't wait for others to do it for us."

My fingers had gone numb. Tuck was squeezing my hands a bit too hard. All that energy behind his words had to go somewhere. Still, I did not dare wiggle my fingers. "There's no way to succeed with this assignment," I said. "I can't be an expert on Edith or anyone else. That's not possible. It's all just observations and conjecture. It's approximations. It's me seeing her through my filters, the biases and baggage and background that none of us can remove when we look at another person. What I see is my version of Edith. I can't get to hers. This is the impossible truth about being human."

"But that's what makes it so beautiful and valuable," Tuck said. "The act of trying to know another person is the ultimate act of love."

"That's not why I write."

"That's the only reason any writer has ever written," Tuck said. "Every book worth reading is an attempt to explain what it means to be human and what it is to try to know another person. That's what literature is. It's humans looking at themselves and trying against all odds to connect with others. Unless of course you're writing a book about rocks."

"Rocks?"

"Not everyone is fascinated by people," Tuck said. "Some people like rocks. Or computers, for instance. Or clouds. Or maybe dinosaurs. Primates. Early man. Spaceships. Coffee beans."

"Hot tubs."

"Stars."

"Skin."

"Nudity."

"Good idea," Tuck said. "Close your eyes." I did. I heard a zipper unzip and the riffling of clothing coming off a body. "OK. Your turn." He had stripped and wrapped a towel around his waist. "I'll meet you there." He opened the door, walked outside, and closed the door behind him.

I slipped off my clothes, wrapped up in a towel, took the cover off the hot tub, and hid my naked parts beneath the surface of the water before Tuck returned with two bottles of beer. I glanced up at the sky as he dropped his towel and climbed in beside me.

"Cheers," he said.

He clinked his bottle against mine. The cold bitter carbonation cooled my mouth, my throat, and the insides of my head that had overheated from overuse. Tuck took a sip, too, and exhaled a long happy, "Ahh." Then he looked at me as he slid closer until our skin was touching. His hand touched my knee and moved up and down across the silky wetness of my kneecap.

"It's OK to love her, Lucy."

Then he kissed me, and we entered a sleepless night, two lovers who danced together under the stars, beneath the sheets, and into and out of one another with the intoxicating bliss of the first time.

* * *

Amy Tatko

The Bend Bugle
"Task #35: Fly an Airplane"
By Lucy Hunt

There is a saying in the world of general aviation: Flying an airplane is as easy as driving a car; landing an airplane is darn near impossible. Edith Small wanted to achieve the impossible.

With less than two months remaining until her seventy-sixth birthday—her own self-proclaimed deadline—she climbed into the cockpit of a single-engine airplane to begin training for her private pilot's license, the thirty-fifth and final challenge on her "Lifetime List of Things To Do." Her goal is to complete the flight instruction and pass the written and flight tests within the next six to eight weeks.

"Oh, it's possible," said her instructor, Spencer McGillicuddy of Moss Beach Flight School. "It's not easy, but I get the sense that Edith isn't interested in easy."

At 0900 hours on Tuesday, their airplane stood ready and revved at the end of the runway. The pre-flight check was complete. With a reporter tagging along to observe the flight, the student-teacher team was forced to fly a four-seat plane. Most of Edith's training will occur in a smaller two-seat airplane referred to as a "trainer."

"Ready?" McGillicuddy asked via his headset microphone.

Edith tugged her seatbelt and checked her headset one last time. Then she gave a single nod to her instructor. About halfway down the runway, the wheels lifted, the wings tipped slightly to the right and then to the left, and the plane began its climb to about 3,000 feet. The morning coastal fog had cleared just after 8 a.m. A 4-knot wind out of the west would not be a factor. The plane inched skyward without a bump, as McGillicuddy narrated every step of the process while Edith watched his hands work the controls and his mouth work the radio.

The spirit of U.S. aviation dates back to the historic and groundbreaking efforts of Orville and Wilbur Wright, whose December 1903 flight charted the course for fixed-wing aircraft. What the Wright brothers discovered more than a hundred years ago was precisely what Edith would be learning in the weeks to come: a reliable method of pilot control as the critical means for solving what they called "the flying problem." Their method was the invention of three-axis control to enable the pilot to steer the aircraft and maintain its equilibrium.

"It's a lot to remember at first," McGillicuddy said before take-off. "But the learning curve is steep, and most pilots get the hang of it by the third or fourth lesson."

For experienced pilots, handling the controls of an airplane is an intimate affair. The nuances of each plane's needs and quirks become familiar, and there is a gut-level sense about which minute correction to make and when. Contrary to popular belief among non-pilots, however, there is plenty of what McGillicuddy called "wiggle room."

"It's not as if you're going to send the plane straight to the ground if you pull back a bit too much or tighten up the flaps too soon," he said. "It's a process. You've constantly got your hands going, moving from one control to the next, checking, reconfiguring, making tiny adjustments."

To the new pilot or anyone without experience in the cockpit, the sensation of handling the yoke, the air term for the "steering wheel," is startling at first. A half-inch in either direction gets an immediate response from the airplane. Yet, sure enough, within minutes of taking the yoke, the experience feels similar to driving a car.

After twenty minutes and a scenic jaunt up the coast toward San Francisco, McGillicuddy was back in command and put the airplane on the ground. The passenger climbed out, and Edith took the co-pilot's seat to begin her formal instruction. By the end of the day, her hands had spent about forty minutes on the yoke and other controls. In about a week, her teacher will begin training her to take off and land the airplane.

"It was exhilarating," Edith said at the end of her first lesson. "I can't for the life of me imagine handling the thing in bad weather or putting it on the ground, but I'm sure I'll get there."

Edith plans to spend two hours in the air with McGillicuddy every day, six days a week. She will read and study on her own every day, too. After about 15-20 hours of instruction, she should be ready to solo, her teacher said. Then she will be cleared to practice flying on her own, adding more hours to her daily routine.

The Federal Aviation Administration requires student pilots to spend 40 hours in the air with an instructor in order to qualify for a private pilot's license. Most students log around 60-80 hours of flying time before taking the tests. Edith's seventy-sixth birthday is on October 26, and she wants to meet her goal of completing her lifetime list at the age of 75. Regional FAA officials at the San Francisco field office said that Edith is the oldest California woman to pursue a private license, though other states have licensed women in their seventies.

"It's a self-selecting bunch," said Buzz Waverly, FAA Regional Coordinator for Northern California. "There aren't many people who start flight instruction but don't get their license."

For those who do drop out or fail to earn a license, money and time are the major obstacles. The average cost to obtain a pilot's license ranges from about $6,000 to $10,000, depending on the airport, airplane, instructor, and student's schedule. Those who can fly more often tend to earn their license on fewer dollars. Those who fly only occasionally make slower progress and pour more money into extra lessons to review procedures and practice.

Edith knew from the start that time and money would not be her problem. Neither would fear hinder her. She did, however, doubt whether she had the mechanical inclination to learn the techniques and tackle the technical challenges of taking off and landing.

"I feel differently now," she said after her first lesson. "I wasn't sure before, but now I know that I can do this. I'll be able to complete my training and pass the test."

Edith's husband, Anthony Rizzo, was waiting on the tarmac when she landed. When she stepped out of the airplane, he handed her a dozen red roses.

"Of course she'll do it," he said. "She's made it this far. She isn't going to fail now."

Edith's son, Billy Small, was also standing by when his mother finished her first flying lesson. He planned to treat her and a few others to dinner that evening to celebrate. He recalled his childhood with a mother who was working her way through a list of 35 lifetime challenges.

"Her list was a part of the air we breathed," he said. "I can't imagine my mom without her list."

The years after his parents' trip to the South Pole, Edith's only hiatus from the list, was a time of restlessness for her, according to her son.

"She just wasn't herself," he said. "She dabbled in this and that. She always kept busy, but it wasn't the same." Billy Small was puzzled that his mother put her list aside for as long as she did, and he was delighted when she resumed her work on it after his father's death. Now he is cheering her on from the sidelines of the airport just miles from his house and not far from the coastal town of his birth and early childhood.

"Of course she'll do it," he said. "I'll be very proud of her when she gets her license."

Yet, earning her license and finishing her lifetime list will be bittersweet.

"I bet she can't imagine her life without the list."

* * *

By the end of the first week, we had fallen into a routine. Tuck arrived before dinner. Sometimes the four of us ate together while Billy was at work, and we took turns cooking in pairs. Edith preferred to use the full kitchen in the house and eat on the back patio. We consented on the evenings when she and Anthony cooked, though the three of us loved Billy's rooftop paradise with its sweeping views of the mountains, sky, and ocean. Some nights Tuck and I walked into town to eat alone together. Some nights Edith and Anthony ate in town, and the two of us had the roof all to ourselves.

We took long walks on the beach at sunset and long soaks in the hot tub after sundown. Billy was co-owner of the animal clinic and the most senior veterinarian. He made his own work schedule and chose four o'clock to ten or eleven most weekdays, with an extra day off whenever he wanted one. He welcomed our visits to the clinic, though he warned us that it got busy. Many locals commuted into the city for work, and evening was the best time for them to take their pets to the vet. Evening was also when most accidents happened, and Dr. Small saw a lot of emergencies, too.

During the day, Billy surfed, ran on the beach, and lounged on the patio and roof with a book. He cooked breakfast for us every day and dinner on the weekends.

Anthony disappeared for hours at a time when Edith was at the airport. No line of questioning could lead me to his truth. He claimed to be busy doing nothing—walking, napping, reading—but there had to be more to it.

I became a regular fixture at the airport, where I read the aviation magazines at the FBO, chatted with the other flight instructors while Spence was up with Edith, and asked for a debriefing at the end of each lesson. Some mornings I rode the red bike beside Edith on the yellow bike. We had come to think of Billy's two bicycles as mine and hers. Sometimes I biked or walked to the airport alone later in the morning.

The rest of the time, I was writing. Billy was right about the desk that he made for his sisters' guest house. There was no place more peaceful and alluring for a writer. I would open the huge window above the desk, and the scent of tree blossoms and blooming flowers would drift in. The eternal summer of California with the aroma of sweet flowers, the breeze tinged with sea salt, and the steady warming of the air throughout the day invited me to sit at the window and write on and on. One day, I reached for a large lined notepad that I kept in my bag. I unplugged my laptop computer and stored it away in its travel bag. There it stayed for the remainder of my time at Billy's. The sensation of the pen moving across the paper lulled me. The formation of full words and complete sentences, as opposed to the abbreviations and scribbles in my reporter's notebook, satisfied me. My eyes drank in the shapes of the letters, and my internal ear feasted on the song of word combinations and melodic phrases. The hum of the machine was gone. The clicking of the keys was gone. I numbered each page and tore it off the pad when I reached the bottom right corner. A plastic folder from a bookstore in Santorini stored the pile of completed pages. The more I wrote, the more I had to write. For hours each day, I added to the growing story, purging from myself the intertwining tales that I had been hearing and seeing for months. Nothing was intended for Cunningham or the readers of *The Bend Bugle*. My intentions were not defined. They did not take the shape of a coherent plan. A force that I had never known, part internal and part external, compelled me to write for hour after hour, day after day. I told nobody, though I knew that Tuck knew.

Playing Cello for the Trees

Toward the end of the second week of Edith's lessons, I needed a break from the airport. As a non-flying aviation expert, I had reached a saturation point that begged me to track down a news story anywhere other than at the airport. I had filed two more daily reports about Edith's progress in the sky, and then I remembered her challenge to me about other people her age and their lifetime achievements. Cunningham found the idea amusing and agreed to let me take it on.

The next morning, after Edith left for the airport, I grabbed my bike and headed in the opposite direction. I had not done any street reporting in ages, and I balked at the notion of approaching strangers and attempting to interrogate them about their personal lives. After the first few interviews, though, the jitters wore off, and I threw myself into it with renewed gusto. I could ask anyone anything, and most of the time, they responded. The simple fact of a reporter with a notebook and pen instilled magic powers. The results were varied and puzzling, but I stuck with my street survey and forced myself to wait to compile and analyze the results later at my desk.

The first dozen gray-haired interviewees labeled their lives as ordinary but then surprised themselves with the lists of achievements that they recited for me. Person number thirteen was eighty-year-old Arnold Johansson, whose answer to my opening question—"What have been the greatest achievements of your life?"—was a jackpot. Johansson, who insisted that I call him Arnie, spilled over with personality and lifetime achievements. He was the first evidence that Edith may have been right. There were others like her. His methodology differed from hers, but the spirit, content, and results were peculiarly similar.

On New Year's Day each year for fifty-five years, Arnie identified one new accomplishment that he wished to undertake and master by the end of the year. He studied foreign languages, played musical instruments, traveled, and read, just like Edith. He also made his way onto a White House dinner list, designed and built a model train powered by solar energy, and ate only fresh locally-grown vegetables and fruits every day for one entire year. He renewed his wedding vows and took his wife on a second honeymoon at the age of fifty. He learned how to stand on his head and do gymnastics in his sixties.

Along the way, he had also ran a marathon, biked a century, and swam across the English Channel.

"How were you able to do each year's task?" I asked him. "Didn't you work a full-time job?"

We were drinking iced tea at a café with outdoor seating. I had thrown my recorder into my bag at the last minute, just in case, and I had placed it on the table when Arnie began talking. It collected one of the best speeches of my short career.

"Sure I did," Arnie said. "I was a banker. I had tons of money and vacation time, plus complete job stability. It was the perfect scenario. Not to have accomplished all that I did outside of work would have been a waste of my life. I would have been irresponsible and ungrateful to live an ordinary life under those circumstances."

I asked Arnie whether he kept track of his achievements, and like most achievers, he referred to a list and a system for logging each completed task.

"I've used the same notebook since the beginning. On January 1, I turn to the next blank page. I write the number of the goal at the top. This year is number fifty-six: Learn about wine and get a part-time job pouring wine in a tasting room. I've lived in California my whole life, and I don't know a darn thing about wine. I drink martinis when I drink, which is about every other night. Or I used to anyway. This year, I'm drinking wine. I like shiraz and riesling, because they taste good to me, no matter what the experts say. I don't give a hoot about that wimpy pinot noir that snooty wine drinkers go on and on about. You meet a lot of snooty people pouring wine, but you also meet friendly folks, too. It's about half and half, with not much in between. I try not to generalize, and I've been a positive thinker my whole life, but that's the truth of it, and there's no way around it. The friendly ones are chatty, because they're kind by nature and they're intoxicated to some degree. Happy drunks for the most part. Giggly ladies and smiley men. They get rather friendly with each other, too, and that can be terribly entertaining. Terribly entertaining, some of the carrying on I've seen in the tasting room."

Arnie started to chuckle and shake his head at the carrying-ons at the vineyard where he had been working since March.

"What about next year? Have you chosen your task?"

"I like to call them endeavors. Endeavor #57: Find a new wife and take a camel ride across the Sahara Desert for the honeymoon. I've been alone for six years, and it's no good, no good at all. We people need to stick together and talk to each other. I get so lonely sometimes I just plain give up and cry right onto my dinner plate. No more eating alone for me. Next year, I'm going lady hunting. She's bound to be a good one, too, because not just any old gal will sign up for a camel-back honeymoon through a desert on the other side of the world—the wilder side."

Arnie raised his eyebrows and jiggled his shoulders at the thought of her. Then he finished his iced tea and stood to leave.

"What's this all about again? You say you're a newspaper report-er?"

"Yes, sir. I write for a paper in Oregon. I'm working on a story about people's lifetime achievements."

"Isn't that nice. Well, you have yourself a good day now."

Arnold Johansson tipped his fedora at me and wandered off down Main Street, whistling and grinning, perhaps as he thought about next year's endeavor. I could not write a word about him until I had con-firmed every fact that he told me and uncovered evidence to support every endeavor that he had claimed to achieve. I biked to the library first, where I did as much research as I could in the archives of the local newspaper and on the internet. Then I spent the rest of the day on the telephone and at my desk back at Billy's cottage. The most ex-citing moment came when a call to a British newspaper confirmed that Arnie had in fact swum across the English Channel, one of only about a hundred and thirty people to do so.

The fact-checking was part of the fun. It separated fiction from real life. Without evidence to support Arnie's claims, there was no news story. That was the problem with news: It had to check out, it had to be real, it had to be truth, or as close to it as we were humanly able to get. Cunningham had grilled me every day over the summer about Edith. Her ticket stubs, boarding passes, language textbooks, ceramic dishes, and other accessories, products, and memorabilia from her work on the list served as ample proof much of the time. I made phone calls to track down her former instructors at schools, in-stitutes, and studios where she took language, music, and art classes. I talked with local old-timers who had worked alongside her on some of the volunteer projects. The boxes that Edith had stored in her attic, the dented and bulging cardboard boxes that housed the remnants of her life with the list, moved to my apartment during the summer and were still there, standing in a row against my living-room wall. Edith never complained about my telephone calls to Rose's house in Vermont to conduct follow-up interviews, confirm facts, and clarify details. In fact, she had suggested that I take the boxes so I could look through them any time I needed more information. Among the piles of evidence and memories, my favorite artifact was her ballet shoes. Women at the age of fifty-two rarely took up ballet. The photographs from her final recital were comical proof not only of Edith's accomplishment but also of her commitment to the process rather than the performance and her love of life rather than a love of ego.

My research on Arnie was done, and I had just finished writing an outline for the story when a familiar hum pulled me out of the cottage. My eyes shifted upward. Edith was buzzing around town at about two-thousand feet. This was hour number eighteen with Spence. He thought that she would be ready to solo by the end of her third week. He called her a natural. That made Edith's eyebrows do their signature jig. The plane banked and cruised out toward the ocean. Edith loved to fly over the water. One recent morning, Spence had spotted a migrating gray whale and pointed it out to Edith. I grabbed my bike and pedaled along the coast, tracking Edith's patterns all the while. The movement, the sea air, the sunshine, and the freedom of the outdoors and the ocean views soothed me and revived me after a day cooped up with reporting and note-taking.

Later that day, after Edith had landed back at the airport, I turned right onto Billy's street and began my final approach toward his driveway. A man was standing near the mailbox with a suitcase beside him.

"Anthony?"

I squeezed the hand brakes and came to a stop inches from his suitcase. He rubbed a hand across his forehead.

"Hello, Lucy."

"What's going on? What happened?"

"Nothing happened."

"Where are you going?"

He looked at me, and then he looked at the sky.

"I can't do it. I can't watch this anymore." He looked at his suitcase. Then he kicked it, but gently, not in a way that had much anger behind it. "I can't be a part of this anymore. She isn't kidding, Lucy. You need to know that. Maybe you've always known that. I can't be here to watch. I won't be a part of this. I feel like an accomplice. I feel like I'm condoning it, and I don't. I don't condone it."

Then he fumbled with his left hand and held out his wedding band. It had not yet earned the scratches and dents that showed the permanent imprint of years of matrimony. I stared at the shiny new ring and kept my hands wrapped defiantly on the handle bars.

"I wrote her a note," Anthony said. "I'm not asking you to tell her. I wouldn't do that."

I shook my head. "You can't leave."

He shook his head back at me. "I can't stay."

"But why?" I said. "Why now? Why did you marry her? You knew from the beginning. She told you exactly what she planned to do, and you agreed to it—to New York and Alice and Greece and Billy and flying lessons and limited time together and her death with or without you. You *promised*, Anthony. You were supposed to stay until the end. Until the very end."

A car engine grew louder behind me. A city cab rolled into Billy's driveway.

"This is my end," Anthony said. "I stop here. I'm finished with this. I can't do it anymore. I won't. I'm sorry, Lucy. You're fantastic. You're better than fantastic. I'll be cheering on you and Tuck from a distance. And if you'll let me, I'll be glad to call you my friend."

He reached for the suitcase, and I threw a leg over the bike seat, released my sweaty grip from the handlebars, and dropped the bike on the grass.

"Anthony, you can't do this."

The suitcase handle was in his left hand, while his right hand reached out again, pleading for me to take the ring. I felt the metal in my palm before I had made a decision.

"Thank you," he said. "Please leave it with my note. Beside the bed. You'll see."

I nodded, and something wet fell to my hand and splattered on the ring. My eyes and cheeks were dripping.

"You don't have to stay either, Lucy. You have a choice."

Anthony reached for me with his free hand and offered half a hug. It was more than I deserved and less than I needed. Then he walked to the taxi. Seconds later, the car moved down Billy's street. The passenger alone in the backseat tried to wave, but his hand was too weak, and his face could not smile. The engine hummed for a while, and then there was a new kind of quiet on Billy's street that followed me into the house, across the patio, and into the guest hut, where writing had never seemed more impossible.

* * *

The drive through the mountains was quiet. I had left a note for Billy on his desk explaining that I had taken his jeep and would be back tomorrow. Anthony's wedding ring was where he wanted it, on his note for Edith in Billy's guest room. She would ride her bicycle home after her flight lesson, and the house would be empty. Billy was surfing. Anthony was gone. I had escaped, too. She would never know what I knew. She would not know that her husband's wedding ring had touched my hand before reaching hers. His note was not sealed, but I would not make a sneak of myself. Its contents could only have repeated what he told me. I should have stayed at the house. I should have grabbed my notebook and recorder and sat ready to capture Edith's reaction when she entered the room, saw the ring and the note, and read her second husband's parting sentiments. She would not cry. She would not express remorse. She would not attempt to call him. She would not ask him to come back to her. What Edith would do—what she had spent her life doing, a life built on enormous volumes of doing—could impress anyone. The news stories were testament to her doing. It was what she did not do that disturbed me.

Edith would spend the afternoon snooping. She would scour the house for evidence of my whereabouts. She would cross the patio and enter the little cottage. She would find nothing, because in our game of chess I had learned to predict her next move. Our months together had taught me how to think like she thought, how to occupy the place inside her mind right alongside her. She would find nothing of mine on her spying venture. Anything worth finding was inside my shoul-

217

der bag or backpack, resting beside me on the passenger seat. She would look through my souvenirs from Greece, nestled among the dirty laundry that lay on the bottom of my half-zipped suitcase. Then she would give up and sit in the empty silence that had replaced her husband of two and a half months.

I stood at the reception desk at the company that employed Tuck. A minute later, I was standing before Tuck, who was wearing khakis and a navy-blue polo shirt, the uniform of a computer programmer. He had on canvas loafers that I had never seen before. His work life and our love life had never crossed before.

"Hi," he said.

"I'm sorry if you're mad. I know I should have called. It's just that—"

Then he smiled, just a little, a work-day smile. "I'm glad. Are you OK?"

He pushed the door open, and we walked down the corporate sidewalk until we were standing in the shade of the building beyond the receptionist's spy zone.

"Anthony left," I said.

"Oh."

"For good."

"Wow. How's Edith?"

"I don't know. She doesn't know yet. He left her a note. And his wedding ring."

"Oh, no," Tuck said.

"Oh, yes." I told him about Anthony's suitcase, the taxi, and the ring. I told him verbatim every word that Anthony had said.

"Jeezums," Tuck said.

"Yup."

"You left before she got home?"

"Yup."

"Oh," Tuck said.

"Don't say it," I said.

"I didn't. I won't."

"I can't believe that I'm doing this," I said. "I can't believe that this story is my job. She's going to do it. She's really doing to do it. I know that now. And she won't try to get Anthony back. When I ask her, she'll make a speech about free will and how love can't wear shackles and it was better to have limited time with him than no time at all."

"Lucy, don't do that."

"I just did."

Tuck looked at the sidewalk and did something weird with his lips and his teeth that he did whenever he did not approve of me, which was never until now.

"Please don't say it." I was begging, and there was an undeniable whining quality to my voice. I did not approve of me either right now. "I know. I know you're right. I can't start assuming that I can predict her thoughts and her reactions and her next move. But the truth is that I can."

"But isn't it impossible to know another human being?" Tuck said.

"If I didn't know you better, I'd think you were playing with me and being cruel, but I do know you better, so I won't answer that question."

Then everything became quiet, because that was what Tuck did best. He let the quiet sit between us when confusion and despair came sidling up to me and hooked their anchor in my gut. He waited, because that was what he did, too. He listened, because he knew more than anyone that listening was a great act of love. He gave me time, because that was what I needed most. I took that time to look at his loafers and his work clothes and remember how real and honest and wise he was and how cynical I could be and how I never wanted to be cynical but it was my worst knee-jerk defense mechanism when I was in pain—and I was in pain, serious pain, because I did not want Anthony to leave and I did not want Edith to let him leave and I knew that she would be dead soon and all of this would be over and I would not be able to watch her life anymore and I would not be able to watch the secondary characters move around the edges of her life anymore and I would miss them and—here came the truth—I would miss *her* so much that I would not be able to find the words to talk about it even to myself, let alone ever write about it or her or anything else ever again.

"I want to see the babies," I said. "Is it time? Is it your lunch break yet?"

Tuck glanced at his watch. "Close enough. I was finishing a report, and then I was going to walk over to the nursery."

My insides had grown so heavy that my belly was folding in half as my knees buckled and lowered me down to the cement. I sat on the sidewalk and waited, and I decided not to let the tears come. I waited some more. He always came if I gave him time. Then Tuck sat down across from me, took my hands in his, and squeezed the right amount, halfway between the firmness of reassurance and the tenderness of love.

"I think it's worth it," he said. "No matter how it ends, there is value in staying with the story and staying with her. Write it to the end. Do it for yourself. Do it for her. Do it for your readers. You have readers, Lucy. That's what every writer wants."

"Today I think I'd rather have any story but this one even if that meant no readers. I would prefer to write in a vacuum. Or perhaps a black hole."

"Some days are like that."

We stood when I decided it was time. Tuck led me down sidewalks and through doors until we reached the rooms where babies cried and gurgled, toddlers screeched and giggled, and older preschool children played with puzzles and blocks. Tuck introduced me to the women in the baby room, and he picked up his favorite baby and showed me how he held him. This one liked the cradle hold. The next one liked to be upright against his chest and shoulder, looking out behind him. When I was ready, I tried one, too. Mine liked to be held close to the chest, lengthwise, with one hand supporting her wee head. She was sleepy, and one of the women said her mother had just come in to nurse her but had to dash off to a meeting. Some holding would be nice for the girl baby. I looked up and saw Tuck watching me as he held his favorite boy baby again. Maybe someday the babies would be our own, homemade from scratch. Standing there with Tuck, holding babies, I let myself imagine the possibility, and it was as pleasant as it was new.

Tuck gave me the key to his apartment, and I spent the afternoon writing after all. Sometimes being a person gets in the way of the writer. The way the person feels blocks the path to the writer's mind. The connections among the world, the writing brain, and the paper become severed. Like a broken bone, though, the connections heal if you set them right and gave them time. Tuck and the babies had set my broken writer's mind, and it was healing rapidly. I wrote at the table in the kitchen. I had good intentions of cooking an appetizing dinner that would be ready and waiting when Tuck walked in the door. I could not stop writing, though, and Tuck would not want me to stop when the connections had been restored. The pages that I churned out that afternoon were infused with more life than most of what I had written so far. The infusion made me nervous. I began to suspect that honest human emotion was an ingredient of good prose. Sentimentality, its trashy alter ego, was the garbage pit of failed literary efforts. I avoided re-reading for fear that my productive afternoon was in fact destined for the garbage pit. The line between honest emotion and sentimentality was often too blurry to locate. I stopped trying to find it. I begged myself not to worry, and on I wrote. I kept writing until the door clicked and Tuck walked in.

"Hey, writer," he said. "It's good to see you back at it."

He slipped off his loafers near the front door. Then he looked at me until I looked up from my notepad. He walked toward me, pulled my chair out from the table, lowered me to the floor, and pressed himself on top of me. We kissed as long as we could. Then we pulled off our clothes and made love under the open windows in the sunlight on the linoleum that left red marks on our skin in strange places.

"Will you stay tonight?" Tuck asked.

"Yes."

"Nobody but me has ever slept in my bed."

"I'm honored to be the first."

"If I'm lucky, you'll be the last."

* * *

Billy's house was empty the next morning when I returned. I walked through Edith's room. Anthony's note and ring were gone. I crossed the patio and entered the cottage, where a note awaited me on the desk: "Lucy – I hope you two love bugs had fun. Please come down to the beach. I want to show you something. – Billy "

I dropped my bags on the floor, walked around the side of the house where Billy stored his gear, and found the red bike. I pedaled toward the beach, and as I came around the last corner, I could see the surfers bobbing on the surface far out where the waves were curved and white-tipped. One started to paddle, then he popped up onto his feet, stood, and danced on the water. This time of year it was only the locals out there. Most lived here as a conscious decision and a way of life, like Billy. Surfing came first, and they figured out how to build their lives around it. When the monster waves came in the winter, the forty-foot waves that attracted celebrity surfers and a world-renowned big-wave competition, Billy would sit on a boulder on a nearby cliff and watch. He claimed not to be a daredevil, but the waves that October day looked mighty to someone who had never stood on a board to dance the ocean.

I leaned the bike against a tree and walked down the beach toward the water's edge. There were about ten surfers out in the water, and Billy was one of them. I sat on the sand and watched. There was far more sitting than dancing, and my patience was almost gone when someone waved from the distance. He turned his head to glance behind him, then he started to paddle. He sprang to his feet and cut tight curves this way and that, back and forth across the curling wall of water. He kept riding, back and forth, tight turns and then wider, until finally he rode the full length of the wave as far as it would take him, slower and slower as his body came into full focus from where I sat on the sand, and then I could see the features of his face, too. He looked across the beach at me and waved again before he jumped off the board.

"Hey. Welcome back," he said.

"Hey yourself. Nice moves."

Billy shook his head, and his shaggy mane sprayed salty drops on my arms and legs. "Yeah. Thanks. Great day."

"They're all great days, right?"

He unzipped his wetsuit and sat beside me on the beach. "Pretty much. That's what it's all about."

Billy's chest was still heaving from his last ride. With his strong build, boyish face, and natural ability to outdo anyone with kindness and affection, not to mention his house, its location, and the meals that he served on the roof, Billy could have attracted a wonderful woman, if he had wanted to. His bachelor status was high on my list of unaskable questions.

"So, good sleepover?" he asked. "First time in Tuck's bed, huh?"

I punched his leg and grinned. Although Billy's candor still surprised me, there was a certain comfort in sitting smack in the presence of honesty with someone that I liked so much.

"Excellent sleepover," I said. "After we got through the bad part. The news." I glanced at Billy, and he frowned. "Anthony left."

"Oh, yeah. Jeez. What a blow, huh? Ma seems alright, though."

"She's always alright. That's the unbelievable and infuriating truth about her. Nothing bothers her. Nothing can even touch her. She's unflappable."

"Aw, come on, Luce. You know that isn't true. I heard her crying through the wall last night. He broke her heart."

"Not before she broke his."

"You can't take sides in love. You got to keep loving them both and let them work it out."

"There won't be any working it out. That's the problem. Your mother will never call him. She'll never ask him to come back."

Billy turned his head away from me and spit salty saliva onto the sand. Then he looked out at the ocean for a long time, longer than a man of words and theories about love usually allowed himself.

"You can leave, too, you know." He looked at me, and I did not turn away. "My mom is an unusual person. You and I both know that. Anthony knew that. It's alright if you want to go, if you've had enough, too."

I dropped my head and stared at my bare feet as they worked trenches in the sand like two little bulldozers.

"How long have you known about her plan?" I asked.

"She told me and my sisters this summer, before you two started out."

"And?"

"Who knows. Who knows what Ma will ever decide to do or not to do. She alone knows that." Then he threw an arm around me and gave me a squeeze. "I am one seriously starving man. Have you tried that sandwich place?"

"Not yet."

"Let's go eat."

Billy left his board with my bike, and we crossed the street into a ramshackle building that made wider-than-your-mouth sandwiches on thick slabs of fresh bread. We sat side by side at a picnic table and watched the waves and the surfers while we ate.

"You ought to try it," he said.

"Me? Are you kidding?"

"Everyone should try it. It's freedom. It's beauty. It's never the same twice. I'll be chasing those waves 'til I'm a dead man."

"My pen is my freedom, and words are my beauty. I'll keep chasing stories, thank you very much."

"Nice." Billy put down his sandwich and tousled my hair. "That's real courage, Luce. Anyone can stand on a surfboard. What you do—that's the real thing."

Then he kissed my head and took another bite.

* * *

The Bend Bugle
"Solo"
By Lucy Hunt

After twenty hours of flight training with an instructor, Edith Small stepped into the airplane alone. She completed the pre-flight check. She opened the window and yelled, "Clear!" She radioed to local traffic and began to taxi across the airfield. At the end of the runway, she ran up the engine. Then she turned the plane around and pointed it at the runway that stretched out before her.

Then, alone at the controls, she and the two-seat airplane with call number N1205 chugged and whizzed down the runway until the wings caught the air beneath them and the wheels left the ground. Moments later, she was airborne, flying solo in the circular pattern around the airport that would send her right into initial approach for landing.

On final approach, Edith's airplane was lined up directly at the end of the runway. Her wings held steady. Her speed slowed under control of the pilot.

"She's looking good," said her instructor, Spencer McGillicuddy, as he watched from outside the flight-school building. "Looking real good."

The wheels touched the ground. The plane slowed down and taxied back to where it had started seven minutes and thirty-six seconds earlier.

"I did it!" the pilot yelled as she stepped out of the plane with two arms in the air for victory.

"Of course you did, Ma," her son, Billy Small, yelled back. He ran toward her, and the two hugged behind the wing of the airplane that she had been training in for less than three weeks.

"She's been working very hard from the first day," McGillicuddy said. "There's a huge advantage to flying every day. Edith has made quick progress. She's quite competent. Her landing was as smooth as they come."

After student pilots complete their first solo flight, they are certified by the Federal Aviation Administration to fly alone with certain restrictions of distance and time as they continue their lessons with an instructor. After an average of 60 to 70 total flying hours, with their instructor and alone, most student pilots are ready to take the oral and flight tests required to earn a private pilot's license.

"It's hard to tell, and it certainly isn't a race or a competition, but I'd guess Edith will be ready at about the 50-hour mark," her instructor said. The FAA requires at least 40 hours of flying before a student takes the test.

Edith pulled off her headset and stood beside the little red and white airplane to pose for the traditional post-solo photo. One copy would be posted on her flight school's bulletin board with her name and the date. McGillicuddy got her permission to include her age, too.

"I sure am proud of her," he said. "It's not often that a 75-year-old comes along and wants to learn how to fly an airplane. She's one of a kind, that Edith is. She's a delight to teach. Razor-sharp mind and tough as they come. An absolute delight."

After posing for the picture, Edith left the airport with her son on initial approach to her favorite restaurant up the road. A champagne brunch was their destination.

* * *

Tuck and I had not spent a night apart since I had read his letter. We agreed that a break was a wise idea, for reasons that neither of us could identify. I joked that a separation of thirty-four hours would increase our anticipation of tomorrow evening.

"Thirty-four?" Tuck said. "You counted?"

"Well, sort of. I guess."

"What do you mean, 'sort of?' Thirty-four isn't sort of. You counted."

"OK. Yes. I counted. Jeez."

"That's true love, Lucy."

"Oh, Tuck."

"I'm the luckiest man in the world. I'm going to count off each of the thirty-four hours. I'll use tick marks in batches of five, like they taught us in first grade."

"Tuck, come on."

"I'm not going to ask the universe whether I deserve to be this happy. I'm just going to take it and go with it. Thirty-four. My new lucky number."

"I'm going to hang up now, you weirdo."

"I'll see you in thirty-four hours."

"Actually, it was thirty-four from the time you left this morning until the time you'll arrive tomorrow evening." There was a pause while I re-calculated. "So, we now have thirty hours left."

"Thirty hours! So many, and yet I must not fear. Parting is indeed sweet sorrow."

"Tuck, you're yelling. Can't your co-workers hear you?"

"Yes! But love cannot imprison me, Lucy. Your love sets me free every minute, even at work in my claustrophobic cubicle."

"Have you been drinking espresso shots again?"

"Not a drop. I'm drinking you, the sweet nectar of Lucy."

"OK. I'm definitely hanging up now. This has been fun and all, but I have groceries to buy and words to write, so."

"I will see you in thirty long bittersweet hours. But don't worry about me. Don't doubt for a minute the strength of my character and the courage in my heart."

"Excellent. I won't. I'll be writing and cooking, like I said. Ciao."

"Ciao, sweet Lucy! Adios! Arivaderci! So long, and farewell."

I ended the call and stared at the sidewalk.

"Oh, no, " Edith said. "He didn't take it well?"

Edith stood outside the restaurant when we had eaten brunch with Billy. I had walked off to a nearby palm tree during my conversation with Tuck. She could not have heard any of my words, but now she saw my face.

"You go ahead and see him, dear. Don't you worry about me. Maybe Anthony will be home today. It can't be much longer, I wouldn't think."

"Tuck is fine. I'm fine. Anthony is gone. Let's go to the store."

"Oh, Lucy, melt that cold heart just a little around the edges, will you, dear? You must let me hope that my Anthony will return to me."

I pulled my bag back onto my shoulder, stepped forward toward Edith, and attempted to smell her breath.

"Are you drunk from the champagne, or are you serious?"

"They're not mutually exclusive," she said. "Anthony will need some time to sort out his feelings, and then he will come back to me."

"Is that what his letter said?"

"Not exactly."

"What exactly did it say?"

"Are you asking me as my friend or as a snooping reporter?"

"Neither. I'm asking as Anthony's friend. I miss him."

"Goodness, Lucy, so harsh with me. Please hold that heart of yours closer to the sun. You've given me a chill now."

"Well?"

"His letter said that he was going north to Washington state to see his family. A pilgrimage back to his childhood home. Our sweet little hometown."

"And he'll be back?"

"Perhaps."

"And what led you to conclude that 'perhaps' he'll be back?"

"The hope in my heart and my faith in our love."

"Oh gods. Not you, too." I started to walk, but Edith stood still. I turned back, grabbed her shirt sleeve, and tugged her along. "Have you considered calling him? You know, something practical like a conversation that might actually make him come back."

"Oh, no. Never," Edith said. "He was very clear in his letter that he is gone forever. Still, I will be waiting and hoping .'"

I missed Anthony more than ever as we walked through town to the grocery store. Maybe I would go up north and look for him later, when I had finally written "the end" on the last page of Edith's story.

We loaded our cart with fresh seafood and vegetables, and we biked home with the bags hanging off my handle bars. Biking under the influence of champagne was enough of a challenge for Edith.

When we got home, I wrote for a few hours while Edith read on the patio and went for a walk on the beach. I wondered what she thought about when she was alone. I wondered how much her thoughts differed from her speech, how wide the gap stretched between her Edith and my Edith. I thought back to the day when I first met her and the quiet strength in her words and her presence as she described to me the husband that she had just lost. Reporters dreaded those assignments. Cunningham liked to send me on death patrol, as we called it in the newsroom. He said my reputation on the city beat meant that locals trusted me. I had been sworn at by grieving mothers, cursed by a widower, and scowled at by in-laws, all of whom wound up inviting me into their homes and telling me more than I needed to know for a five-hundred-word story that could not possibly have captured all of what they wanted the world to know about their deceased loved ones. Edith was different. She had breathed steadily as she stared at the mountains that day on her porch swing. She waited until she had captured the essence of Henry herself, and then she opened her mouth to describe him to me in careful words that she knew I could not improve upon and therefore would not change. From the very beginning, she had orchestrated everything with care. Each stop along our way had been a goodbye. Now she was preparing for her aviation tests and walking the beach alone with whatever thoughts visited her at a time like this, a time like no other. I could not guess at the contents of her mind, and that was enough to make me slam down my pen and burn every page that I wrote.

When I finished writing that afternoon, I pulled off my clothes, walked naked across the patio, and sat alone in the hot tub. The wind whispered through the leaves the names of the people that I had been writing about, the lives that I had attempted to sketch with words.

Perhaps it was not wind but ghosts moving through the trees: my mother, Surat, Alice, Anthony, Zalira, Rose, Carter. Ghosts of animate objects fluttered through the leaves, too, that afternoon: Alice's dresses hanging in her closet at work, the private jet that she and Surat flew to Washington, Zalira's apples, Rose's weeds, the little red house and the trickling brook, the pancakes and maple syrup that Daisy and Samantha allowed me to eat, the bar stools where Carter and I sat, the beer glasses that we lifted to our mouths, Anthony's cello and his trees, my suitcase wheels clicking along the stone path to the cliff house in Greece, Tuck's suitcase wheels doing the same, Billy's jeep and his surfboard, my red bike, Edith's yellow bike, her headset, the little airplane, the heels of the woman hurrying to work on Edith's fortieth birthday, the scrap of newsprint that floated out the window like a flying carpet, the list that had charted a course thirty-five years ago with only a month now remaining. I stared at the sky and listened to the wind whispering through the leaves.

Then I stepped out of the hot tub and got dressed for dinner. Soon, Edith and I stood side by side and chopped tomatoes, green beans, carrots, avocados, asparagus, and a plethora of other fresh vegetables to sauté or toss in a salad. Edith stirred the sizzling shrimp and scallops in a pan of butter on the stove. Then we sat across from each other at the table too large for two and spread with the bounty of the sea and the local fields. A pitcher of herbal iced tea stood between us, and I poured some into glasses for each of us.

"Do you ever miss teaching?" I asked.

"I don't miss anything," Edith said. "I've had the right amount of everything already. I taught one class almost every semester, 'An Introduction to Philosophical Thinking.' My absolute favorite. The students' faces would come alive when they understood it. Like Billy and Shakespeare. They couldn't believe that something so old could be relevant to them. It really fascinated some of them."

"How long did you teach?"

"Until I was seventy. I never officially retired, though. One year I didn't teach either semester, because my class was not offered. Then I got busy with travel. Henry had retired by then. At some point, I realized that I was done teaching."

"Do you ever regret not teaching full-time? Not making academics your career?"

"Heavens, no. I loved it to the tune of one class per semester. I appreciate the life of the mind as much as anyone, but I'd have felt like a caged bird if I had taught full-time."

"In the end, has your list been enough? Did it let you do everything you wanted?"

Edith wiped her mouth and looked at me with a gentle affection.

"It was the map for my perfect life. It guided me to every place, idea, and experience that I wanted to explore. I have no regrets. Not one. I gathered knowledge and wisdom from everything I tried. I have a full heart and a full memory. The failures and pitfalls along the way are as much a part of me as each item that I crossed off the list."

We refilled our glasses and ate more food. Then we cleaned up dinner and sat on two cushioned chairs with candles lighted on the side table between us. We talked about flying and Spence, Billy and cooking, jeeps versus bicycles, and whether to try a surfing lesson. We talked about my childhood and my family. Edith asked me many questions about my mother's death, and I answered them all. We talked about Alice and her broken heart. I asked how a mother can stand to see her child in pain, and Edith explained how she had endured it. We talked about the Greek thinkers that I had just read for the first time and that Edith had known all her life. We argued about the wisdom of Stoicism and debated the merits of the various translations of Homer. We talked until the moon rose high above us and our eyelids could no longer stay as open as our minds, two minds that did not cease to find askable questions and explorable subjects in one another's company.

* * *

On October 17 at 0900, Edith pulled the seatbelt across her shoulder and placed her headset on her ears. To her right in the co-pilot's seat was the FAA examiner who would decide her fate. The back seat was empty. Spence, Billy, and I sat at a picnic table outside the FBO. Edith had passed the written examination before her first solo flight, as required. The flight test was the final step to obtain her private pilot's license and complete item #35 on her list. I listened to the hum of the airplane and wondered whether she had checked the other two items off the list. I imagined a black check beside the rings of ruby ink. I wondered, too, whether she would check the final endeavor off her list, whether it would matter to her after her exam today to make a black check mark next to the last red circle.

The plane started to roll along the taxiway. Billy and Spence chatted behind me, but my senses were fixed on the airplane, as if my full concentration could affect Edith's performance. I watched as the flaps went up and down. I listened as the engine roared during the final run-up. Though I did not doubt Edith, I was nervous on her behalf. She had not expressed one iota of jitters that morning, so I valiantly took it upon myself to suffer anxiety on her behalf.

The engine went quiet for a long moment, and when it grew louder again, the airplane started down the runway and left the ground. Edith had flown alone dozens of times in the last few weeks. Taking off, landing, and guiding the plane through every maneuver that appeared on the list for the practical examination was routine for her by now. Spence went inside to check on his appointments for the day. Billy sat beside me.

"You look nervous, Luce."

"Who? Me? Nah."

He elbowed me in the side. "I'm telling you, kiddo. You look nervous."

"She'll be fine. She's a great pilot. We all know that."

"Yes, we all know that. My mother the pilot."

The plane had shrunk into a distant dot, and I dared to take my eyes off it and look at Billy. "It's not like you weren't prepared for this. It's been on her list for thirty-five years."

"Yeah, well, some things you can't prepare for, I guess, no matter how long you've had." Billy was wringing his hands in a way I had never seen.

"I think it's amazing," I said. "I'm proud of her. Did you know she was nervous in the beginning?" Billy shook his head. "She told me the day before her lessons started that she didn't think she could do it. She thought her mind wasn't suited for anything highly mechanical."

Billy laughed. "That's ridiculous." Then his face turned serious. "Actually, it's wrong. She was the handyman in our family. She made it a personal challenge never to call a repair man. She fixed the vacuum cleaner, the toaster, even the washer and dryer. She changed the oil in her and Dad's cars, too."

"That's very weird. She told me she didn't have a mind for mechanics."

"That *is* weird. Are you sure?"

"Of course I'm sure. I'm not kidding that she said it, and there's no reason she would lie. Why would she lie to me about that?"

Billy shrugged. "Got me. Ma is a lot of things, and not all of them good, but a liar she is not."

"And yet, it seems she lied to me about this," I said.

Billy was content not to decipher the meaning of Edith's strange claim. The dot was getting closer. Spence called to us from the doorway, and we both turned our heads. He was gesturing to us to come inside. Another instructor had brought in doughnuts and coffee in honor of Edith. I glanced back at the sky, and the dot was gone again.

"It's gonna be awhile," Spence said. "They'll be at least an hour."

Billy and I had planned to sit outside and wait, but watching an empty sky and listening to the absence of an airplane engine was proving less eventful than either of us had expected. We went inside, ate doughnuts, and talked with Spence and the other instructors and students who were arriving for lessons. After a while, only Billy and I were left in the waiting room. We got lost in magazines, reading about aviation with the distant curiosity of two who would never experience the thrill that Edith had.

About an hour later, we sauntered back outside to the picnic table and sat down. The sun was high and hot, and I had forgotten a hat. I pulled my sunglasses from my bag, and when I saw my notebook, I pulled it out, too, and scribbled details about the day. The plane appeared and then went out over the ocean and almost vanished from sight again before returning to the airport. I knew the pattern. I watched as Edith circled around on initial approach and then made the turn into final approach, lower and lower, engine quieter and quieter, plane slower and slower, down, down, down onto the runway for a pretty landing that would earn her a license from the FAA and the thirty-fifth and final check mark on her lifetime list. Spence was standing behind us with his arms crossed.

The airplane came closer and then stopped. The pilot turned off the engine. The propeller turned more slowly and then came to a halt, nothing but a piece of metal with the power to twirl fast enough to lift a pair of wings and a metal box off the ground.

Edith pulled off her headset and stepped out of the plane with one thumb pointed skyward. The three of us stood and clapped. The FAA examiner stepped out of the plane, patted Edith on the back a few times, and smiled at us to confirm what we already knew.

"That's one fine pilot you've trained, Spence," the examiner said. "Come on inside to sign the papers, Ms. Small, and we'll get that license to you within the week."

Of all the achievements that Edith had collected, this one meant the most. She stood beside the airplane with the grin and confidence of a champion. She was like a marathon runner who had trained long, hard, and well, never doubting that she would cross the finish line and yet in a state of exalted disbelief nonetheless when she did. Her marathon had spanned a lifetime, and though there had been two husbands, three children, two granddaughters, a reporter, an editor, and a slew of readers beside her along the way, she was in spirit and in essence a soloist. She had designed her list alone. She had paced herself to move through it with steady determination alone. Although we were there to congratulate her and celebrate her, she was alone in her final endeavor, too. A solo artist, a champion of free will, and a loner, Edith could love, but she also could leave.

* * *

There were six of us at dinner on the rooftop terrace that night. Tuck arrived after work. Spence came with a bouquet of flowers for Edith and a pin of silver wings, two gifts that he had never given any other student in all his years of teaching. This was what Edith did to people, without even trying. As we mingled and lounged on the cushioned chairs, an unfamiliar face popped up through the hole in the living-room ceiling.

"Hello," came a voice with the tinge of an accent.

"Oh, hey." Billy turned from the kitchen counter and fairly flew across the patio to greet the mystery guest. "Welcome."

He kissed her on the cheek, and she handed Billy a bottle of wine. "It's your favorite," she whispered loudly enough for all to hear. She had short red hair, dark shoulders, and a body shaped by hours of some form of exertion.

"Hey, everyone. This is Veronica. She owns the wine shop in town, and she also owns Mr. Nilsson, my favorite patient."

Veronica smiled and waved her hand through the air to greet us. Billy stood beside her and made the introductions. He saved his mother for last, and Veronica stepped forward to shake Edith's hand and offer her congratulations.

"My mom was a pilot in the U.S. Air Force," she said. "One of the first. She was based in Germany when my dad happened to be there on business. The rest is history."

"So your father is not German?" Edith asked.

"My father is Italian, but he was a diplomat, so I was raised all over the world. When I started high school, we settled here for good. My folks still live in San Francisco."

"And you live here in town?" Edith asked.

"I do. Just up the road."

"Veronica will be happy to field more questions during her press conference after dinner, Ma, but for now let's offer her a seat and a glass of wine," Billy said.

Everyone laughed, and Spence moved to the end of the sofa to make room for Veronica. She sat down and talked about aviation with Spence and Edith, leaving me and Tuck to chat with each other. All I could think about, though, was how long Billy had been hiding Veronica from us and why.

I waited through dinner, while the pilots talked about airplanes.

I waited through dessert, while the wine lovers talked about vineyards.

I waited until Spence said good bye and left.

I waited until Edith said good night and left.

I waited until Veronica looked at her watch, kissed Billy's cheek, and left.

I waited until Tuck stopped quizzing Billy about surfing.

"Why didn't you tell me?" I asked at last.

Billy lifted his beer to this mouth. "There's nothing to tell. It's not like that."

Tuck and I looked at him. "Oh, come on," Tuck said.

234

"She's terrific," Billy said. "No doubt about that. I'm teaching her how to surf, and she's teaching me about wine. We have lunch sometimes, dinner sometimes. It's all good, but it's not what you think."

"How could you do that to her?" I said.

"Do what?" Billy said. "I'm not doing anything. We're friends. We're hanging out. She's cool with it. Come on, you two, knock it off."

"I'm a dozen years younger than you, and I know that's not cool," Tuck said. "Even I could see the way she was looking at you."

Billy stood up and walked his empty bottle to the kitchen. "OK, you little love birds. Just because you found one another doesn't mean the whole world is falling all over each other. We're friends. We hang out."

"Billy, you're forty years old. How much longer do you plan to 'hang out?'"

"Aw, Luce, don't turn mean on me now. I'm a happy guy. Veronica is a nice woman. And now, I'm going to sleep."

"This conversation isn't over," I said. He was walking past us to the staircase, and he did not bother to stop for a hug. Rooftop dinners always ended with a hug. "Just so you know."

He kept moving toward the stairs, and he waved one hand at us in a final goodbye. His feet disappeared down the stairs, then his body, and finally his head. Tuck and I looked at each other.

"I can't believe—" I said.

The head reappeared through the hole, gopher-style. "I did it for Ma. You know what today means. I invited Veronica because I thought maybe Ma would stick around if she knew I had somebody, if she thought there might be a wedding or more grandkids." He looked at us and waited. "Stupid, right?"

"Not stupid," I said. "Hopeful."

"Loving," Tuck said.

"Nah," Billy said. "Wishful thinking." He looked across the floor to where I was sitting. I wished he were closer. I wished there would be a hug. "Now I'm supposed to get into my bed and close my eyes and try to sleep, not knowing whether she'll still be here in the morning. And if she is, then I have to do it again tomorrow night."

"Have you tried asking her?" Tuck said.

"Who are you kidding, my friend? This is Edith Small we're talking about." Billy shook his head and turned to go, but then he stopped and looked at me one last time. "Have you tried, Lucy? Have you? Because you're the one who could do it. You're the one who could get through to her."

I shook my head. "I gave her my word at the beginning. I agreed only to observe and not to influence. That was what she asked of me. That was her condition."

Billy nodded and disappeared down the hole.

Tuck and I sat in silence and looked at the sky. A wide swath of thick milky clouds had covered most of the stars. There was nothing pretty to look at anymore, so we disappeared through the hole, too, to get into bed, close our eyes, and try to sleep, not knowing whether she would still be there in the morning.

* * *

The next morning, Rose called again. She and Alice had called the afternoon before, to hear the news and offer their forced congratulations. This time Billy took the telephone into his bedroom and closed the door. When he emerged a half-hour later, he handed the phone to Edith, who was drinking tea and reading on the back patio. I was writing at the desk with the window open when I heard her voice.

"Oh, honey, that's wonderful! Congratulations to all of you! Are you hoping for a boy this time or another girl?"

I could have asked to talk with Rose. I could have made myself take on the newest question from the list of unaskables and try to find out whether her pregnancy was real, and if so, whether she actually wanted a third child or whether this was a plan of the Veronica type. Instead I sat by the window, eavesdropping and deciphering, until I heard Edith say goodbye.

About an hour later, the telephone rang again. Billy was still home, and I was still home, because Edith was still home. Vigilance was running at an all-time high. Again Billy shut himself into his bedroom, and again he brought the phone to his mother on the patio where she was reading American history, the colonial period.

"Oh, sweetheart, I couldn't be happier for you. He sounds lovely. Yes, I'm sure Billy would love to have you both join us. I'll leave the details up to you kids."

I could not have talked with Alice. I could not have asked her about the sudden change of her status from eternally alone to dating and apparently in love. I could not have asked her whether and why she was lying to her mother. Although I could not have asked Alice anything, I did not need to. Back-to-back phone calls from the Edith's daughters were no coincidence.

Edith ate an early lunch. Then she poked her head out her bedroom door to where Billy and I sat reading on the back patio, keeping watch with extra focus, each of us believing that we were serving as top security detail with the other as back-up.

"I'm off to the airport," she said. "Ta ta." She flittered her fingers at us and tapped the flight bag that was hanging on her shoulder and across her chest. The pin from Spence was secured to the collar of her blouse. I squinted at her with deep-rooted suspicion, as she turned and headed for the yellow bike.

I looked at Billy. He had not said a word. I looked until the weight of my stare raised his eyes from the page to meet mine.

"Should I follow her?" I asked.

He shrugged.

"Are you going to follow her?"

He shook his head.

"This is ludicrous," I said. "This can't go on. We can't keep this up forever."

He nodded.

"I don't know what to do," I said.

"I don't know either, Luce."

He returned to his book, and I walked around the house for the red bike. I rode slowly along the streets between Billy's house and the airport. I arrived at the FBO and chatted with Spence. I sat on the picnic table and watched Edith practice landing and taking off, "touch and goes." When the plane shrank into a dot far in the distance over the ocean, I pedaled home and wrote for the rest of the afternoon and into the evening.

* * *

When I woke up the next morning, both bicycles were gone but the surfboard was not. I drank too much coffee while I tried to read on the back patio. About an hour later, Billy appeared.

"Where's your mother?"

"She's in the house. Guess what I did?"

I shrugged.

"I went flying with Ma."

"Wow. Why?"

"To buy us another day. It was amazing. She's an excellent pilot. Didn't crash once. And I didn't have to use my parachute either." He winked at me. "I booked you for tomorrow. I told her you wanted to fly with her but hadn't had a chance to ask yet."

"Gee, thanks. You're a true friend."

"It buys us another day."

Billy looked self-satisfied with his new method for distracting his mother from other activities. He would probably ask Tuck to fly with Edith, too, and maybe even Veronica and Mr. Nilsson.

"Is this how you plan to spend the rest of your life?"

"It's just for one week. We need to get her through one week, and then Alice will be here."

"And then what?"

I was staring at Billy when a second face appeared beside his.

"Hello, Lucy. I hear it's your turn tomorrow."

"Apparently."

"Excellent," Edith said. "Now, in the meantime, I've made plans for the three of us this afternoon. I'll meet you out front after lunch. We'll need your car, dear. And Lucy, please bring your notebook and recorder."

By early afternoon, Edith was navigating to an address that Billy did not know. We pulled into a parking lot with a sign that said, "The Palms – Care With Dignity." When Billy turned off the engine, Edith looked at him and then at me in the back seat.

"No questions," she said. "And I do mean none. I will be your tour guide, and I will provide the narration. There will be no discussion after we've left. Understood?"

Billy and I nodded and followed Edith into the building.

"Wait here," she instructed us.

She walked through a doorway labeled "office," and we waited in silence as old people muttered in the living room and traipsed through the corridors with walkers, wheelchairs, and oxygen tanks. A few minutes later, Edith reappeared.

"Come," she said.

We walked single file down a long hallway until Edith stopped outside a room.

"Lucy, your notebook and recorder."

I pulled them from my bag and found a pen, too.

"Not a word from either of you. Understood?" Edith said.

We nodded. Then she walked into the room. There were two beds parallel, like in a hospital room. The furniture and décor resembled a hospital, too. The smell, though, was worse.

"This is Margo," Edith said. "She's seventy-nine. She had her first stroke when she was seventy. Then for four years, she lived with her son. When his marriage and family were just about destroyed from the stress of trying to care for her while raising teenagers, he moved her here. A year later, she had another stroke. Since then, she hasn't spoken. She doesn't move. She has lucid thoughts, though, the doctors say. She watches television for an hour at a time, then she sleeps for about two hours, then television again for an hour, then sleep for two hours. Everyday it's the same. At night she's restless and sometimes calls out as if in pain. The doctors can't find the source of her pain. They say it's mental. She has lived like this for three years now. "

Edith took a step back and gestured for us to step forward. Billy and I stood side by side at Margo's bed. Her white hair looked like spider webs. Her eyes were closed, and the lids were veiny. The knuckles on her hands were gnarled and knotted like a diseased tree. She was three years younger than Edith.

"Write," Edith said, when I glanced at her.

I put the pen to my notebook, but nothing came. We stood for another minute, and then we heard the sound of Edith's shoes moving toward the second bed. I turned and saw a man for the first time. I had missed him on the way in.

"This is Richard. He's seventy-seven. He had a heart attack at the age of sixty-eight after a life of red meat and beer. A few years later, he got lung cancer, probably from the second-hand smoke he breathed at the garage where he worked as a mechanic for forty years. His wife tried to take care of him at home for a few months, but it killed her. She collapsed one morning while trying to help him in the shower. He's been here ever since. His cancer goes into remission sometimes. He's had four major surgeries in the past six years. He sleeps because he wants to be dead but nobody will help him. He asks me every time I come in if I will bring him something. Last week when I came in, he said, 'If you can't get pills, maybe you could get a gun.'"

Edith stepped back and gestured for us to step forward. "Please, Lucy, write. I've done all your reporting for you. I've come three times each week the entire time we've been in California. Please, do your part now."

When I finished scribbling, I looked up at Richard. He was snoring, and his rising chest and belly barely moved the covers. The days of beer and meat were too far gone to have left much flesh on him. The cancer had eaten everything right up to the amount required to keep him alive.

Edith's shoes clicked against the floor again. We left the first room and entered another. Edith stood over a bed. The woman was knitting and did not look at us, though she smiled slightly, as if she had been prepared for our visit.

"Susan never had a stroke or a heart attack or cancer. She's had nothing. No medications, no surgeries, no health problems. She's eighty-seven years old, and she's been here for ten years. After her husband died, she lived with her daughter for almost ten years, but one day, her daughter looked her in the eye and said, 'Ma. I'm done.' The next day, her daughter dropped her off here. The daughter visits once a month. Susan knits and sings, and sometimes she plays bridge in the lounge with the others. She told me she is done living, but she doesn't want to suffer any more than necessary, so she tries to enjoy life's simplest pleasures. Knitting, singing, playing cards. I asked her the other day what she wants most, and she said to see the ocean. Her daughter lives in the city and refuses to take her anywhere outside the nursing home. Susan has nobody else. Her husband dropped dead of a heart attack twenty years ago. Her son was killed in a car crash before that. The same day that she told me about the ocean, I went to the office, signed her out, loaded her in a rental car that I got up the road, and drove her to the beach. I got her out of the car and rolled her wheelchair through the parking lot to where there's a clearing in the trees. She took one look at the ocean and wept at its beauty She said it sounded like God's symphony. Those were her words, Lucy. Isn't that right, Susan?" Susan kept her eyes on her knitting, smiled, and nodded. "I can remember words, too. The good ones, anyway. I promised Susan we'd go every afternoon that I came to The Palms. That's all she wants. To see the ocean. So we go every day, don't we dear?"

Susan nodded again. Edith took a step back and gestured for us to take a step forward. Unlike the others, Susan was awake and moderately alert. Everyone else we saw was sleeping. After all her visits, Edith knew that most of the nursing-home residents dosed off in the afternoon. Edith clicked her shoes across the floor, down the corridor, and into the next room.

"This is Joe. He was overweight most of his life and had diabetes. After his wife died, he stopped taking his medication, stopped going to the doctor, stopped taking care of himself. One day the mailman noticed that the mail had piled up in the mailbox, and he knocked on the door. When nobody answered, he called out loud enough that his voice carried through the open bedroom window in the back of the house. The mailman called 911, and an ambulance got Joe to the hospital just in time to save his life. He lost both feet, though. And he lost his mind, too. Most of the time he stares at the television. He likes old westerns. As soon as the television goes off, he starts to mutter that he wants his feet back. He says it over and over. He's seventy-six years old, and he's been here for a year now."

When Edith looked at us, Billy turned said, "Enough, Ma."

"Oh, no, honey. We're just getting started. I have fifteen friends here, all over the age of seventy-five, and I'd like you to meet them all."

"I can't, Ma. I get it. You've made your point. "

Billy walked past her and left the room. I looked at Edith, and she raised her eyebrows, but I was done, too, like Anthony, like Billy. I walked past her and out the front door. When I reached the parking lot, Billy was sitting in the driver's seat staring straight ahead. I walked over and looked at him. He looked at me. For a long, long time, we looked. We looked at each other's faces in search of an answer that we knew did not exist. We searched each other's glassy eyes for an explanation that would never come. We looked and looked, and in the looking there was comfort. Then I climbed into the back seat.

Edith appeared a few minutes later. "I told Susan I'd be back later. The home has been so generous in lending me a car for our trips to the beach. When the manager found out I'd been renting a car, he wouldn't have it. Lovely people here."

Billy and I did not look at her. He started the engine.

"Our next stop is not far from your clinic, dear."

"We're not going to another nursing home, Ma."

"That's right. We're not." She smiled at him and then glanced back at me and winked.

Soon we arrived at a house like any other. The door swung open, and a middle-aged woman with a round face and round middle greeted Edith by name and let us in.

"This is Joanne," Edith said. "She's a hospice nurse."

"Nice to meet you both," Joanne said with a bright cheery smile.

"She works with families who are bringing their loved ones home from The Palms to die. That's where we met, at the nursing home. Some of her patients have never been in a facility. Some go straight home from the hospital."

In the living room was a hospital bed, and in the bed was a wrinkled woman with closed eyes. Our tour guide stepped toward the bed and gestured for us to gather round.

"This is Doreen. She's been living here with her sister for many years. When her sister died last year, her daughter came up from Los Angeles to take care of her. Doreen is eighty, and her daughter just lost her job, so she has time to care for her. She plans to go back after. It's been just the two of them, and the daughter doesn't have much physical strength, so home health aides have been coming in twice a day for the past year. Since the age of seventy-five, Doreen has had a stroke, heart disease, and two hip replacement surgeries that were routine, but the anesthesia really took a toll. That was four years ago. She hasn't been lucid since. When the home health aides noticed a change about a week ago, they called Joanne."

We looked at Joanne. She smiled sweetly again. "I'm so grateful for the chance to help folks pass peacefully. It's joyful work, really."

Something moved beside me, and then the door clicked open and closed. I took a deep breath and smiled the best I could at the woman who did the joyful work of helping people to die. Then I followed Billy's lead and left the house. I climbed into the back seat again and watched the clouds. Billy was inspecting the steering wheel in silence.

When Edith got into the car, she did not speak.

Nobody spoke on the drive home.

When we pulled into Billy's driveway and the engine stopped, Edith opened her mouth, but for once I was faster.

"I'd still like to go with you tomorrow," I said. "I'd like to fly with you. It would be an honor."

She reached out her hand and patted my knee. "Of course, dear. Of course we'll go."

* * *

I tightened my seatbelt and adjusted the headset from Spence. The time was 0900 hours. Edith completed the pre-flight check, yelled "Clear!" through the window, and taxied to the end of the runway. She checked the wing flaps and ran up the engine. Then she turned to me and said, "Ready?" I smiled and gave her a thumbs-up.

We chugged along the runway for the first few hundred feet, and then we were racing, the asphalt jumping at us as the wings waited for the magical moment. The speed increased until at last the air caught the wings, and they lifted the airplane off the ground. We were high and free, able to move anywhere, no lines, no signs, no traffic, nothing between us and the sky and the ocean.

Edith turned a knob and pushed a lever and the plane began to level off. She banked hard to the left, to the west, and a sheet of green-blue-gray spread out beneath us. We went a short distance out over the water, and then she turned back toward shore, always aware of the glide ratio in case her single engine sputtered to a halt, always aware of her passenger's mental comfort. We flew over Billy's house, and Edith tipped my wing to give me a closer look. There was the rooftop paradise where we had spent many hours and enjoyed many meals, conversations, and laughs. There was the miniscule roof of the sisters' guest cottage, my home for now, the writer's hut. There was the driveway, and there stood the jeep. Edith turned toward the inlet, and I saw the black dots of surfers. We flew over the town and spotted the animal clinic. I remembered Doreen in her house up the road, and I looked in the other direction and admired the hillside instead. Up, up, up Edith pointed the plane, gaining altitude to clear the mountains. There was the road that connected Main Street to the two-lane highway, and then we were on the other side of the mountains, above the long low roofs of Tuck's software company. Several blocks to the east stood his apartment building.

Onward we flew, two birds in the never-ending sky with not a cloud to obstruct our view. We flew without a bounce, gliding through the air on metal wings, propelled by a twirling metal stick, and moved by an engine that we did not even need, I had learned, for a safe landing on a runway or elsewhere.

The Golden Gate Bridge came into sight, and Edith pointed and grinned, even as I nodded in reassurance that I saw it, of course. Then Alcatraz in the distance. Then the breaking waves below us. Then ocean and more ocean, wide open deep-blue water that stretched on and on. The beach came closer until we were on final approach, the familiar pattern that I had watched Edith's airplane fly many times from the picnic table, vigilant, wondering, worrying because she was not, anxious for what could happen.

The wheels bumped once, twice, three times against the asphalt, and the little two-seat trainer, call number N1205, with its newly licensed pilot and her passenger returned to the ground.

* * *

After dinner, I sat at my desk and began to write. Tuck got into our bed and read his book. At some point Billy turned the music off on the roof and headed into his bedroom for the night. I wrote after Tuck whispered goodnight, turned out the reading light, and went to sleep. I wrote to the rhythm of his breathing. I wrote after Edith clicked off her reading light, too, and the yellow glow through the back window of the house disappeared. I wrote while the crickets sang in the neighbor's garden on the other side of the fence. I wrote as the full moon traveled through the black sky and cast shadows on the patio. I wrote until there was nothing left to write, and I was lost in a trance, far away in a place where a voice that was not mine but came from me could find its way through me and onto the page.

And then, at last, I set down my pen. I stepped out into the night to feel the cool air. Tomorrow had already come, and so I was less afraid.

* * *

When I opened my eyes later that morning, the sun was high and warm. Tuck was gone, and in his place was a note:

Dear Sweet Writer – Do not apologize. Your writing is a part of you. I hope to spend many more hours in the quiet with you as you write. See you tonight. Love, Tuck

I pulled on shorts and a T-shirt and walked across the patio, through Billy's bedroom, and into the kitchen. Nobody was home. I could not eat. The time was 0845 hours. Take-off was soon.

I walked to the front door. The jeep was gone, but Billy was not surfing. He was somewhere else. This morning he would want to be alone.

I went to the guest hut for my sandals and sunglasses. I left my notebook behind. I would not need it. Then I stopped in Billy's bathroom to brush my teeth and my hair.

I walked outside and around the house, where I saw Billy's surfboard and the two bicycles. Edith had walked today. She had never walked before. I rolled my red bike out of the shed, closed the door, and pedaled up Billy's road toward the beach. The breeze was gentle and brushed past my cheeks without ruffling a hair. The sun was high already. I pedaled slowly, and at last I arrived. I leaned my bike against a tree, pulled off my sandals, and walked toward the water.

When I reached the edge of the ocean, I turned north and walked along the shore. I gazed up the open expanse of the beach. There was not a soul for miles, for all the miles that I could see. I heard the buzzing and looked up to find the little airplane moving toward the ocean. She flew at an angle out over the water and behind me. I stopped walking and stood in the wet sand. The plane was following the shoreline about a hundred feet out from where the water lapped my feet. She flew straight past me, headed north now, and as I waved up at her, she tipped her wing once and then again. I breathed the moist salty air and kept walking as the plane grew smaller up the coast.

Playing Cello for the Trees

I watched her bank hard to the left, make a tight turn, and begin her return down the shoreline toward me. She began to climb, higher, higher, higher. Then she moved farther out over the water. Then even farther. By the time her airplane was directly across from where I stood, there were a thousand feet between us and several thousand feet between her and the water's surface. I stopped and looked. I waved again, and again she tipped the wing: once, twice; hello, good-bye.

The engine stopped. The nose tipped downward. She fell into a direct plunge with the grace of a swan, the confidence of a woman who had charted her course thirty-five years ago, and the calm of a pilot who had complete control of her airplane.

The impact was swift and mighty. I tried hard not to close my eyes, because I knew she wanted me to keep them open, but there was a moment, one fraction of a second, when the splintering and crashing and disintegration was more than my eyes could look at. When I opened them again, I saw the debris floating on the surface. A pile floating on the water. It could have been a boat. Or maybe a whale.

I looked up the beach and then down it.

I turned and looked behind me.

I was alone.

When the time was right, when I was ready, I took the telephone from my pocket and dialed 911 to report the crash. Then I sat on the beach for a long, long time until I was ready to leave that place and that moment.

* * *

When Spence walked into the FBO after his first lesson, another instructor told him. He shook his head, as if shaking off a fly. Then he walked out to the picnic table and stared at the runway. He had never lost a student. She had been one of his best. He moved mentally through every part of the airplane to check for a problem and diagnose the mistake.

Billy found me sitting on the front step when he got home that morning. He looked at me from behind the steering wheel of his jeep. He knew without asking. Then he sat beside me, and we held hands for a very long time, and nobody said a word.

Tuck was sitting at his desk at work when the telephone rang. He heard the news in my voice in a fraction of a second. He hung up the phone, told his boss that there was a family emergency, and arrived at Billy's house twenty-five minutes later. We were still sitting on the front step when he arrived. He sat on my other side and slipped into our silence. He was the first to cry, and his tears let me cry, and mine let Billy cry. In silence together we wept, and nobody said a word, because the time for words had not yet come.

Later, Billy called Rose and told her. Rose would decide for herself what to believe. When her daughter was born several months later, she considered naming her Edith, but in the end she understood that each new life must chart its own course.

Billy called Alice and told her. Alice would decide for herself what to believe, and forever she would be able to believe in the accident, the mistake, the mishap that took her mother's life. That was the kind of mother that Edith had been, after all. There was care in her planning. There was love—her kind of love—in her decision, despite everything.

Veronica heard the news from Billy's partner at the clinic the next day when she took Mr. Nilsson in for an exam. She walked back to the wine shop in a daze with the monkey on her shoulder. She had read the stories in *The Bugle*. That was part of loving Billy. She wanted to know everything there was to know about him, including his mother and her list. Now that Veronica was no longer a prop, she hoped to become something else to Billy. She wondered whether hoping for something like that at a time like that made her a bad person.

Anthony received a box in the mail a month later. Its contents were the same as the box that Billy received and Rose received and Alice received. Rose showed hers to Carter, and she would show Daisy and Samantha and their little sister, too, when the time was right. Two boxes went to Oregon, one to my father and the other to Cunningham. One box flew all the way to Africa to Zalira. Three boxes stayed in Minnesota, one for my brother, one for Tuck, and one for Uncle Lewis. Theirs were hand-delivered, since we were living in Minnesota by then.

Anthony was back in Vermont. He had enjoyed his trip to his childhood town. He liked seeing his family after so many years away, but he missed his home and his cello. We spoke on the telephone several times before he received the box. When he opened it, he saw what the others saw, too. There was a handwritten note on top, a few lines from the scribe penned for each reader, each unique. Anthony read the note, and then he saw the title of the manuscript that lay beneath. He read the words in silence inside his head before he opened his mouth and read them aloud for everything and everyone, nothing and nobody, to hear.

"*Playing Cello for the Trees*," he said. "By Lucy Hunt."

Then he turned to page one and began to read.

THE END